CORPORATE AMERIKKKA

BLACC TOPP

Published by: BlaccStarr Media Group
Written by: BlaccTopp

For information contact:
BlaccStarr Media Group
P.O. Box 9451
Port St. Lucie, FL 34985-9451

blaccstarrbooks@gmail.com
www.facebook.com/deanswift
twitter...@novelistblacctopp
instagram...@novelistblacctopp

Other Novels by

BLACC TOPP

This book is dedicated to

T.M., R.S., M.J., and G.W. and the company that you guys represent!!

PS. I'm still spending that lawsuit money, thanks to your racism and my raw ass lawyer!!

Acknowledgements

To my readers, I hope you guys enjoy Corporate Amerikkka as much as I enjoyed writing it. You guys make this dream possible and I couldn't do it without you. I would love to name each of you individually but that's a book within itself. I want to say thank you and as long as I have feeling in my fingers and characters in my head I will continue to write. Patrice McKinney there are no words to describe my love for you. I love you, I love you, I love you with everything in me. Michelle and Nate Davis, you guys are topnotch and I am thankful to have you guys in my and my family's lives. Faye Wilkes, well partner, another one down, sixtyleven billion more books to go!! I love you Midget!!

K'wan man, wow.... I don't even know where to begin, every day is like a crash course in advanced learning and I'm forever grateful #1050-CERTIFIED, #ML-Executive life!!!

On the real, thank you to each and every person that I've encountered on this incredible journey and remember this is just the beginning. If I left your name out and you're feeling some type of way, just know that it was not intentional.

Oh before I forget: To my son Kalil, man I love you with my entire soul and now that you're in school, you amaze me EVERY DAY!! Your intellect and drive give me life and it serves to make my drive that much stronger!! The sky is no limit for the things that you can achieve!!

Prologue

My name is Tristen Graham and I've murdered and maimed. Contrary to popular stereotypes, my mother wasn't a whore or a crackhead. My father didn't run out on us when I was a child. I didn't drop out of high school to get a job to care for my four siblings. I didn't run with a rough crowd who encouraged me to drink and do drugs. No, I was raised by both parents in a staunchly Christian household with a wonderful upbringing. My mother, Ruth Graham, is a Professor of Law at Rutgers University. My father, Chester Graham, is a Brigadier General in the United States Air Force at McGuire Air Force Base.

My earliest recollection of my technical abilities date back to my seventh birthday, when my parents threw me a surprise birthday party and one of my gifts was a new remote-controlled Jeep. I loved that Jeep; it was an exact replica of my father's red Jeep Wrangler. I noticed early on that the Jeep went a little too slow for my tastes, so later that night, after the party was over, I snuck into my father's workshop and got a few of his tools. I don't know how I knew how to change the speed regulator, but I knew. The next day my father was outside with me when I tested out what I'd done. He was so surprised that it caused me to chuckle a bit, but when he asked me how I'd made the car so fast, surprisingly enough, I was able to explain it step by step. And that's how it started. My parents nurtured my love for electronics and it grew from there. My entire life I studied to get ahead. My tenacity and hard work earned me a full academic scholarship to M.I.T., where I exceled in my studies.

Anyway, just for clarification, I need to explain that I don't fit the typical nerd profile. Not to stereotype my brainy brethren, but you know when people think of the intellectually superior, they envision them with thick bifocals, pocket protectors, and ill-fitting clothes. They often equate with them their penchant for robots and calculators. I was thankfully none of those things. Although I never considered myself any sort of Adonis, early on I was aware that I was blessed with strong features and a lean, toned body. I was often mistaken for an athlete versus a mathlete and there was never a shortage of women. It was always my choice to forego the girls and concentrate on my school work and I was rewarded handsomely for it. Make sure you let everyone know that I don't regret any of my decisions. My only regret is believing that the world had changed and could actually accept a black man with an Ivy League education. My mother and father believed in me when no one else would. I let them down, and for that, I'm truly sorry. I allowed my anger to push me to the point of no return, and for that, I must pay the price.

Chapter 1

The sound of jovial laughter could be heard from the street in front of the Graham household. Chester and Ruth Graham had worked hard to raise their only son in a loving and productive environment and it had paid off in a big way. Tristen Graham had just graduated from M.I.T. at the top of his class and he'd managed to do it in three years because he'd double majored. Now, their family was celebrating his graduation from one of the most prestigious Ivy League colleges in the nation. They were also celebrating the fact that he'd been offered a senior position at one of the largest software companies in Texas called CrossTech. Tristen had walked out of his college graduation with not only the honors of having the highest GPA in M.I.T. history, but he was walking into a position as a Senior Software Architect. At twenty-two years old, Tristen was the youngest executive ever hired at CrossTech, not to mention the only African American in an executive role. It wasn't hard for them to convince him to choose CrossTech as his first choice of employment. His starting salary would be a whopping $125,000 annually. They'd discussed salary, but as the company had explained, there were many perks of being an employee of CrossTech in addition to his salary. They had agreed to send a plane for him to meet with them on Monday, but for now, Tristen would party.

Another round of robust laughter erupted from the living room of the Graham household. Chester Graham was in the middle of the floor, trying his hardest to imitate the breakdance moves that had been so popular when he was a young man. His wife Ruth, although a professor, was still hip hop at heart. She walked to the iPod dock, flipped it to her old school list, and stepped out to the middle of the floor.

"Watch out, Pops, let me show you how it's done," she said. Run-DMC flooded the speakers as she posed in her best B-Girl stance.

Now Peter Piper picked peppers and Run rocked rhymes.

Humpty Dumpty fell down in these hard times.

Jack be nimble (what) nimble, and he was quick,

But Jam Master Jay……..

Ruth Graham was now in full breakdance mode and her small but loving family cheered her on as if she were a contestant on *America's Got Talent*. "That, my good sir, is how it's done," she said to her husband.

"C'mon, Tristen, show your mother how it's done," Chester said. He sat stoically, refusing to move with a twisted smirk on his face. Truth was, he wasn't much of a dancer – hell, he couldn't dance at all - but he had never once in his life rejected a request from his mother.

"Alright, Miss Lady, if you insist," he said.

Tristen stood and walked to the middle of the floor. His family watched in anticipation and curiosity as he silenced them with a wave of his hand. He pointed to his favorite cousin, Toby Graham, who in turn moved to the iPod docking station and put on Tristen's favorite song. "All I do Is Win" by DJ Khaled wafted through the speakers and Tristen's family was silent. His once shy persona had given way to a skilled and graceful dancer. His body was popping and locking, ticking and sticking, and he krumped until his family exploded in laughter and applause.

Ruth ran to meet Tristen in the middle of the floor just as the song drew to a close. She hugged his neck and kissed him on the cheek. She held him at arm's length and looked into his eyes. Ruth Graham had been worried about being a productive parent when she'd initially learned of her pregnancy. As a pair of twenty-eight-year-old parents, she and Chester had been comfortable with their modest but stable lives. Chester had already been enlisted in the military for ten years, working his way up the ranks. Ruth was working towards her Juris Doctorate and they both held unbelievably busy schedules. They had felt blessed, though at age twenty-eight, they'd naively believed that their daughter or son would be starting kindergarten. Ruth smiled to herself; that had been twenty-two years earlier. She'd honestly believed that God hadn't blessed them with a child until He felt that they were both comfortable with their ambitions. Then it happened. Tristen had come bursting into the world kicking and screaming. And here he was, her baby boy, a grown man, standing tall and proud as his father had taught him to do.

"Why are you looking at me like that, Mother?" Tristen asked.

"I'm just really proud of you, baby. It almost seems unfair that we're so blessed. I mean, for the most part you've never given us any problems and you're my joy. I feel blessed and honored to be your mom."

Tristen blushed. He both hated and loved when his mother got mushy, especially in front of Toby, who thought his cousin to be somewhat eccentric, if not soft. To see Toby and Tristen together was like watching a bad episode of *The Odd Couple*. They were polar opposites in every sense of the word. The only commonality that they seemed to share was their love for one another. They were more like brothers than cousins with their constant ribbing of one another. Their fathers were brothers and had been extremely close until Grady Graham's untimely death. There was a running joke in their family that Grady and Chester must have planned to get their women pregnant at the same time because the boys had been born only hours apart.

Toby's life was a walking stereotype and he knew it, but it never deterred him. His mother was undoubtedly the worst mother to ever give birth in his eyesight and his father had taken him from her when he was only two years old. He couldn't remember his mother much, only what his aunt and uncle chose to share with him. What he did know was that she hadn't tried to contact him while his father was alive or after his death. Grady Graham had been gunned down robbing a liquor store when Toby was an impressionable twelve years old while Toby waited outside on his bike. He hadn't known why they went to the liquor store; his father had only told him that they were going to get some money from some friends. He hadn't tried to rob for dope or any habit. He'd merely been a desperate father trying to feed and clothe his only child and had been too proud to ask his brother for help.

Early on, Toby and Tristen had been taught to always take care of one another and they had wholeheartedly taken it to task. When Tristen was being teased, it was Toby who stepped in and came to his rescue. Likewise, when Toby fell behind in his studies, it was Tristen who either tutored him or simply did the homework for him. After Grady's death, he'd come to stay with his cousin and his parents. They never seemed to make a difference between the boys until they were older and Toby started to get into trouble. They hadn't kicked him out as he'd expected. No, they showed *more* love and became stricter.

Now to see Tristen graduate from college and move into a cushy job gave Toby mixed emotions. He was happy for his cousin because he knew that he'd worked extremely hard to get to where he was, but a small part of him felt as though he were losing a piece of himself. If Tristen took the job in Dallas, he would be a world away, not just down the hall like he'd been throughout their lives. He looked at Tristen standing there and hugging his mother and felt a pang of jealousy. He caught Tristen's eye and nodded towards the front door. Tristen kissed his mother on the cheek and made his way towards the front door.

"You boys don't go too far now, Tristen. I want you to cut your cake soon, baby," Ruth said.

"Okay, Mother, we'll be right out front."

"Okay, Mother, we'll be right out front," Toby mimicked playfully. "You're a fuckin' mama's boy, Tristen. What you need to do is pull Aunt Ruth's titties out ya mouth and grow up, nigga," he added.

"First of all, don't ever in your black-ass life call me a nigger again. You know I hate that shit. And second, don't talk about my mother's titties. Say milk pockets or moo bags, anything but titties," Tristen countered. They both laughed heartily.

"Goddamn, I'm proud of you, bruh! You showed all of them uppity ma'fuckas over there how to get that paper. You know what I think? I think you're a mutant, nigga - I mean, brother. How else can you explain being so damned smart? Like I think Unc 'n'em made you in a laboratory on the Air Force base, dude," Toby said.

Tristen shook his head. He was used to Toby making jokes about his intelligence so it didn't bother him. That was his way of showing admiration.

"On the real though, bro, I am really proud of you and I know you're gonna do great in Texas," Toby said.

"Why don't you come with me, bro? I'm going to be making more than enough money for the both of us. Shoot, I can get you a job at CrossTech with me."

"Nah, dawg, it's your time to shine. Plus, what the hell would I do there? Sweep floors and shit? Nah, I'm good, I'll just stay here and keep grinding. Besides, somebody gotta stay here and keep an eye on Aunt Ruth and her big-ass titties," he said, laughing. He took off running just before Tristen could connect with a left jab. They walked into the house laughing like a pair of old friends fresh into port after a long journey at sea.

Chapter 2

Tristen stepped off of the Boeing 747 and headed to baggage claim. He stood patiently waiting for his Nautica duffle bag to make its way around the conveyor. He grabbed his bag and was surprised to see a sight fresh from television. A tall, gangly white gentleman held a cardboard sign with bold lettering - TRISTEN GRAHAM - scrawled on it.

"Excuse me, sir, I am Tristen Graham," he said.

The man gave Tristen a once over, examining him as if in disbelief that the young man could actually be the patron for whom he waited. "Right this way, sir," he said, taking Tristen's bag.

The heat hit him in the face like a ton of bricks. It was only nine o'clock in the morning and the temperature was scorching hot. The chauffeur showed Tristen to a limousine parked at the curb. He climbed into the back seat and looked around in disbelief. He'd only been inside of a limo on one other occasion and that was at the funeral of his Uncle Grady. As they pulled away from the curb, the partition window separating him from the driver was lowered.

"Excuse me, sir, but there are soft drinks in the ice chest and the control for the stereo is overhead. We should reach your destination in a little under an hour, sir." The driver didn't wait for a reply; he simply raised the window and continued to drive.

Tristen was too nervous and excited to drink anything. To a certain extent he felt like a lame for acting as if he weren't used to things. His mother and father had given him everything that he needed and most of the things that he wanted. This was different though. Tristen would be earning his own money and the fact that this company wanted him was intriguing, not to mention flattering.

The limousine pulled into the parking lot of an elegant glass-structured office space in the Turtle Creek section of Dallas. It looked like one huge, oddly-shaped mirror. There were only three stories, but the square footage was massive. Tristen had done a little research of his own when they'd offered him the job. CrossTech had been built from the ground up by Hayden Cross in the garage of his childhood home. He'd turned a $10,000 loan into a global software company worth upwards of five billion dollars. Tristen Graham's thesis had been based on a more efficient approach to CrossTech's already flourishing infrastructure. He wasn't exactly sure how his thesis had landed on Hayden Cross's desk, but he was grateful.

Tristen smiled silently to himself. He could hear his father's booming voice talking to him from across the dinner table. *"Show me a man that doesn't like to work and doesn't eat pussy at home, and I'll show you a man whose job and wife that I can have!"* His mother hated when his father talked that way, but it was true. He always ended by telling Tristen that in life, a man had to make the tough choices and Tristen embraced those choices.

Tristen grabbed his briefcase and exited the limo as the driver held the door for him. "Good luck, sir," the driver said.

Tristen nodded and made his way towards the large mirror-like doors. He tried not to look around. He refused to look like an anxious tourist at Disney World, but it was next to impossible. As he neared the doors, he noticed that the entire building seemed to be built not with mirrors, but rather, it had been constructed with thick, reinforced glass. The employees had a view of the world outside, but from the outside, no one could see in. The sound of cars whizzing by came to an abrupt halt as he entered the building. The entire building was soundproofed, more than likely to ensure that the employees had the most conducive work environment possible.

"Excuse me, sir, my name is Tristen Graham. I have an interview with Mr. Cross today," he said to the security guard sitting behind a large, semi-circular workstation.

The guard thumbed through a list in front of him and pushed the list towards Tristen. "Sign by your name, please," he said as he began riffling through the *Guns & Ammo* magazine that he'd been reading.

Tristen took his action as rude, but decided against saying anything. The last thing that he needed or wanted was a confrontation on perhaps the biggest day of his life. He simply signed the list and slid it back to the guard, who in turn handed him a visitor's pass.

"Take the elevator to the third floor."

Tristen exited the elevator and approached the receptionist's desk. As he opened his mouth to introduce himself, the secretary interrupted him.

"Right this way, Mr. Graham, they are expecting you."

Tristen tried not to stare, but she was gorgeous. Her skin was smooth milk chocolate and her eyes were a smoky dark brown. Her hair was cropped short, but styled bone straight. The only hint of makeup that she wore was a light, clear lip gloss. Her attire was business chic and her blouse and skirt seemed to hug every curve on her ample body. She displayed a timeless beauty, the kind of beauty that made it hard to believe that she could possibly be a secretary. Her demeanor and her stride said that she took her job very seriously and was proud of the work that she'd done at CrossTech. Tristen watched her hips sway seductively as she led him to where his new employers waited.

"Behind this door is your future, Tristen Graham; don't blow it. And the next time that you meet a woman for the first time, don't stare. Instead, make small talk. We like that." She smiled and winked at Tristen as she opened the door. "Gentlemen, I present to you Mr. Tristen Graham," she announced.

"Thank you, Natalie, that'll be all. Well, Mr. Graham, are you ready to begin the rest of your life?" Hayden Cross asked.

"Yes sir, I believe that I am."

Hayden motioned for Tristen to take a seat at a large cherry wood conference table overlooking a pond and common area. In addition to Hayden, there were two other men present. Caleb Weeks was CrossTech's Vice President and COO and Raj Patel was CrossTech's CFO. Raj had nurtured the company's finances to Fortune 500 status and was a no-nonsense Hindi financier from the old country. Caleb Weeks had come along from when CrossTech was a fledgling business of only six employees. He'd started as a glorified errand boy and had fought his way to the top. His business practices were legendary; Caleb Weeks was both feared and revered. He had proven his loyalty to Hayden Cross ten times over as his right hand man and had been rewarded handsomely for it.

"Mr. Graham, I am very interested in hearing you expound on your idea of integrated logistics for CrossTech," Caleb said.

Tristen stood and reached into his briefcase and produced four folders. They contained a detailed analysis of his ideas, taken directly from his thesis. He handed a folder to each man. "As you will each see, I have given a comprehensive breakdown of the numbers. I've actually run the numbers multiple times. We are a global enterprise software company with upwards of thirty-five hundred employees. For the last twenty-five years, CrossTech has shown a steady increase in profit. However, that profit could be increased exponentially if we implement these techniques. Let me explain," Tristen said.

His delivery was smooth and eloquent, leaving no stone unturned in explaining his plan. By the time that he was finished, each of the men present was in awe of the fresh-faced Tristen Graham. Raj Patel could see dollar signs, Caleb Weeks saw raw talent, and Hayden Cross saw the future of his company in his new hire.

Hayden stood and cleared his throat. "Tristen, if this new software of yours works, then you, my young friend, will be a very rich man; I'm going to make sure of it. Raj will show you to HR so that you can sign your employment contracts, after which Caleb will show you around the complex. Now, if you will excuse me, I have a flight to catch," he said, extending his hand.

Tristen shook his hand sternly. "Mr. Cross, thank you for the opportunity, and I promise you won't regret your decision," Tristen said.

"I'm sure that I won't, son, I'm sure that I won't. Caleb, I will call you when I land in California. Remember that we have a conference call at 4:00 p.m. Central time."

"Sure thing, boss," Caleb said, walking Hayden to the door.

The door opened and Tristen caught a glimpse of Natalie before Caleb closed the door. He'd never been a womanizer, but he wanted to know more about Natalie. There hadn't been many black women at M.I.T. and the one's that *had* been there weren't interested in him. He was too dark for their tastes. They'd wanted Caucasian men with trust funds and demure demeanors. For some reason, they believed that the darker the man, the more aggressive. That couldn't have been further from the truth, but it had served to keep Tristen dedicated to his studies. He hadn't felt the need to prove to anyone that he was worthy of their attention. Natalie seemed to be different. She seemed to be a genuinely nice person and he wanted to get to know her better. Tristen tried to convince himself that it had nothing to do with the fact that she had an amazing body.

"Mr. Graham, you're going to be a star here at CrossTech if this software works. I'm astonished at the sheer brilliance of the idea. Shall we?" Raj said, showing Tristen to the door.

They walked out into the third floor foyer and headed towards HR. Inside, they sat and the Human Resources Director gave Tristen a packet containing everything he needed to get him started on his journey at CrossTech. It explained his salary and his perks. He was also to be given a bi-weekly stipend for six months until his finances were stable. He smiled as she explained to him that his living arrangements had been taken care of by CrossTech. Every senior level executive in the firm stayed in what was affectionately known as Billionaire's Row. It was a lavish high rise condominium complex owned and operated by CrossTech. Any amenity that a person could think of was supplied in Billionaire's Row. The staff fought for a spot in the high rise and it was rumored that the waiting list to get into the complex was two years long. Many of the employees that fought for those spots never made it to Billionaire's Row because they didn't last that long. The work load at CrossTech was heavy and very demanding. Most of them had either quit or were hospitalized from the stress, only to be terminated as ineffective when they returned to work. With more than three thousand employees globally, it was easy to understand how the pressure could mount.

By the time that he was finished conversing with HR, Tristen's head was spinning. This job was too good to be true and the old adage kept playing over in his head: *if it sounds too good to be true, then it probably is*. Tristen stared down the long glass corridor and sighed in relief. The statement that Hayden Cross had made only moments earlier was truer than he could've known. This was the beginning of the rest of his life.

Chapter 3

Natalie Sinclair had been working at CrossTech for six years and loved every minute of it. Besides the old black janitor Mr. Wilkins, Natalie had been the only African American at the firm until Tristen had come along. She'd made her share of mistakes since she'd been hired - namely, Brennen Goldstein. He was the project manager over in the IT department and had his choice of any number of women within the confines of CrossTech. He was twenty-nine years old and probably one of the most eligible bachelors in the firm.

Brennen was from old money; his grandparents had come to the United States from the old country and settled in New York City like so many other immigrants. His grandfather and grandmother both had been accountants for the Mafia with a penchant and ability to skim money from them without their knowledge. This practice, although dangerous, had proven to be very profitable. They'd opened business after business until their money had swollen to unbelievable heights. Brennen Goldstein carried himself with the same cocksure swagger that had proven fatal to his grandfather. His dark features and docile demeanor belied his shark-like tactics. He was known as an asshole throughout the company and he seemed to thrive on it. Brennen was young, good-looking and rich, a mixture that served him both financially and sexually.

Natalie had unwittingly fallen into his charming snare, and by the time she'd realized that she was being used, it was too late. After Brennen, she'd vowed to keep her eyes open and her legs closed. He felt like Natalie belonged to him and she found it quite amusing. Even after his intentions had been made evident, he'd still had the audacity to call her relentlessly and show up at her apartment unannounced. He'd even cornered her in the hallway of her apartment building, drunk and professing his love.

"My parents would disinherit me if they knew that I was in love with someone like you. I don't care though; let's make a baby," he'd said.

"Brennen, you're drunk and you're crazy. I'm not making a baby with you."

"You should be happy I'm giving you the time of day. What do you want me to do, pay for it? How about if I get you a loft on Billionaire's Row, would you like that?" Brennen asked. His words were slurred and he reeked of liquor. He groped her repeatedly, causing her to drop her bags to the floor.

"Brennen, you really need to go home and sleep this off. I know it's hard for your little ego to grasp the fact that I'm not interested, but sweetie, I'm not interested in the least bit."

"You know you want this!" he said. He stepped back and unbuckled his belt, allowing his slacks and boxers to fall to the floor. His flaccid penis barely cleared the bush of brown stringy hair that surrounded it. It resembled a small grub worm wearing a flesh-colored turtleneck sweater. Natalie burst into hysterical laughter. "Aww, look at it, Brennen, it's so little and cute. Pull your pants up; you're embarrassing yourself," she said sarcastically.

"Either fuck me or look for another job, you black bitch!" he spat.

His words burned into her flesh like a hot knife sliding through butter, but she refused to give him the satisfaction of seeing her discomfort. Again she laughed, but this time when she spoke, her words were cold and ruthless. "Listen, you little Jewish prick, my building has security cameras. How will you explain this in court while I'm suing you for sexual harassment? Your best bet would probably be to go home and sleep it off as I suggested. I'm going to forget that you called me a black bitch and you're going to stay away from me. If you see me walking down the street, you'd better cross to the other side, because if I get the feeling that you're being anything less than a gentleman, this tape will go straight to my lawyer and I will own your gefilte fish-eating ass. Now scram!" she barked.

Natalie laughed to herself. That had been an eon ago and Brennen Goldstein was terrified of her. Tristen Graham was a welcome sight in the world of tech-savvy gurus. There were whispers about CrossTech having a thin veil of racism hanging over it. With the exception of Brennen Goldstein, she hadn't witnessed any of it personally. Tristen was the African American messiah of CrossTech, and Natalie hoped that he could breathe some much-needed life into the predominantly white corporation.

Chapter 4
June

Tristen's head was spinning as Caleb escorted him throughout the CrossTech complex. The building was equipped with everything that a person could imagine in order to have a productive work day. The multiplex not only held the common workplace maze of offices and cubicles, but there was a gym with all of the latest equipment, an indoor Olympic-sized swimming pool with a Jacuzzi, a full basketball court, and a sauna for relaxation. There was a large café on site that catered both breakfast and lunch. CrossTech even offered free child care on site, which made for less excuses and more convenience. After they'd toured the entire building, Caleb led Tristen to his new office. Every piece of wood in the office was made of the finest walnut and the large picture windows not only wrapped around the office but stretched from floor to ceiling. The furnishings were Euro chic and very modern, with accentuated curves and lines.

"What do you think, Tristen?" Caleb asked.

"It's nice. I can see the whole complex from this office."

"I must warn you, you'll probably get a lot of dirty looks. This particular office is a hot commodity. It sits between my office and Raj's office and is directly across from Hayden's office, so the suck-ups are going to be out for your blood," Caleb said.

Tristen gave Caleb a puzzled look. He hadn't counted on making enemies, let alone on his first day. He hadn't exactly taken the job to make friends either, but he didn't want to come in making waves. "If the guys are going to ostracize me because of corporate's choice of office location, then that's their choice." He shrugged and walked to the plush leather high backed swivel chair behind his desk. He turned his back to Caleb and stared out of the window.

"Why don't I let you get acquainted with your new office? I will come back for you at lunch time. By then I should have your security badge and amenities."

"Amenities?" Tristen asked, turning to face Caleb.

"Yes, amenities. When our upper level employees start, we give them certain things to make their experience here at CrossTech more…how should I say…pleasurable."

Tristen turned again to gaze out of the window. He heard the sound of Caleb quietly closing the door. *Damn, if they are hating on an office, wait until I put this mind to work*, he thought.

Tristen leaned back in his chair, running his hands along the curves of the soft, luxurious leather. He swiveled in his chair much like a child might upon visiting his father's office. He looked around his office, mesmerized. Tristen had by no stretch of the imagination come from poverty stricken origins, but his parents had never lived an ostentatious lifestyle either. He felt rich, he felt luxurious, and most of all, he felt powerful. He would do as he always had: work hard to prove himself and make the doubters angry.

His philosophy was different than most of the young people his age. They believed that there was plenty of time to pick a career. But Tristen thought the opposite. He wanted to settle into a position and solidify himself as a leader at an early age instead of slaving away his entire life. He, unlike his young counterparts, didn't believe that he had haters. He'd heard it so much throughout high school and college that he was numb to the word. Haters didn't exist; only jealousy, envy, and greed existed. He believed that people disliked you because they were jealous of you for whatever reasons, but they didn't hate you.

His cousin Toby swore that everyone on the face of God's green earth was hating on him. If he got a new pair of sneakers, people were hating. If he started dating a new woman, people were hating. He said it so much that Tristen had actually gotten used to it. Before he could finish speaking, Tristen was usually completing his sentences. "Man, you see how that bitch nigga looking at these new J's?" Toby would say.

"Let me guess, he's hating, huh?" Tristen would counter sarcastically.

After their brief exchange, they would both burst into raucous laughter. Tristen laughed at the memory. He hadn't been gone a full twenty-four hours, but he missed his family tremendously.

A light tap at his office door brought Tristen out of his daydream. "Come in," he said.

"Hello, Mr. Graham, is there anything that you need?"

"Call me Tristen, and no, Natalie, there is nothing that I need," he said.

"So how do you like it so far? Have you had any problems yet?"

"I haven't had an opportunity to move around enough to have any problems. Should I expect problems?"

Natalie stared at Tristen as if trying to see into his soul. In actuality, she was trying to gauge whether she could trust him or not. If Tristen was an Uncle Tom, he would run immediately to Caleb Weeks and she would probably be fired. With as much time as Natalie had in at CrossTech, she was privy to a lot of information, some of which was unintentionally obtained, but she had it just the same. "Tristen, can I trust you?" Natalie asked.

"What do you mean? I mean, if you have something to say, then it goes no further than this office."

"Okay, I believe you. Listen, you're a very bright young man with an even brighter future in front of you, so I want to be completely honest with you. This is a fantastic company, but there are some things that you have to watch out for," Natalie said.

"Yes, Caleb kind of pre-warned me about the hatred that I'd receive because of the office."

"It's deeper than that, Tristen. Caleb is okay, but he tends to operate with blinders on, and in my opinion, that makes him just as guilty as the rest of them," Natalie said, shaking her head.

"You make it seem like it's some type of great conspiracy or something."

"It's not a conspiracy; it's cut and dried. There are some racist-ass people in this company that will do all that they can to make sure that you don't advance in CrossTech," Natalie said. Her voice was a hushed whisper, dripping with caustic foreboding.

"Well, I appreciate your concern, but I believe that my education and innovative ideas will outweigh all of that."

"If that's what you believe, then more power to you, Tristen but at least keep your eyes open. There is a lot of money to be made with this company, and as Biggie said, 'more money, more problems'. You may want to write this down," she instructed.

Tristen smiled. Her tone was firm but gentle. He reached into his briefcase and retrieved a leather-bound notepad and gold Cross ink pen. "Okay, so what am I writing down?"

"Write these names down: David Ganzelle, Brennen Goldstein, Sean Westbury, Frances Trimble, and Caleb Weeks. These five men are dangerous, Tristen, and it would behoove you to pay close attention when in their company," Natalie whispered.

"I don't understand. I - " he started, but a knock at his door stifled his questions.

Natalie stood and straightened her clothes. She walked to the door and opened it and there stood Caleb Weeks, surprised that Natalie was opening Tristen's door. "I will have a list of car dealerships in the area ready for you by the time your lunch hour is over, Mr. Graham. Will there be anything else?" she asked, winking at Tristen.

"Yes, Natalie, a short list of clothiers here in Dallas would be great, thank you."

"No problem. Enjoy your lunch. Excuse me, Mr. Weeks," she said as she slithered past her employer.

Caleb Weeks smiled at Natalie. He was rather fond of her. She brought a much-needed ray of sunshine to CrossTech. He didn't trust her, but he liked her. "Here you go, Ace: a company supplied laptop, iPad, iPod, and a company phone. The phone is to be kept on your person at all times. This is your security card to get into CrossTech and these are the keys to your condo." He put all of the items onto Tristen's desk.

The two men walked towards the cafeteria, making small talk along the way until a large room just shy of the café caught Tristen's attention. "What room is that, Caleb?" he asked, pointing to the area.

"That's the auditorium. At certain times, Hayden or I may need to address the company as a whole, so we use the auditorium. It's large enough to hold everyone in the Dallas office and it's also patched into our remote offices by satellite. So we're able to address everyone without the need to hold multiple meetings. We call it The Slaughter House. Come on, let's get some food before these mongrels eat it all."

When they stepped into the café, Tristen couldn't believe his eyes. It was as if he'd stepped into a five star restaurant. It was sectioned off by meats, fresh vegetables, fresh fruit, breads, and desserts. There was even a section for those on their obvious health kicks. The sign read "The Green Room" and it held dishes like kale shakes and low calorie tofu cakes. Tristen winced from the thought of the taste. He was an old-fashioned type of eater; meat and potatoes would suit him just fine. He rubbed his stomach. He hadn't realized that he was so hungry, but his stomach growled loudly over the chatter inside the cafeteria.

"You must be hungry, Ace?" Caleb asked, smiling.

Tristen nodded. He didn't know why he was so embarrassed by the comment, but he was. An array of hired servers, mostly Caucasians that stared at Tristen as if he'd somehow wandered into the wrong area, served him as he pointed out what dishes he wanted to try. Caleb led Tristen to a large round table where four other men sat with Raj Patel. He was introduced to David Ganzelle, Brennen Goldstein, Sean Westbury, and Frances Trimble, the very same men that Natalie had only moments ago had him scrawl down on a list for safe keeping. They joined the men for lunch and he listened intently as the six men shared stories of things that had happened at CrossTech in the past.

When Brennen Goldstein began to mention Natalie as if she were somehow his property, Caleb Weeks shot him a knowing glance. He hadn't thought that Tristen picked up on it, but he had. Tristen let it slide off of his shoulders because as far as he knew, Natalie could have been the company slut. She hadn't presented herself as such, but Tristen was intelligent enough to realize that first impressions were usually overseen by representatives; their truer selves were revealed later.

"Okay, Tristen, let me get you over to the condo so that we can get you settled in," Caleb said.

"Settled in? I don't have any of my things here from home. I was under the impression that today was like an interview and I would have time to go back to Jersey to get my things."

"Anything that you need will be supplied by CrossTech. Feel free to have one of your family members bring anything else down that you need. We will pay for travel, of course, but we need for you to be working by the morning. We have a contract pending with the government that you could be very instrumental in pushing through. Now if you don't mind, let me show you to your apartment," Caleb said.

Tristen didn't utter a word, but his disappointment showed clearly on his face. He had wanted to return home and spend time with his parents. He was silent as they rode to Billionaire's Row in the back of the limousine.

When they arrived, they pulled up to an enormous high rise building. The white stone building with its baroque style ornamentation gave the structure a very expensive feel. Tristen stared up at the building in awe. They walked into the lobby, where brass and marble adorned the lavish atrium. Sheer white curtains flowed and billowed from ceiling to floor. With its long, rustic marble countertops and perfectly-dressed concierge staff, the lobby looked more like an exquisite hotel than a condominium tower.

They walked to the elevators and were greeted along the way by an overly courteous staff, which Tristen found to be pleasant, but they were too animated. Their smiles were plastered across anxious faces eager for either tips or compliments, and Tristen found it hard to distinguish which. The polished brass elevator doors slid open and a woman's voice came to life over the loud speaker.

"First floor," she sang.

Tristen and Caleb stepped to the side to let a tall, lithe blond with oversized breasts exit. Tristen stood motionless, gawking at the woman as if hypnotized.

"That's Casey. You like that? She's a nympho too, nasty little freak that will let you do anything that you want to her - for a price, of course," Caleb said with a sly grin.

Casey sauntered away clad in a black and fuchsia two-piece legging and sport bra set. Her fuchsia Air Max sneakers squeaked along the intricately-designed marble floor, undoubtedly en route to the fitness center.

Tristen stepped into the elevator and leaned against the mirrored wall. He peered at the control panel. There were thirty-eight floors in the building, not including the large P that he assumed must have meant penthouse. Subconsciously, he counted the buttons and noticed that there was no thirteenth floor. "Why is there no number thirteen, Caleb?" he asked.

"Most people see the number thirteen as bad luck. Architects are people too, so it stands to reason that they would have their share of superstitions. I have never been in a high rise building and seen a thirteenth floor, have you?"

Tristen thought for a long while before dismissing the question. There had been too many field trips and errand runs to recollect every building's elevator control panel. Caleb pushed a button and they began their ascent to the thirty-fifth floor.

"Mr. Cross is in the penthouse. There is no way to get there unless invited or unless Mr. Cross gives you an access key, which I doubt, so don't get caught in the penthouse," Caleb warned.

Tristen was silently fuming. Caleb's warning for him not to be caught in the penthouse seemed like a veiled implication. He wasn't one to jump to assumptions, so he quickly let the statement pass. "Thirty-fifth floor," the automated voice said in her melodic tone.

Caleb led Tristen out into the foyer of the thirty-fifth floor. The same decorative tile that titivated the lobby of Billionaire's Row lined the floors of this floor. The heels of Caleb's Tom Ford loafers clacked and echoed against the cold stone tile as he made his way to the door of 3502. He opened the door and handed the keys to Tristen. They walked inside and Tristen was breathless.

When HR had talked to him about the condominium, he had envisioned a small one or a two bedroom apartment, but he was in no way prepared for what his eyes beheld. The space was huge, approximately 3900 square feet, and opened up to the Dallas skyline. There were two large windows that ran the length of two walls and opened the apartment up to the brightness of the scorching Texas sun. Tristen fell more and more in love with the place as Caleb gave him the tour. There were four larger than life bedrooms with three bathrooms. The master bedroom had its own private bath unlike anything that he'd ever seen. There was only a frosted glass wall between the bedroom area and the bathroom. The sink and toilet were in their own space while the shower and tub were also separated by a frosted glass partition. The tub was raised and freestanding, and although Tristen found it to be very elegant, the shower is what caught his attention. The shower head hung from the ceiling and there were also water jets that sprayed from two directions. The water was remotely controlled and there were no knobs to control the water in the bathroom.

They went into the living room, where Caleb opened the sliding glass door leading to the balcony. Outside, Tristen walked the balcony, noticing that he could almost see the entirety of his enormous condo from the balcony. He looked over the hand carved, waist high stone wall onto the street below. The cars and people on the street underneath them looked like ants as they scurried along going about their day.

"So what do you think, Tristen?" Caleb asked.

"I love it; it's a really nice place. It seems a little expensive though. I'm not sure if I can afford it."

Caleb's hearty laughter wafted through the afternoon air. His throaty chuckle was a little uncalled for, but Tristen was more confused than annoyed. "May I ask what's so funny?" he asked.

"Mr. Cross is a very wealthy man, Tristen. It was easier for him to simply purchase this building to house his employees than to have them spread out. So you see, you have no rent, no utilities, not so much as a cable bill. You merely have to produce for us at CrossTech and you're taken care of," Caleb said.

Tristen's head was spinning. He walked inside and looked around. He couldn't believe his ears or his eyes. He walked to the bookshelf, which looked more like a fancy centerpiece, and thumbed through the selection of books. *The 48 Laws of Power* by Robert Greene caught his attention. Also among the selection were *The Prince* by Niccolo Machiavelli, *The Art of War* by Sun Tzu, *The Communist* by Karl Marx, and *The Social Contract* by Jean Jacques Rousseau. The selection excited him.. He'd on many occasions listened to his father give micro dissertations on many of the same titles. He was eager to dive into the pages of one of the books as soon as he was able to get rid of Caleb. As if sensing his eagerness to get settled in, Caleb walked to him and put his hand on his shoulder.

"Why don't I let you get settled into your new place? Do you smell that, Tristen? Can you smell it?" he asked.

A look of confusion washed across Tristen's face. "Smell what, sir?"

"Success, my friend, success! Welcome home; welcome to CrossTech."

Chapter 5

Toby Graham sat in the small smoky room, sweating profusely. He stared at the cards in his hand and wiped the sweat from his brow.

"Well, Toby, lay it on the line. What you got, playa?" Esco asked. He was a short stocky man with a scar running from the center of his forehead to the tip of his nose. It was rumored that he'd been killed when he was in his early twenties and that he'd been too mean to die. Whatever the case, Toby knew that there had to be some truth to it because Esco was, by any definition, the devil himself. Along with Toby and Esco were Creep and Stacks, two more unsavory characters with the reputations to match.

"Yeah, my nigga, run that shit!" Creep said.

"Read 'em and weep, son," Toby said. He laid his cards on the table. He had scored the highest possible hand that he could get in poker: the infamous royal flush. The Ace, King, Queen, Jack and ten of hearts all spread nicely on the table before him.

The three men at the table stared at the cards in disbelief. Toby had always been the brunt of many jokes in New Jersey's gambling underworld. He had to be perhaps one of the unluckiest people to ever gamble, but he kept coming back for more punishment. After all of his own money was squandered, he would always borrow, which in turn led him to do other unlawful things in order to pay back the money that he'd borrowed to fuel his gambling addiction. He'd never been a big time criminal, maybe a petty theft here and there, nothing serious enough to warrant a huge amount of jail time. His luck, it seemed, had finally turned around and he was sitting around a table with three gangsters with a total pot of four thousand dollars. Pretty damned good, considering that he'd only come to the table with the one hundred dollars that he'd borrowed from Tristen before he'd left for Texas.

Toby smiled greedily with his eyes trained on the array of bills strewn before him. He reached in and raked the bills towards him with trembling hands. "Well, my niggas, it's been nice, but I think I'm out," he said, stuffing his pockets with money.

"You finally had a decent night and you're just going to dip like that? You're not going to give us an opportunity to win some of our money back?" Creep asked.

Toby stood up from the table and smiled at the men as he backed up towards the door. Nervously, he reached behind him in search of the doorknob that would lead him to freedom.

Esco produced a small caliber handgun and placed it on the table. "Hold up, Toby, let me ask you a question. How is it that you spread a royal flush with the Ace of hearts, but I got the Ace of hearts in my hand, bitch nigga?" he asked, turning his Ace over.

Toby's face dropped. He'd hoped that by the time his iniquity had been discovered, he would've been long gone. His hand reached the doorknob at the same time as Creep and Stacks reached for their pistols.

"You cheated, nigga?" Stacks barked.

Toby slid through the door and slammed it behind him. He'd barely let the knob loose when the first shot pinged through the thick metal door. He ducked low, looking down the alley toward the Newark city lights. He ran in the opposite direction, towards the darkness. He was tired of losing, tired of being the butt of their jokes, and he'd finally gotten even. He heard the door burst open and then he heard the men shouting. Their words sounded like a jumbled mess of curses, taunts, and threats. Toby heard a boom coupled with the sound of bullets ricocheting off brick whirring past his head. The slugs dinged the metal of lowered fire escapes and the crackle of the gunfire seemed to be getting closer.

"You're a dead man, Toby! I want my fucking money!" Stacks shouted.

Toby's legs felt like jelly as he ran, but he had to keep pushing. The three men chasing him would have no problem killing him if they caught up to him and he had no plans of dying any time soon. He turned a corner and then another and still another, and when he looked back, there was no one there. Ahead of him, he could make out what appeared to be a trash dumpster tucked into the darkness. In the distance, he could hear footsteps approaching so he made his way silently to the dumpster and slithered inside. Toby lifted the lid a couple of inches to see if he could spot his pursuers. They stood at the intersection of the alleyway and the street, looking around in bewilderment, guns in hand.

Toby lowered the lid carefully and burrowed underneath the trash in the bin, leaving nothing exposed but his eyes. The smell of the garbage was horrible and he retched, vomiting in his mouth a little bit. The rancid odor of rotting fruit and stale bread invaded his nostrils, but he didn't dare move for fear of death. Something was crawling on him, making its way up his pants leg, slowly foraging through the hair on his legs, but he remained still. In the quiet of the dumpster, there were only two sounds present: his heartbeat and God's voice.

Toby had never been an overly religious person, but he knew how to listen. He remembered his Aunt Ruth telling him that when things got bad, really bad, God had a way of revealing things to you. Toby had wanted to know, as he and Tristen sat on the edge of their beds late one night, why God had to wait until things were bad to reveal them. She'd said that it wasn't that He waited until things were bad; it was that man had a bad habit of not really listening until things got bad and that God had to catch us just before we fell the hardest. She said if you got still and listened, really listened, that everything you needed for a healthy, prosperous, blessing-filled life was always in front of man. She said that man had to learn to listen to God and stop relying on the words of each other, and she had always been right.

So Toby got even more still and listened, but that voice never came. He did, however, hear the sound of footsteps approaching. Gravel and broken glass crackled under the weight of slow steps. The footsteps stopped in front of the dumpster, and moments later, the lid was yanked open and Creep peered inside. Toby could see him as clear as day. As he lowered the top, Toby chuckled inwardly to himself. He thought of some of the corny phrases that he and Tristen had used as children. They'd play their childhood games and whenever they didn't want to die, they'd always say that they had their force field on. He felt as though the trash had been his force field - a shield made of rotten vegetables, old tampons, maggots, and utility bills.

Somewhere between the time that Creep had peeped into the trashcan and now, Toby had fallen asleep amidst the half-eaten sandwiches and candy wrappers. A sliver of daylight pierced the small gap between the dumpster and lid, beaming on Toby's eyes. He tried to turn to snuggle deeper into his bed until he realized where he was. The brevity of his situation hit his mind. He needed to get home and tell his uncle and aunt what had gone on. Neither of the hoodlums knew where he stayed, but it wouldn't be that hard to find out. People on the street were hungry, and for the right price, they would give up their own mothers.

Toby lifted the lid slowly and looked around. Toby climbed out of the dumpster and walked towards Broad

Street. He touched his pocket for reassurance that the previous night hadn't been some type of nightmare, and the money was really there. Both of his pockets were lined with the $4,000 that he'd cheated the men out of. He reached into his back pocket, removed his cell phone, and dialed Tristen's number. It was early, but Tristen would be awake. Since they were children, Tristen had always had the same schedule: wake up at five o'clock, shower, eat, go jogging, workout, shower, eat, and start his day.

A groggy-voiced Tristen answered the phone. "Hello?"

"Damn, Cuzzo, Dallas got you lazy already, huh?" Toby said cheerfully. His demeanor belied the fact that he carried the putrid odor of fear and garbage.

"Nah, we are an hour behind y'all. It's still mad early here."

"My bad, dawg. Listen, I need a favor, my G," Toby said. He never liked to ask Tristen for favors, but in this instance he *needed* him.

"Name it, Cuzz. You know if I can do it, you got it."

"I need to disappear for a while. I have to get the fuck out of Newark, Cuzzo. I've gotten into some heavy shit that could cost me my life. Plus I don't want Auntie Ruth and Uncle Chester getting involved, you feel me?" Toby said.

"You got money for the plane? I can wire you some money for a ticket if you need me to."

"Nah, I'm straight, bruh. I'm going to go home and pack and I will be on the first thing smoking up outta here today. I will call you later with the details," Toby said.

"Alright, just let me know. I get off at five o'clock - six o'clock your time."

"Fa sho', Tristen, thanks, my nig," Toby said.

"Not a problem, hit me later."

Toby hit the end button and put the phone back in his pocket. Dallas would be different for him. He wanted to go there because besides his cousin, nobody would know him. He could get a fresh start, a new lease on life.

As he rounded the corner, he saw a mass of confusion, women in housecoats with head scarves on, men in pajamas and basketball shorts, mothers holding crying infants, all standing by watching something. Toby could see police officers and ambulances as he got closer. On the corner of Broad Street and the alleyway, two bodies lay sprawled out. They were both dead, crumpled on top of one another. The blood that had been running from their wounds had now began to coagulate and had turned a deep, dark, purplish burgundy. Their bodies were riddled with bullets, and as the police tried to disperse the crowd, the entire picture came into view. It was Stacks and Creep, and just at the base of their feet, written in their own blood, were the words TOBY YOU'RE NEXT.

Chapter 6

Tristen had dozed off after he talked to Toby, but now a thunderous knock jarred him from his peaceful slumber. He staggered to the front door and looked through the peep hole. "Who is it?"

"It's Natalie. Open the door, Tristen, you don't want to be late on your first official day," she said in a chipper tone.

Tristen opened the door to see Natalie standing at his front door dressed for business. Her navy blue and white sailor's dress seemed only to accentuate her curves and her breasts jutted forward, threatening to burst through the thin material. Her ebony skin glistened and her eyes beamed from excitement. Natalie's navy blue Christian Louboutin stilettos only served to make her derrière seem larger than life.

She walked in and handed him a cup of coffee from Dunkin Donuts. Tristen hadn't noticed his morning hard-on until he followed Natalie's gaze. "You'd better do something with that monster, Tristen," she said seductively.

He blushed from the embarrassment. He'd never met a woman as forward and as open as Natalie. Her personality dripped sexuality. The way she walked, talked, and moved turned Tristen on and his manhood throbbed with lustful anticipation. He sipped his coffee and headed for the shower. "Give me a few minutes and I will be ready," he said, disappearing behind the frosted glass.

Tristen stepped out of his boxers and started the shower with the remote control. Tristen bathed quickly, afraid to touch his genitals too long for fear of an explosion. He let the hot water cascade over his shortly-cropped hair, lifting his face to meet the warm moisture.

When he opened his eyes, Natalie was standing in the doorway of the bathroom with a lustful smirk on her face. Her eyes alternated between his eyes and his penis. Tristen's manhood pulsated uncontrollably, bouncing upward towards his stomach as he reached for a towel to cover his nakedness. Natalie giggled at Tristen's shyness. She'd never witnessed a grown man react that way about being naked in front of a woman.

"We might need to have a quickie before we leave for work," she said, licking her lips with her eyes trained on the bulge in the towel.

"Yeah, that is most definitely not going to happen," he said.

"And why is that? Are you gay, Tristen?"

Tristen ripped the towel from his waist to reveal himself. The full length of his penis was massive and thick veins coursed through it from the base of his shaft to the tip of it. "Do I look gay, Natalie? If I was gay, then your body, although fully clothed, wouldn't have me so erect."

"I don't know, it's a lot of that down low stuff going on."

"Well, I assure you that I am not gay," Tristen said.

"So what is it? Don't you find me attractive, Mr. Graham?"

"You're very attractive and I'm attracted to you, but I can't," he said.

"Why not? Do you think I'm not good enough for you?" She pouted. Natalie knew that she had a nice body. She didn't have any children and she took care of her body. She worked out in the gym two hours a day and she made sure that she ate healthy. Natalie was by no means promiscuous or easy, but she wasn't used to being turned down by men. She usually did the turning down.

"Why are you pouting? Well, if you must know, I'm a virgin," he said.

"Bullshit!"

"No, seriously! I guess between my studies, church, and my morals, loose sex just wasn't high on my priority list," Tristen said sarcastically.

"I didn't mean it like that," she said, moving towards him seductively, taking his phallus in her hands. "I just meant that it seems a shame to let all of this, um, deliciousness go to waste." She could feel Tristen's heartbeat pulsating through her fingertips. It beat rhythmically against her soft skin as she began to stroke it gently.

Tristen pulled away slowly and dropped his head. "With all due respect, Natalie, I don't want to do this. To you it may sound old fashioned and naïve, but I want to save myself for the woman that I fall in love with."

Natalie kissed Tristen on the cheek and left him to get dressed. Actually she didn't think that it was old fashioned; she thought that it was cute. She'd never met a man quite like Tristen Graham. He was handsome, motivated, smart *and* a virgin. She would respect the fact that he wanted to wait on his Mrs. Right, but his honesty had caused a self-imposed catechism. His candor had given her plenty to think about and the old adage rang true: *out of the mouth of babes.*

After Tristen was finished dressing, they exited his apartment in silence, each wrapped in their own thoughts. Natalie's thoughts were centered on trying to undo the damage of her unwanted advances. Tristen fought with himself internally. He wanted Natalie in the worst way. She was beautiful, had an incredible body, and she was attracted to *him*.

The elevator reached the garage and Natalie scurried towards her car. Her heels clicked against the concrete floor and echoed hauntingly. Tristen caught up to her and touched her arm gently just as she made it to her vehicle.

"Natalie, wait. I hope things aren't going to be weird between you and me."

That statement was precisely why she was somewhat intimidated by him. She had only known him twenty-four hours and she'd violated him. She sat behind her steering wheel and lowered her head. "No, Tristen, things won't be weird. I just don't want you to be mad at me."

Tristen looked at Natalie as if she'd somehow lost her mind. He'd never been in this position and it made him squirm uncomfortably. For some strange reason beyond comprehension, he felt it necessary to explain his mindset. Natalie navigated towards CrossTech as Tristen talked. "Natalie, let me explain something to you. I know that I think differently from most young men my age, but this is the way I see it. We spend our entire lives as humans, running from person to person in search of the perfect mate. Along the way, we give those people tiny bits and pieces of ourselves and by the time we finally meet our soulmate, we're unable to give them one hundred percent of ourselves because we've scattered those pieces around the universe to all of the wrong people. I just want to make sure that I am totally able to not only give my true love my one hundred percent, but also give her the gift of my mind, body and soul. I know it sounds corny, but that's who I am," Tristen said, shrugging his shoulders.

Truth of the matter was, she didn't find it corny at all; she found it to be extremely sweet and sincere. But rather than sound disingenuous, she chose to remain silent. She smiled to herself. *I guess I will just have to make Tristen see me as his one true love*, she thought. She not only saw him as a challenge, but she also had never been with a virgin. Men spent their entire lives on a mission to conquer women; it was her turn now. She would have him no matter the cost.

Chapter 7

Toby squeezed into the middle seat between two women and tried to settle in. He pulled his *XXL* magazine from his backpack and thumbed through the pages. The flight from Newark to Dallas would take a little under three hours and Toby wasn't looking forward to it. Beside him next to the window was a young woman barely twenty years old that had obviously had too many donuts and not enough time on a treadmill. Toby eyed the woman curiously. To see her perched uncomfortably in the small seat was painful to witness. She wiggled awkwardly in her seat, trying unsuccessfully to find a comfy position. On Toby's left was a hefty, thick-necked woman with snow white hair that looked as if she only answered to the title of "Big Mama". She stared into the pages of her King James Bible, her eyes darting from word to word as if to refresh her mind with material that had already been memorized. She hummed a spiritual hymn quietly to herself, lulling Toby into a tranquil state. Unbeknownst to him, he had begun to rock softly in his seat to her spiritual melody. Big Mama noticed his rhythm and patted him gently on his hand.

Her touch startled Toby and he jumped slightly. "It's okay, child, when the spirit moves you, you s'posed to move," she said gently.

Something about her touch eased his mind, which was clouded with thoughts of the future. On one hand, Toby wanted a change; he wanted to use Texas as his new start. But on the other hand, he still had his gambling bug. In gambling houses, there was always chatter about where the best gambling dens were and South Dallas had come up in conversation on more than one occasion. He closed his eyes and tried to relax.

Toby could hear the engines of the plane roar to life and soon they were backing out of the terminal and taxiing down the runway. The flight captain's voice came over the loud speaker and began to speak, but Toby could barely hear him. The sound of the plane's tires beating against the thick concrete airstrip all but drowned out the sound of the captain's voice. As Toby leaned back in his seat and tried to settle in for the flight, he felt the familiar feel of the old lady's soft touch on his skin.

"Do you know Jesus Christ, child?" she asked.

"Yeah, I know him. I know that He never gave a damn about me. I know that He likes to play cruel jokes on the unsuspecting."

"Rest your mind, child. If it's got sin in it or wrongdoing, it ain't Jesus. He's a loving and compassionate God. He's a miracle worker and healer of souls, baby."

"Yeah, I hear you," Toby said. He shifted in his seat uncomfortably and opened his magazine to escape her truth.

"If you don't mind me asking, son, why are you so angry at the Lawd?"

Toby thought for a long while before answering. He'd dealt with enough holy rollers in Jersey to know that no matter what he said or what his reasoning, she would talk until her point was proven. He had every right to be angry, but no one really understood. *Maybe I don't express myself properly because people don't seem to get it,* he thought. "Ma'am, with all due respect, what kind of God allows a two-year-old little boy's mother to leave him, and then, just when he's getting over that bullshit, snatches his father's life too? My whole life is a waste. I ain't shit and ain't gonna never be shit. I'm just biding my time on this rock until somebody takes me out of my misery."

"You're hurting and I understand perfectly, but Jesus loves you. He will never put a burden on you heavier than you can bear. All you have to do is believe in Him, give Him your life, child, and He will make it better. Do you want to be rich?" she asked.

At the sound of the word, Toby perked up. "Yeah, who doesn't want to be rich?" he asked.

"Riches await you, baby, He can make you richer than you've ever imagined, but you have to work for it. You have to have faith in Him, and if you take one step towards Him, He'll take two steps towards you. But you have to believe. Do you believe that Jesus died on the cross for your sins?"

"Honestly, ma'am, I don't know what I believe. I think I'm cursed and God doesn't know I exist." Toby's eyes welled over, threatening to expel his pent-up tears.

She rubbed his hand softly, regretting that she was unable to hold him close and soothe his troubled soul. She reached into her purse at the base of her seat and rustled around until she located a small, crumpled business card. "This is my card, baby. I am an elder at New El Bethel Baptist Church. When you get to Dallas, if you need anything, make sure you call me. We have a wonderful youth ministry outreach program and I would love to get you involved. If you allow me to, I would love to show you some of God's wonderful works. My name is Mattie Daniels, but everyone calls me Mother. Now get you some rest, honey, we have a long trip ahead of us."

Toby closed his eyes, but there was no rest. He needed to know what she meant by riches beyond his wildest dreams. *Is it really as simple as believing in a God that you can't hear or see to become a rich man? If so*, Toby thought, *I really have been wasting my time and my life.*

Chapter 8

Frances Trimble dressed slowly and watched his wife's reflection in the mirror. She snuggled deeper into their Martha Stewart down comforter, trying to escape the faint noise of her husband's morning ritual. Frances - or Frank, as he preferred to be called - looked at his wife with a mixture of adoration and disdain. Adoration because she was a quarter century his junior and she was gorgeous; disdain because she was lazy. She refused to work and she couldn't cook. In the five years that Frank and Heather had been married, she'd had a total of thirty-two jobs, the lengthiest of which had only lasted two months. Her idea of cleaning was just to move things from one place to another and it irritated Frank, so much so that he'd hired a maid to come in three times a week to clean and cook his meals. His friends, although sympathetic to the fifty-two-year-old's plight, often questioned his undying love and loyalty to Heather Trimble. To hear him tell it, she was the best thing to ever happen to him. He would swear to anyone that would listen that she was smart with incredible ideas and a heart of gold. In reality, she used her body and sexual prowess to control him and he knew it. She was Hollywood gorgeous and held a classic timeless beauty, but her heart was impure. She'd done and said things to her husband that the average man would've found difficult to accept, but Frank loved Heather to no end.

He'd met her in Hard Body's Gentleman's Club at the ripe age of twenty-one. Frank had used the same line that he'd used time and time again with countless other strippers before her.

"You're too pretty to be in here dancing, baby girl. Don't you want something better for your life?" he'd asked during a lap dance.

"Who wouldn't want something better than men pawing all over them?"

"You need a man that can take care of you, that's what you need."

"Yeah, well, I'm sure your wife won't let that happen, so why even talk about it?" she said as she gyrated on his lap seductively.

"I've never been married, so there is no wife. No illegitimate children running around either."

"So you're going to take care of me, is that what you're saying?"

"If you'll let me. My name is Frank, by the way."

"Well, as you know, my stage name is Heaven but my real name is Heather. Where are you from, Frank? Do I hear a little country twang in there?"

"I'm originally from Alabama but I been here for about five years now. Moved here for a job. I've got the house, the car and the money. All I need now is a beautiful wife and I'd be happier than a hog in slop."

And that had been that. Two months later they were married in a courthouse ceremony with Hard Body's manager Bobbi Rae and a stripper by the name of Champagne as witnesses. Frank had agreed to take his bombshell bride to any locale that she wanted for their honeymoon and she'd chosen Jamaica. He hadn't wanted to go there but had reluctantly agreed because he'd given her his word that she could go wherever she wanted to. Frank Trimble was a self-admitted racist and the idea of spending his honeymoon surrounded by foreign blacks was not idyllic.

They'd stepped off of the plane and gone immediately into party mode. They'd both consumed massive amounts of Guinness Stout until they were beyond inebriated and passed out. They'd performed this ritual night after night until Heather had grown tired of doing the same things. During the day they had snorkeled, gone scuba diving, and gone shopping, but as soon as nightfall came it was back to barhopping for the newlywed couple.

Their last night in Jamaica had been extremely taxing on the budding marriage. Frank had watched his wife get a little too friendly with some black vacationers and he was not a happy man. She lay across a table in a local tavern and allowed them to take body shots from her radiant skin and Frank was livid. After multiple shots of tequila and bottle after bottle of Guinness Stout, they'd both fallen asleep in a drunken stupor - or so Frank had thought.

The bright Jamaican sun had come beaming through the wicker blinds of the honeymoon suite of the Secrets Wild Orchid resort. Frank stirred, trying desperately to hide his eyes from the brightness of the summer sun. His head pounded as if someone had beaten him about the skull with a baseball bat. Even in his confused state and alcohol-infused euphoria, his hearing was sharp. He heard a woman in the throes of passion, professing her undying love to her suitor. Frank reached to the other side of the bed towards where his wife lay. Hearing the woman scream in delight had caused an instant erection. He felt for her, but she was not there. He sat up in bed, trying to shake the wooziness swimming in his head.

At first he panicked, fearing that some of the locals might have kidnapped his wife, but there was something familiar about the voice on the other side of the wall. He leapt from the bed with a start, scurrying over to the far wall of his hotel suite to hear the voices clearer. Frank's heart almost stopped as he realized that the voice that he was hearing, the cries laden with ecstasy, belonged to none other than his wife. His new bride had dishonored the sanctity of their marriage and they'd been married less than a month. Frank cringed in horror, not wanting to believe what he'd heard. He frantically made his way to the door, fumbling to find the doorknob through his rage.

Frank stood in the hall, contemplating knocking on the door next to his. It sounded like Heather, but he had to be sure. Just as he built his courage enough to knock, he heard the faint creak of the doors hinges slowly spring to life. Heather backed into the hallway wearing only a towel. Her arms were flung carelessly around her lover's neck as they embraced in a deep, sensual kiss. Her body seemed to melt with every twist of his magical tongue. *She never goes limp like that when I kiss her*, Frank thought, seething with rage. He watched as the man's hand disappeared underneath the towel and seemed to bring his wife to instant orgasm. She bucked and writhed against his fingers until an audible gasp of pent-up sexual frustration escaped her lips.

Heather's lover was regal in his stance. His dreadlocks hung low, framing his massively muscular shoulders. Lines and ripples cut sinuous paths throughout his chiseled body. Pearly beads of sweat dripped from his taut skin as he breathed huskily, towering over Heather's 5'2" frame. He resembled an African chieftain with his dark chocolate ebony hue. His presence was commanding and his mane was reminiscent of that of a lion. His hand was still buried deep beneath the towel, threatening to bring Heather to yet another climax, while his other hand gripped her round, firm buttocks tightly.

Frank was frozen from both shock and fear. Not only could he not believe that his wife would violate him in such a manner, but he was afraid of what the black man might do to him if he moved. He gave the man a once over, trying to convince himself that maybe, just maybe he could take him. And then he saw it.

Heather ripped the towel from his waist to expose the full glory of his manhood. She pawed at it lasciviously, stroking it as though she were a starved cannibal. "Oh my God, you're huge! Can I have it again please?" she begged. She still hadn't noticed her husband standing there, trying his hardest to blend into the wall of the hallway. "Please, Jamal, please!" she screamed.

He removed his hand from her moist, wet love nest and brought his fingers together as if testing her moisture. "It seems like it's just about ready," he said, grabbing a handful of bleached blond hair and dragging her back inside of his suite.

Frank's pulse quickened. He didn't know whether he should beat on the door and make his presence known or just wait for her to finish her tryst. As most cowards would, he returned to his room and waited. He could hear Heather continuously profess her love to Jamal as he undoubtedly ravaged her innards with his grotesquely oversized member. To think about it caused a shiver to ripple through Frank's soul. It was at least two inches in diameter and a foot in length, truly a sight of magnanimous proportions, to say the least, which only served to further Franks own male inadequacies. As a youth growing up in rural Alabama, he and his friends had often made off-color remarks concerning the stereotype of the African American phallus, but he'd never seen one in the flesh, so to speak.

Sweetwater, Alabama was a small town built on the backs of slaves. In the small town of less than three hundred residents, he never saw black people unless he went to nearby Huntsville. The close-knit community of mostly relatives, whose families had been there since its founding, viewed blacks as lazy, arrogant, and overbearing. Somehow the belief that black people hadn't deserved their freedom had embedded itself within the lore of the small, inept community. Those values had been passed on from generation to generation until it was so deeply rooted that the children growing up in Sweetwater, Alabama felt a sense of entitlement having been born of Caucasian decent.

As a child, Frank would sit for hours listening to his father and mother, uncles and aunts, even his grandparents sit and expound on the good old days when "niggers knew their place." For him, it was not uncommon to refer to grown men and women of color as boys and girls. According to the mindset of the whites in his rural Alabama enclave, blacks were seen as chattel, personal property, beasts of burden put on God's green earth to be used by and for white society for whatever means they saw fit. Frank Trimble had grown up with those values and beliefs instilled in him and he would die with that mind frame.

He sat at the edge of his hotel bed, trying to make sense of his wife's behavior. She had not only slept with another man, but with a *black* man. His stomach turned, threatening to expel his bowels. He felt himself gag at the vision of Jamal making love to his wife. Thick saliva caught in his throat and his tongue felt excessively wet. Frank cradled his head in his hands and rocked back and forth. The tears had begun to flow freely, but he was more angry than hurt. His first instincts were to go next door and to kill them both, but Frank had never been a violent man - at least not alone. He'd always been with his hooded buddies whenever trouble had occurred with blacks. The anonymity of being an associate of the KKK had always been the fuel to drive his anger. A face to face confrontation with no back-up was suicide and he knew it, especially after seeing the size and demeanor of Jamal.

Heather walked in, trying to be as quiet as possible, until she noticed Frank sitting at the edge of the bed. "Morning, baby, I didn't know you were awake," she said. Her voice was perky and chipper and it grated on Frank's nerves.

"Don't 'morning' me, Heather, where the fuck have you been?"

"First I went and sat out by the pool and had a Bloody Mary to try and get rid of my hangover, then I went for a walk on the beach, and now I'm back."

Frank sprang to his feet. "You're a fucking liar, Heather! I saw you with him, I heard you telling this nigger how much you loved him!" he screamed.

"Are you sure that it was me, Frank? I'm not the only blond white girl in Jamaica, Frank!"

For a split second, he almost second guessed his own eyesight, but just as quickly he dismissed her denial. "I know what I saw, Heather, I'm not stupid. If you'll lay with a nigger, you'll lay with anything. When we get home, I want you out of my fucking house."

"You don't mean that, baby, think about what you're saying!" she protested.

"I know exactly what I'm saying! I don't need this shit. I do way too much for you for you to treat me like this."

"Where are you going to find another woman like me?" she said, dropping her towel.

Frank felt his manhood stir. He hated the way that Heather made him feel. She looked down and saw the bulge in his boxer shorts and moved closer. Frank took a step back, but she reached out and grabbed his penis and massaged it gently.

In reality, Frank repulsed her. He was simply her means to an end, her personal ATM, but there was no sexual attraction. She slept with him out of pure obligation and had never been satisfied by her husband. His manhood was at best an unimpressive five inches when it was erect and was as thin as a pencil. Even cunnilingus was excruciatingly boring with him. But he was all she had, financially.

Heather dropped to her knees and took Frank's penis into her mouth. He stumbled and collapsed onto the bed, and just before he climaxed, she stopped. Frank's eyes popped open. He'd been instantly snapped out of his state of euphoria.

"I don't know why I'm doing this. You're just going to leave me like everyone else does," she said. She'd managed to conjure up crocodile tears to reinforce her point. "I've never told you this, baby, but I have an addiction to sex. I can't help myself. Some people are addicted to drugs, but my addiction is sex and I need help. I don't want to lose you, but I understand if you want to turn your back on me!" Heather cried. Sobs racked her body as she crumpled to the floor. Heather wept uncontrollably, not because she was overcome with grief about her imaginary sexual condition, but because she was afraid of losing her meal ticket.

"Don't cry, baby, we will get through this situation together. I love you, Heather, and I don't know what it's going to take, but whatever you want me to do, I'll do," Frank said.

And just like that, she'd reeled him back in.

That episode had been at the beginning of their marriage, but Frank was certain that it hadn't stopped. There was no concrete evidence to support his thoughts, but with Heather at home day after day, it made it hard for him to work a complete shift without worrying about whether she had a stray man in his bed. He wanted to leave, and he knew that he needed to leave, but he was in love with his wife. In his own twisted and warped sense of reasoning, he'd rather have a piece of her and share her with everyone else than to not have her at all.

Chapter 9

Natalie and Tristen pulled into the gates of CrossTech and parked. She was still somewhat embarrassed, but managed a weak smile. "Tristen, I want to apologize again for making you feel uncomfortable. If it's the last thing I do, I am going to make it up to you," she said.

"It's okay, honestly, Natalie. If you want to make it up to me, I have just the thing that you can do for me."

"And what's that?" she asked.

"My cousin is coming in this morning and I don't want to take off work just yet. Can you go and pick him up for me?"

"How am I going to know who he is? You expect me to hold up one of those signs like I'm a limo driver or something?"

"No, just look for a guy that looks like me. Knowing Toby the way that I do, he'll probably be wearing Timberlands."

Natalie kissed him on the cheek. "I'm sure I'll find him. Tristen?"

"Yes, Natalie?"

"Do you think you'll ever give me a chance to prove to you that I am a good woman?"

"No one knows what tomorrow will bring, but I will tell you this. My ideal woman has all of your physical characteristics, but loyalty and intelligence rank high on my list too. Just stay the same and we will see what happens, deal?"

"Deal…on one condition." Natalie was willing to take a "maybe" versus a "no" any day.

"What condition is that?"

"You let me take you and your cousin out to dinner tonight at a little place called Rosewood Mansion Bar. We can have dinner and a couple of drinks - my treat," she offered.

Tristen nodded as they walked into CrossTech. He wasn't sure what Natalie's angle was, but he needed a friend.

When Tristen stepped into his office, both Hayden Cross and Caleb Weeks were waiting for him. He hesitated slightly because they'd startled him, but he quickly regained his composure. "Good morning, gentlemen, is there something that I can help you with?" he asked.

Hayden stood and crossed the room in long strides. As he reached Tristen, he extended his hand and cupped Tristen's shoulder. "It's been brought to my attention that you are without a vehicle, my boy, is that right?"

"Yes sir, that is correct. I haven't had the opportunity just yet to find one."

Hayden gave Tristen's shoulder a slight tug as if leading him toward the window. As they approached the window, Hayden put his arm around Tristen's shoulder and pulled him close like his father had done on so many joyous occasions. "Tristen, I don't know what's in that beautiful mind of yours, but whatever it is, I have a feeling that you are going to usher this company into a new era - and make yourself a very rich man in the process. Now if you'll direct your attention to the parking lot…" He pointed down to the jumble of BMW's, SUV's and Hybrids. "Which car do you prefer, Tristen? If you had your choice of any vehicle - reasonably priced, of course - which would you choose?" Hayden asked.

Tristen raised his hand and rubbed his chin, thinking and contemplating for a long while. His brow furrowed, searching the parking lot for his perfect car. The truth of the matter was that he didn't really have a preference. "Honestly, Mr. Cross, I don't really have a particular choice."

"That's not what your mother and father said. They said that your dream car was an Acura TL and that your favorite color is blue. So I ask you again, Tristen, do you see your car in the parking lot?"

Then he saw it, sitting alone in the light of the Texas summer sun: an Acura TL with the dealer's sticker still taped to the window. The sunbeams gleamed and shimmered across the metallic blue paint, matched only in beauty by the glimmer of lust in Tristen's eyes.

"Now that that's done, what exactly do you have in store for CrossTech?" Hayden asked.

Tristen walked to his desk and opened his briefcase. Inside was a manila folder marked NR613. He handed the folder to Hayden and Caleb and took a seat behind his desk. The two men stared at the schematics in dazed amazement.

"If this is what I think it is, then you may be able to write your own ticket, Tristen," Hayden said.

"It's exactly what you think it is. It's a neuro-remote control. Although mechanical in nature, it has purely medical capabilities. Do you guys have any idea what this could mean for the medical community?" Tristen asked excitedly.

Caleb seized the opportunity to chime in. "Why don't you explain how this works, Tristen?" He had no idea how it could possibly work, but he didn't want to look like an idiot in front of Hayden. Instead, he took an air of supremacy.

"What you're seeing here is an exploded view of the NR613. The actual device is only about the size of a grain of rice. It would be injected into the brain via the temple or the base of the skull. After injection, the NR613 will crawl its way through the brain until it reaches the frontal lobe, where it'll attach itself to the neuro-proteins in the brain. Once the device is stationary and planted in the frontal lobe, the controller would only need to enter preprogrammed short codes for access and control."

"And what would be used for the remote control?" Caleb asked skeptically. He squinted to study the schematics more closely.

"As of now, I'm working on coding for iOS systems. So as long as the controller is within a ten mile radius, they could control the device with their iPhone."

"Do you know what you've done, Tristen? You've created an effective method of mind control," Hayden said. His wheels were turning. If there was one thing that Hayden Cross had always been, it was an opportunist. He knew how to turn nothing into something and Tristen Graham had come to him with *something*. The thought of a medical breakdown was not even a remote thought. He was thinking government contracts - defense contracts, more specifically. Military weaponry contracts always paid huge dividends and Hayden knew that they could be staring billions of dollars in government funds in the face.

"That's assuming that it works," Caleb said.

His skepticism didn't go unnoticed. Tristen's initial impulse was to defend his brainchild against Caleb's onslaught, but he thought against it. There was no sensible reason to make enemies with his new boss. Tristen was intelligent enough to know when he saw jealousy and it was etched deep into the furrows of Caleb Weeks's face. He could only hope that the CrossTech veteran would allow him to display his talents without hindrance. Just as soon as the thought had crossed his mind, Tristen cursed himself for his easygoing personality. *I need to tighten up and start standing up for myself*, he thought.

Hayden noticed his young golden goose fidgeting nervously and decided to get back to the business at hand. "Tristen, how long do you think it'll take to have a functional prototype?" he asked.

"With a lab and the proper tools, Mr. Cross, I'd venture to guess that I could have a prototype with an initial round of testing done by mid to late fall."

"Perfect, absolutely perfect. Caleb, see that Tristen gets everything that he needs. Brennen is barely using the space that we've allotted to him, so make half of that lab Tristen's work space," Hayden said.

"Hayden, I don't think that Brennen is going to be too thrilled about sharing his space. I think - "

But before Caleb could finish his sentence, Hayden raised his hand to silence him. "Last time I checked, this was *Cross*Tech and I'm Hayden Cross. I have always respected your opinion, my friend, but this is non-negotiable. If Mr. Goldstein has a problem accommodating Mr. Graham, then perhaps I should expect to see Brennen's resignation on my desk by morning," he said, winking at Tristen.

"I'm sure he will more than accommodating to Mr. Graham, sir."

"Well then, there's nothing further to discuss. If you need me, I will be in my office. Better still, Tristen, come with me. I will show you to your lab personally," Hayden said.

The pair walked out into the hallway, leaving Caleb Weeks standing alone in Tristen's office, befuddled as to what had just happened. Hayden put his arm around Tristen's shoulder. "Tristen, let me explain something to you. There are three types of men in this world; men that wish that they could do, men that actually do, and then men like me that do whatever the fuck they want to do. I want to groom you to be a man that's able to do whatever he wants, a man that operates with full impunity, if you'll let me," Hayden said. He added, "First thing we must do in order for that to happen is to grow you a pair of balls."

"Grow a pair of balls, sir?"

"Yes, a pair of balls. Caleb disrespected you and you never stood up for yourself. If you allow people to walk all over you, Tristen, they will make a habit of it."

"I'm new, sir, and I don't want to cause any waves. What strategic advantage would I gain by making myself appear defensive and argumentative?"

"You, my young friend, have a lot to learn. Men will test you simply for the fact that they realize that you are intellectually superior to them. Remember I told you that I recruited you for CrossTech because I believe in your talent and intellect, but you're of no use to me if you're stressing about making waves, as you put it. You know what I think you should do?"

"What's that, sir?"

"First I think you should can the 'sir' shit. My name is Hayden. And second I think you should say fuck a wave. I think you should cause a tsunami in CrossTech. I think you have the heart and the intellect to run this company someday."

"Really, sir?"

"Hell yes, really!" Hayden said, opening the door to a swank, modern laboratory.

It was a huge open space with clinical white and glass walls. Everything in the lab had a sterile look to it. The overhead lights were in the shape of honeycombed panels that cast a bright, almost blinding glow over the room. Brennen Goldstein sat crouched over a stainless steel lab table, staring into his computers monitor.

"Brennen, I see you're hard at work. Why don't you take a break so that I can introduce you to someone?" Hayden asked.

Brennen turned to face Hayden and his face dropped immediately. Brennen Goldstein wasn't exactly a racist; he loved black women. Black men, however, were a totally different story. He didn't particularly *hate* black men; he just didn't understand them, and most of all, they scared him. He'd been beat up so many times by blacks as a child growing up that he'd developed a natural dislike for them as a people. He stepped to Tristen and extended his hand. "Hello, I'm Brennen - Brennen Goldstein."

"Hi, I'm Tristen, nice to make your acquaintance."

"Well then, I will leave you two great minds alone to get acquainted. Brennen, Tristen will be sharing the lab with you, effective immediately," Hayden said as he exited the lab.

As the automatic glass doors slid shut, Brennen turned back to his work but began to speak. "I'm not particularly happy about splitting my space with you, but it is what it is. Just stay out of my way, don't touch any of my shit, and don't play your jungle music in here." He snorted.

"Excuse me, jungle music?"

"You heard what I said! Let's get one thing clear: I'm not going to pretend to like you and you don't have to pretend to like me. Like I said, just stay out of my way!" Brennen barked. He put his ear buds in his ear and ignored Tristen.

Tristen was dumbfounded. Although this was one of the men that Natalie had warned him about, he didn't seem dangerous - a dick, yes, but dangerous? Tristen didn't see it. He walked around quietly, examining the laboratory closely, trying desperately not to disturb his new neighbor.

Chapter 10

Natalie knew immediately who Toby was as he stepped off of the plane. Not only was he dressed differently, but he and Tristen actually favored each other a lot. For a split second, she thought about Tristen's rejection of her advances and giggled at how he would feel if she slept with his cousin. She just as quickly dismissed the notion. She was a freak, but she was nobody's whore. "Excuse me, are you Toby Graham?" Natalie asked.

"Who wants to know?"

"I'm a friend of Tristen's and he asked me to come and pick you up."

"Oh shit, my bad, ma! I didn't mean to be rude, you feel me?"

"Yeah, I feel you. Well, if you get your luggage, I'll show you to the car so that we can go."

"Luggage? Shit, this duffle bag is all I got, shorty."

Natalie shook her head. Toby and Tristen couldn't have been more different. Tristen was smart and reserved whereas Toby seemed to have a nervous edginess about him. He had most definitely been in the streets; she could sense it. Her days of loving bad boys had long since been over, and as much as Tristen and Toby resembled one another, she found Toby to be less than attractive.

"I'm sorry, I didn't catch your name," Toby said.

"My name is Natalie; I work with Tristen."

"Oh, okay. So what's the story?" he asked as they made their way to the parking garage.

"What do you mean what's the story?"

"I mean, are you and my cousin fucking or what?"

"Wow, did you really just ask me that? That has to be the lamest thing that I've heard a man say in quite some time. Well, if you must know, no, we aren't fucking, we're just friends."

"Lame? Well shit, if my cousin ain't tapping that, then you might as well put me in it! That nigga ain't gonna fuck nothing anyway; he's saving himself," Toby said.

Natalie burst into a hysterical fit of laughter. *Is this kid serious?* She thought. "Little boy, listen, number one, you probably couldn't handle this if I gave it to you, and number two, you're not really my type. You just got off a plane with a duffle bag, for God's sake. I'm not a gold digger or anything, but I would at least like to have a man with some type of direction."

"Well damn, babe, you sure do know how to make a nigga feel like a peasant," he said. They both burst into riotous laughter at that point. Toby stared out of the car window as they drove away from DFW International Airport.

"I'm sorry if I hurt your feelings, Toby."

"It's not that. I mean, honestly, you made a valid point. I'm just tripping off of something that I heard on the plane."

"You care to share?" Natalie asked.

"Not really, it's just some things that I have to work out for myself. Let me ask you a question: where is Martin Luther King Jr. Blvd?"

"It's on the south side in the hood. Why?"

"Because no matter what city you go to, MLK Jr. Blvd is always in the hood. I'm a hood nigga so I like to know my surroundings, that's all."

"I understand that; just be careful. South Dallas isn't for everyone. No south side for you yet. I want you to go to Tristen's and chill. Try and get some rest, because I want to take you guys out for dinner and drinks tonight," Natalie said.

The rest of the ride was fairly quiet, both of them lost in their own thoughts. They pulled into Billionaire's Row and Toby's eyes beamed. He knew that his cousin had taken a cushy job, but he had no idea that he had it like this. Natalie said a few words to the doorman and handed him a crispy fifty dollar bill as Toby looked on from the car. Moments later, she returned and instructed him to follow the doorman.

As Toby neared the door, Natalie called out to him, "Toby, Tristen and I should be here at around 6:00 p.m. so try and be ready."

Toby couldn't believe his eyes. Their family was by no means poor, but the sheer beauty of the condominium took his breath away. He stepped out onto the balcony that wrapped around the corner unit, breathing in the muggy summer air. All around him were tall buildings, and below him was the everyday hustle and bustle of people on a mission. Toby took a deep breath as if trying to inhale cleanliness and exhale his troubles, but to no avail. The old lady that he'd met on the plane had really touched him and made him think.

Could Jesus really fix my life? Toby wondered silently to himself. What could God possibly see in a sinner like him. He'd never intentionally hurt anyone and he wasn't a hoodlum. He was a gambler and an avid weed smoker; those were his only vices. Not bad by a long shot, but there was an emptiness inside of him that he could not quell. There was something missing that no amount of loose sex, marijuana, cards, or dice could replace.

Toby sighed heavily. He felt like a bastard child - no mother, no father, and no siblings. He only had his Uncle Chester, Aunt Ruth, and Tristen. Nobody else in their small close knit family really dealt with Toby. The sins of his mother were his, according to his family, and to a certain extent they blamed him for not doing something the night his father was killed. He had harbored that guilt for as long as he could remember and it frightened him.

The fright came from the thoughts that crept into his head almost daily, suicidal thoughts of blowing his own head off. He missed his father terribly. Grady Graham had given his son all that he could before his death. When Chester was teaching Tristen how to ride his bike,

Grady was teaching Toby the three card Monte. While Tristen was learning and excelling in mathematics and science, Toby was learning and excelling in street life. Although his father had taught him how to survive on the street, he had been adamant that Toby *never* sell drugs. As Grady had put it, any hustle that intentionally hurt people was no hustle at all. Drugs, in his eyesight, were detrimental to society. It ruined homes and created zombies and Grady wanted no part of it. Robbery, murder, and burglary created victims and were to be strictly avoided or they could have dire consequences. Grady had gone against his own word by trying to rob the liquor store and had been killed in the process. That alone was enough to make Toby feel as though his father was a prophet, and because of that, he'd stayed away from drug dealing, robbery, and burglary. He had been trained well by his father, and although he'd tried to follow his uncle and aunt's rules for fear of being put out onto the street, he'd still held his father's words dear to him.

"Book smarts will only get you as far as a desk job, Toby, but street smarts and common sense can help you survive," Grady had said and Toby believed him. It had proven true and helpful on more than one occasion.

Toby walked through Tristen's home and settled at the bookshelf, staring at the unfamiliar titles. He let his fingers slide along the spines of the books until it came to rest on Robert Greene's *48 Laws of Power*. He turned to Chapter 1, "Never Outshine the Master". He went into the guest bedroom and plopped down on the thick goose down comforter draped across the bed. He began to read:

"Always make those above you feel comfortably superior. In your desire to please and impress them, do not go too far in displaying your talents or you might accomplish the opposite—inspire fear and insecurity. Make your masters appear more brilliant than they are and you will attain the heights of power."

So far, so good. Toby liked the sound of attaining power. How he would manage to do it, he had no clue, but he liked it. He read until he could no longer keep his eyes open and drifted off to sleep.

Chapter 11

Natalie and Tristen walked slowly toward the cafeteria in deep conversation. "He said what?" Natalie asked.

"You heard me! He said don't play jungle music in the lab," he said, laughing. "I'm sure he didn't mean anything by it though," he added.

Natalie was furious. She knew exactly what Brennen meant. He and his little merry band of Klansmen tried the intimidation factor with any and all minorities that came through CrossTech. They'd been successful with most and only a few had stood up for themselves. Many of the ones that had stood up for themselves had met with accidents and it was a running rumor that the five horsemen had all had a hand in the *accidents* that had befallen their coworkers.

The old black janitor Mr. Wilkins had been one of those victims. He'd been brazen enough to call Sean Westbury out as the racist he was, accusing him of intentionally giving him any shit job that he could think of in the hopes that he would quit his position at the company. It was common knowledge that Mr. Wilkins loved to drink, so when he didn't come to work the Monday after July 4th one year, people naturally assumed that he'd gone on a drinking binge - that is, until his daughter had come to CrossTech to give them the news that he'd been beaten within inches of his life. She said that after they'd cooked that Friday for the fourth, he'd left and hadn't called when he made it home, which was unusual, so she immediately started calling hospitals and jails. She'd found him at Baylor Hospital with four broken ribs and a fractured skull and his hip had been shattered. His face was almost unrecognizable when she'd seen him and the police didn't have much to go on as far as who could've been responsible for her father's beating. Months later when he'd returned to work, he looked different. Whereas he'd previously always been a happy man with kind words and a pep in his step, he now had a lisp, a lazy eye, and he walked with a limp. He never spoke of what happened, but body language didn't lie. He wouldn't make eye contact with any of the five horsemen and when forced to talk to them, his gaze stayed affixed to the ground. His demeanor was docile and broken. Work was no longer a joy, but rather a necessity, and it showed in his actions.

"Tristen, the shit isn't funny. Remember what I told you about those guys? I was serious when I told you that these assholes are dangerous, so don't underestimate them."

As they walked into the café, Brennen, Frank, David, Sean, and Caleb sat huddled around a large round dining table. They walked into the buffet line under the close scrutiny and hateful gaze of the five men. Tristen noticed, but didn't speak. Natalie, on the other hand, seized the opportunity to rib the men. She knew that none of them were bold enough to disrespect her. Not only would she sue their asses, but her brother had already made his presence known to Brennen Goldstein and she was sure that he'd spread the word to his cronies. She stopped in front of their table, put on her biggest smile and danced a quick jig, making sure to flail her arms and wiggle her fingers much like the old tap dancers would do during minstrel shows.

"What's your problem, Natalie?" Caleb asked.

"I figured since you guys were watching us, I might as well give you a show."

"Yeah, well, this isn't Showtime at the Apollo so you're wasting your time," Brennen said sarcastically.

"Awww, Brennen, are you still bitter because you came up a little short?" Natalie said, bringing her index finger and thumb together in his face.

Brennen made a move to stand but Frank grabbed his arm. "Move along, Whoopi Goldberg, nobody wants you here," Frank sneered.

"I'm sorry, Jamal - I-I-I mean Frank - you're absolutely right. You fellas have a nice day," she said as she walked away. She took Tristen by the arm and giggled impishly. "That should get their juices flowing."

"Who is Jamal?" Tristen asked.

They made their way through the line silently, and once they were seated, Natalie began to recount the events of Frank's wife Heather's infidelity as told by Brennen Goldstein during pillow talk. By the time their lunch hour was over, Tristen knew it all. Frank's wife had a thing for black men.

Brennen Goldstein was Jewish and Natalie had briefly carried on a torrid affair with him, but only because he'd come across as a nice guy. Although sexually inadequate, he gave good head so she'd dealt with his egotistical and somewhat narcissistic fascination with himself. Brennen fancied himself a gangster due in large part to his Jewish roots coupled with too many reruns of old gangster flicks. His family's past association with the Italian underworld gave him an inflated sense of self-worth. He wore expensive Italian suits, his shoes were handmade, and he drove the finest car. His finances, however, suffered because of it and he was constantly struggling to make ends meet. His façade of the successful Italian ladies' man had just about bankrupted Brennen, but none of his friends were the wiser. To hear them tell it, he'd come from old money, which was partly true except for the fact that the old money had long since dried up.

David Ganzelle, on the other hand, was just the opposite. He didn't have a lavish lifestyle at all. He was housed in Billionaire's Row, and to Natalie's knowledge, his only extravagance was scotch - the more expensive the better. As a matter of fact, according to Natalie, David had grandiose tastes when it came to his scotch, shelling out a whopping $20,000 for a bottle of Glenfiddich scotch. His most prized possession was a bottle of eighty-seven-year-old Macallan scotch that cost him $75,000. David Ganzelle was an expensive drunk and everyone knew it.

Natalie went on and on, telling Tristen about the five men that he needed to avoid like the plague. Sean Westbury often lied about being married with a small child but, everyone knew the truth. He was only married to his lifestyle - with men. It was supposed to be a big secret, but Sean and Brennen were best friends. There was no need for Tristen to guess how she'd found out; he just let her talk. Sean Westbury had a thing for boys, the younger the better, and he thought that nobody knew. But Natalie knew. She said that she'd seen him on several occasions watching the men in the fitness center with his lustful gaze. Brennen had told her of his infidelity, but she hadn't believed him because Sean had said that he was married, plus he was somewhat handsome with a very nice body. It wasn't until she'd gone to Grapevine Mills mall and saw Sean getting rather cozy with a young college boy that she believed it. They looked like two star-crossed lovers sitting in the food court and she'd made sure to go undetected.

Last on her list was Caleb Weeks. She painted him as Hayden Cross's bitch. He catered to Hayden, not in a sexual way, but in an overly admiring way. He wanted to be Hayden Cross, from his rugged good looks to his bank account. Caleb idolized Hayden, but he envied him also. Caleb Weeks had helped build CrossTech and he felt as though he deserved more, even though Hayden had given him plenty. Caleb earned almost $400,000 a year in salary plus bonuses. He'd been given cars, watches, property, name it and Hayden had given it, but Caleb was still not satisfied.

"If Caleb is making money like that, then why is he so envious of Mr. Cross?" Tristen asked.

"Because men aren't like women. See, as long as we have a nice place to live, our hair and nails stay done, we have a nice car and money in the bank, then we couldn't care less about what another person has. Men, on the other hand, want what the next man has all the time. If he has more money, he wants that. If he has a finer woman, he wants that. If his dick is bigger, he wants that. It's human nature," Natalie explained. She stood and tapped the face of her watch with her manicured nail. "It's about that time, cutie. I told your cousin that I'm taking you guys out for dinner and drinks tonight. I'll be over about 6:00 p.m. so be ready, okay?" she said. She grabbed Tristen by the wrist and pulled him from the table, intentionally locking eyes with the men at the table across the cafeteria.

The five men sat livid, each silently brooding over Natalie's blatant disrespect. "Caleb, why do you let that black bitch get away with running her mouth that way?" Brennen asked.

"For a few reasons that none of us, including your cocky ass, can afford to ignore. She will sue this company, first of all, and second of all, have you forgotten who her brother is? And lastly, she answers to Hayden Cross, nobody else. If you have a problem with her, you'll have to take care of it personally, but there is no firing Natalie. If you want her gone, then you'll have to kill her," Caleb said.

Each man sat deathly still, afraid to speak or move, waiting for a sign from either Caleb or Brennen, but neither of them spoke. Caleb Weeks examined Brennen's face closely. For all of his bravado and flashiness, he was a stone cold coward.

"Just as I suspected. The thought of doing something on your own terrifies you, Mr. Goldstein. My advice to you is to not worry about things that are far above your pay grade. She will be taken care of in due time, along with her new jiggaboo, showoff boyfriend," Caleb sneered.

None of them noticed Mr. Wilkins sweeping around the cafeteria only a few steps from where their sinister conversation was taking place, soaking in every diabolical word that was spoken.

Chapter 12

Esco sat in his car in long term parking at the Newark Liberty International Airport, fuming. He'd been running all over town trying to find out where Toby lived and when he'd finally found out, he'd watched the house religiously for days. There were only two older people coming and going from the home. His first impulse was to tie them up and beat them until they told him what he wanted to know, but the plan that he'd come up with had worked flawlessly. Esco had gone to the Graham's residence dressed in the finest Goodwill suit that he'd been able to find. He'd parked in front of their home and when they both arrived, he made his way to the front door and rang the doorbell. He wasn't sure whether the woman that answered the door was his mother or not, but Esco turned on his finest charm.

"Hello, ma'am, my name is Kevin Muncy. How are you today?" he asked in his most respectful and contrite voice.

"I'm fine, young man, how may I help you?"

"I am trying to locate a Mr. Toby Graham. He came to United Plumbing and Heating some time ago in search of a job and we have room in our mentorship program," he lied.

"Since when do companies make house calls?"

For a split second, Esco felt his adrenaline rush. He didn't want to kill anyone, but he would if he had to. Panic almost set in until Mr. Graham came to the door.

"Young man, Toby has left the state for a while. Is there a number that we could pass on to him?" Chester asked.

"Well sir, actually, depending on the state that he's in, we may still be able to use him." Esco had settled comfortably into his lie. He avoided Mrs. Graham's eyes. Her piercing gaze made him uncomfortable, but not in a fearful way. It was a way that made him want to grab her by her hair and beat his fist with her face. But Esco was on a mission. He hadn't come for a confrontation and if they told him what he wanted to know, there wouldn't be one. "We have locations in almost every state except North and South Dakota, Wisconsin, Wyoming, and Utah but other than that, we're everywhere, sir," Esco added.

"Well, if you have an office in Dallas, Texas, then I'm sure Toby would be more than happy to sign up for your mentorship program," Chester said.

The look that his wife shot him said that he'd gone too far. Ruth Graham was very protective of both her son and nephew - more so her nephew than her son. She didn't worry much about Tristen because he was incredibly intelligent, and although Toby wasn't a complete idiot, Ruth worried constantly about his decision making process. With Toby having neither one of his parents during his most impressionable years, he had been susceptible to more of the streets than Tristen, oftentimes bucking their strict rules and rebelling openly. The more he rebelled, the more love the Grahams tried to show him, hoping that someday he'd come around. She'd been afraid that she'd lost him for good when he'd explained that he was going to Texas to live with Tristen.

She'd abruptly told him, "This is a big opportunity for Tristen, so don't go down there and blow this opportunity for him."

Toby had been heartbroken, pleading for her to have a little faith in him, and then he'd hung up in her face. She wasn't sure about this Kevin Muncy though. His eyes were shifty and he moved nervously.

Esco, however had gotten the information that he needed. He didn't say another word. He simply turned on his heels and walked towards his car. Ruth and Chester Graham both stood dumbfounded, wondering what had just happened.

"Mr. Muncy? Excuse me, Mr. Muncy?" Chester Graham was still calling after Esco as he drove away, smiling ominously and watching them both through his rearview. Esco's smile gave way to shrill laughter as he thought about the pain that he would inflict on Toby Graham.

That was a few days earlier and he hadn't been asleep since. He'd stayed up gambling, trying to get enough money together for his hunting expedition. Now Esco was about to board his flight with no idea what to expect on the other end. There were things that he would need in order for his mission to be a success. He would need to find the hood, and once there, he would need to find the nearest back room gambling shack to make some quick cash, just in case his money ran low. He would also need to find and buy a throwaway pistol. He wasn't about to take the chance of packing it in his luggage.

One thing that Esco knew for certain was that if he found his way to the ghetto, anything he needed was as simple as asking. He was the consummate gangster and he wore his impoverished pedigree like a badge of honor. Esco had gone as far as dubbing himself Mr. Ghetto Pass USA. There was an unspoken language among men from less than well-to-do areas. Real recognized real no matter where life took them and they were able to spot one another from what seemed like miles away. The soul of a man could be read through his eyes. There was something about the emptiness and pure frustration in a man's gaze that made his plight that much more recognizable. Esco had grown up hearing that it took one to know one and there had to be truth to it because he could spot whether or not a man was willing to kill for what he believed in. In essence, it took a killer to know a killer and Esco was indeed a killer.

"Ladies and gentlemen, we are now boarding group three for flight 914, destination Dallas/Ft. Worth," a high pitched voice bellowed over the loud speaker.

Esco passed the flight attendant his ticket and smiled broadly. "Welcome to United Airlines, sir. I hope you have a wonderful flight," she said, handing Esco his boarding pass.

"Thank you, ma'am."

Esco walked the long, shaky corridor leading to the plane and stopped just short of boarding. A great sense of foreboding overtook him. It wasn't that he was afraid of flying - no, he'd done extensive traveling in his forty plus years. The problem was that he'd never taken a trip without saying goodbye to his daughter. Thirteen-year-old Enid was as smart as a whip and the love of his life. He'd always made sure to at least call her to say that he loved her and that he'd see her later. She was being raised by her mother, who'd abruptly filed for divorce five years earlier when Esco had left his job and made gambling his full time career. "Find and do something that you love and you will never work another day in your life", he'd been told, and it was true. He was very good at gambling and he'd actually managed to make a lot of money. When he hit, he hit big, but the same could be said of his losses, because when Esco lost, he lost big.

Hence his anger with Toby's cheating ass. He didn't like the kid and it was no secret. To Esco, Toby was a young punk who didn't know a poker chip from a potato chip. He seemed to always pop up wherever the high rollers were gambling and it irritated Esco to no end. Toby was such a joke on the underground gambling scene that the older players had jokingly nicknamed him Easy Money, so when the opportunity had presented itself for Esco to take some easy money from Easy Money, he'd jumped at the chance.

He made his way down the aisle in search of his seat. He silently giggled to himself as he shuffled past the first class passengers. The look on a lot of their faces was smug, as if somehow spending a few extra dollars on their seats made them better than the rest of the passengers on board. The only advantages of being in first class instead of coach, as far as Esco could tell, was boarding and disembarking the flight first and more elbow room. He found his seat, Row 20 seat F. Esco squeezed past a petite Oriental lady with a little too much swagger to be the traditional subservient Asian that stereotypes dictated. He took his seat and stared out of the window onto the runway. The sun beamed and ricocheted across the thick concrete slab. Luggage handlers grabbed and tossed baggage, seemingly undaunted by the brutal New Jersey heat.

"Excuse me, are you going to Dallas?" Miss Oriental asked.

"As a matter of fact, I am, why? What's up?" Esco waited for her answer, but it never came. He settled back into his seat, trying to get comfortable.

The captain's voice crackled across the loud speaker and flooded the small, confined space with his deep baritone. "Good evening, passengers, and welcome to flight 914. Weather conditions in Dallas are a humid ninety-six degrees. Our estimated travel time is two hours and fifty-four minutes. Please fasten your seat belts and enjoy the ride."

After he'd finished his introduction, it was time for the flight attendants to explain airplane procedure. In the event of a waterborne landing, please blah, blah, blah. Esco tuned the stewardess out as she spoke. He couldn't care less about the meaningless conversation. Truth of the matter was, if the plane went down, everything that they'd told the passengers in preparation for the event would fly right out of the window with everything else. Panic would set in and all hell would break loose.

The whir of the plane's tires against the runway could be heard and then moments later, the colossal steel bird was airborne. Esco stared out of the window, mesmerized. As much as he traveled, he was amazed each time at the strength and dynamics of the airplane. How something so gigantic and heavy could take to air was beyond his comprehension. He watched as the people and cars got smaller and smaller until they were mere miniscule grains of sand sprinkled on earth's massive surface. He wondered how God saw man. Did God honestly look at man as his greatest creation or were they just specks of dust on his celestial canvas?

Again, he heard the familiar twang of the tiny Asian woman, who seemed to be trying desperately to conceal her accent. "Are you going to Dallas for business or pleasure?" she asked.

"Business mostly."

"Oh, that's too bad, maybe you should try a little bit of both," she said flirtatiously.

"And how much is this little bit of both going to cost me?"

"What makes you think that it's going to cost you anything? Do I look like a whore to you?" she asked.

"Looks can be very deceiving, and furthermore, it's not your look, it's your conversation. You speak like a woman with a ton of game, but to answer your question, no, you don't look like a whore."

She dropped her head and smiled demurely. She'd done a wonderful job of changing her life for the better. After her pimp had been arrested for murder and ironically murdered himself while awaiting trial, she and the remaining whores in his stable had taken and divided his assets. She'd taken her portion and relocated up north. First she'd gone to Manhattan, but the cost of living was beyond expensive, so she'd gone across the bridge to Newark, NJ. Once there, she'd opened the Serenity Day Spa and had employed a stable of some of the most beautiful Asian women that money could buy. She'd paid cash for six young women to be smuggled into the country, and although most people called it slavery, she called it opportunity. Over a period of close to six years, she'd managed to amass close to a million plus dollars, a far cry from her days working for Yellow Shoes the pimp. Unlike him, her girls were taken care of. They weren't all made to stay in the same house, but rather the girls had their own lives. Some of them had even settled into families and had gone on to start businesses of their own.

Yummi had made sure to train her girls for more than just hooking and hand jobs. She hadn't been on Dallas soil since Yellow Shoes's death, but out of all of his whores, Candy was the only one that she'd kept in touch with. When they were whoring, Candy hadn't been too fond of her and Yummi knew it, but they had come to terms with it. Now Candy was lying in Parkland Memorial Hospital dying of full-blown AIDS. She'd hooked up with a pimp named Silky Slim while Yellow Shoes was in jail. Yummi had received a call from her saying that she needed her. Her first thought was that she just needed money or that she wanted to get away from her pimp, especially after Yummi had let it slip about how much money she was making as an independent. No, Candy had explained it play by play to her and she was livid. Silky had been given AIDS by an unknown rapist. Candy was supposed to believe that he'd been overpowered by some female and sex had been taken from him. He'd given all of the girls their walking papers because, as he'd put it, with his condition worsening he didn't want to drag them down with him. He still had dope money coming in, but he preferred to die in peace. Candy had sucked her teeth and rolled her eyes at Silky Slim and accused him of sleeping with men. He'd laughed it off and assured her that that wasn't the case, but after all of the other girls had gone on their way to restart their respective lives, he'd beaten her with the butt of his pistol and then raped her.

After he came inside of her, he lay there taunting her, saying, "Welcome to the disease that there is no cure for." He smiled a hollow smile of pain and degradation as he recounted how one of his enemies had hired two gay men with full blown AIDS to rape him and then let him go. He'd been too embarrassed to tell his girls what really happened, but he'd thought enough of them to let them go on with their lives. He'd cried on her chest and apologized, but the damage had been done.

Three months later, Silky Slim was dead and Candy had been left alone to watch herself waste away to nothingness. Yummi sighed heavily. Candy had made her re-evaluate her entire life. She'd convinced herself that she was made for whoring. She had been repeatedly raped by her uncle as a child and it had severely damaged her. He'd started raping her when she was an impressionable twelve years old, sneaking into her room while her parents were asleep. When she'd tried to tell her parents, they'd abruptly shut her down, accusing her of lying and intentionally conspiring to dishonor their family. *Honor, honor, honor, everything is about fucking honor with my people*, she thought. She'd run away at sixteen after being savagely raped for four years and then she'd met him.

Yellow Shoes had come into her life like a knight in shining armor, treating her kindly and not forcing her sexually. It wasn't until months later that he'd come to her and explained that keeping her around was costing him a fortune and that unless she could help him recoup some of the money for her expenses, he would have to put her out on the street. She'd offered to get a job, but Yellow Shoes told her he had a way for her to make twenty times more than she could ever expect to make at any job. He took her to the Aristocrat Hotel in downtown Dallas and had her sleep with five different men in one night. Afterwards, she'd felt dirty and useless - that is, until Yellow Shoes had taken her shopping and convinced her that whoring was what she was made for. He said that he was still getting phone calls from the men saying how much they loved her and how she was the best that they'd ever had. That had made her spirit soar, like she mattered to someone. She had found her purpose in life - bringing men pleasure and helping them escape the reality of their otherwise mundane existence. Yummi was beautiful, but Yellow Shoes had broken her spirit and given her low self-esteem after years of making him a rich man. She wanted a love of her own, the kind that they spoke of on television, so change was paramount in order to obtain that which she wanted most. No more lies and no more games was the way that she wanted to live her life from now on.

"What's your name?" she asked.

"My name is Esco. What's yours?"

"My given name is Yo Mi Ling, but my friends call me Yummi," she said, extending her hand.

Esco shook her hand and let his eyes roam over her body. Although slender in size, she was very curvy and her breasts seemed larger than he would have imagined for a woman of her ethnicity. Yummi leaned over to get close to Esco and whispered seductively, "Can I tell you something? I'm not a whore, but I used to be. If you promise to treat me right, I'll be anything that you want me to be."

Esco smiled. He had her and he knew it, but what could a young, beautiful girl want with him? His battle scars showed clearly on his Puerto Rican skin and he'd gained a few pounds. They talked the entire flight about life, death, and the pursuit of happiness. By the time the plane landed in Dallas, they were joined at the hip. They walked hand in hand to Avis rental car where Yummi rented a car, vowing to show Esco all of the benefits that Texas hospitality had to offer.

Chapter 13

Natalie, Tristen, and Toby walked into the Mansion Bar in Turtle Creek in very high spirits - Natalie especially. She enjoyed hearing Toby and Tristen recount the days of their youth. She had merely witnessed their surface differences, but their differences went far beyond dress code and attitude. Although they had grown up in the same household, their thought processes couldn't have been more different. After watching and observing them, Tristen was Ricky to Toby's Dough Boy.

The trio walked in and were immediately seated by the maître d. They sat and talked for a while before Tristen excused himself to use the men's room. Moments later, he returned with an amused look on his face.

"What's up, Cuz? Why the smirk?" Toby asked.

Tristen didn't answer. Instead he looked at Natalie and smiled his most charming smile. "Guess who I saw when I went to the bathroom?" he asked.

"Don't even say it. For real?"

"Yep, all five of them. What is this? A company hangout or something?" Tristen asked.

"Actually, it is. A lot of upper management come here to unwind because it's so close to Billionaire's Row. Did they say anything to you?"

"No, I mean, unless you count what they were saying with their eyes. If looks could kill, I'd still be lying back there," he said.

"Well, let's go straighten that then!" Toby exclaimed.

"It's not that simple, man. My boss is back there, and the last thing I need to do is get fired because my cousin checked my boss," Tristen said.

Toby understood, but he didn't like it. Tristen was like his brother and he felt he owed his loyalty to him. After all, Tristen had been the one to really champion his cause when his father had been killed. His parents were always planning to take Toby in, but they needed to *talk* about it. Tristen had been there with his confident, intellectual preteen swagger to sway his parents towards expediting their decision. He'd said to them, "Mom, Dad, I know I'm a kid and my opinion probably doesn't matter much. I mean, you two are obviously more equipped to make major life-changing decisions better than me, but Toby is our blood so I'm confused about what you guys need to talk about. You've taught me that family is always first and I've always listened. Hopefully you guys keep that in mind when you render your decision."

Ruth and Chester Graham sat motionless, staring at one another, trying to figure out whether their son had just checked them. They'd agreed that Tristen was absolutely right and had welcomed Toby with open arms.

"Alright, Triz, if you don't want me to say anything, it's going to cost you," Toby said.

"Cost me what?" Tristen asked knowingly. As kids, whenever Toby said it was going to cost Tristen, it generally had something to do with drinking.

"It's going to cost three shots of Grey Goose - apiece," Toby said sternly.

"Okay, I can do that. Natalie, are you down?" Tristen asked.

"Um hmm. Tristen, are you trying to get me drunk so that you can get my goodies?"

Tristen didn't answer her. He just smiled his boyish grin and winked at her. He wasn't ready and he knew that she knew it, but it was flattering nevertheless to have her so attracted to him.

"My name is Pierre and I will be your server for the evening. Could I start you guys off with some drinks?" the waiter asked.

"We'll have nine shots of Patron chilled and three Grey Goose with orange juice, please," Tristen said.

"Right away, sir."

"Oh shit, so you're big time, huh? We are doing Patron shots instead of Goose shots? Okay, okay, I see you, big balla," Toby said jokingly.

"Patron shots go down a lot smoother than Grey Goose and I have to work tomorrow," Tristen said.

They laughed as they drank. They both found Natalie to be enchanting and hospitable, although Toby saw her as more. He looked up from his glass feeling particularly tipsy and noticed the five men at the bar staring in their direction. There was an older man there with them who raised his hand to wave them over.

"Y'all know this clown?" he asked, pointing to the man at the bar.

Natalie and Tristen both turned to look in that direction. "Yeah, those are the men that Tristen was talking about. Let's go over and say hi," Natalie said with a devious smirk.

They walked over to where Frank Trimble, Caleb Weeks, Sean Westbury, David Ganzelle, and Brennen Goldstein were waiting.

"Good evening, gentlemen. I believe you've all met Tristen, but this is his cousin Toby. We're here celebrating Toby and Tristen calling Dallas home now," Natalie said.

"Well then, this calls for a toast! Bartender, bartender!" Frank said. "Let me have five Bud Lights for me and my friends and three grape sodas for the coons," he said.

Toby made a move towards him, but Tristen blocked his path. He leaned in towards Toby and whispered in his ear, "Don't let this clown knock you off of your pivot, cousin. He's not worth it. Watch this. Excuse me, bartender, the grape sodas won't be necessary. Instead we'll take three Sagres please," Tristen said.

"Do you want regular, Bohemia, or Negra, sir?"

"Negra, please."

"Frank, why do you always have to be an asshole? Our new friends are here celebrating and you're making jokes. The drinks are on me, guys," Caleb Weeks said.

"You'll have to forgive Frank. He's not the most cordial person alive. What are your plans for the rest of the night?" Sean Westbury asked.

"They'll probably go home and run a train on this skank that they're with," Brennen Goldstein said sarcastically.

"Brennen, you sound so bitter. Actually, they are with me, not your mother, you piece of shit! You strut around here like your shit doesn't stink, like you have it going on, but try paying for a round of drinks and watch your credit card decline," Natalie retorted.

Brennen's blood was boiling. He wanted to smack her, but the last thing he wanted to do was deal with her brother.

"Man, let's go before I have to mollywhop one of these bitch-ass white boys," Toby said disgustedly. He wasn't used to the blatant racism that he was witnessing.

It made him both angry and nervous because the white men seemed to have absolutely no respect. Not only did they lack respect, but they seemed to have nothing to lose.

"Don't leave yet, Kunta Kinte. We were just about to go can kicking," Frank said nastily.

"What the fuck is can kicking and who the fuck are you calling Kunta Kinte?" Toby asked.

Up to that moment, David Ganzelle had remained quiet, but he cheerfully chimed in, "You've never been can kicking? Oh, it's the best thing in the world. We're going to kick the shit out of some Mexi*cans*, some Afri*cans*, some Domini*cans*, some Puerto Ri*cans*…do you get the picture now, jiggaboo?"

Tristen's normally calm demeanor was now replaced with anger and anxiousness. "I don't understand why you dudes are being so racist, but it's cool. C'mon, Natalie and Toby, let's go," he said. After they were outside, Tristen exploded. "Man, this is bullshit! Did you hear what they said? That shit was beyond disrespectful! It's cool though. I am going to HR tomorrow morning about all of their asses."

"What the hell do you think HR is going to do, Tristen? You're in Texas, boy, and that means good old fashioned racism coming directly from the good ol' boy network. See, the difference between Texas and other places is that at least in Texas, you *know* that they're racist. In some of these other states, the racists throw rocks and hide their hands," Natalie said.

"So we're supposed to just deal with it? Fuck that shit! I'm from Jersey, kid. Those white boys were outta line. Triz, you should have let me handle that, son," Toby said.

Tristen felt like Toby was right. Maybe a good ass whipping was exactly what they needed, but he wasn't trying to lose his job. No, he would wait until the next morning and deal with it head on.

The night was warm and crisp as they strolled the short distance from the Mansion Bar to Billionaire's Row. The liquor had taken its toll on them all and soon their irritation had been traded for laughter and drunken merriment. Natalie took Tristen's hand in her own and snuggled in close to him. It surprised Tristen, but he did not pull away. He wasn't sure if it was the liquor or seeing Natalie in her tight jeans or both, but whatever it was caused his attraction to her to manifest itself. He stopped and turned to her and gazed deeply into her eyes. He pulled her close and kissed her passionately. He'd finished kissing her and Natalie still stood motionless with her eyes closed and her mouth open as if waiting for more.

Toby, in his drunken stupor, began laughing hysterically, which caused Natalie to open her eyes. "Damn, Natalie, that fool's tongue must be magical! You look like you busted a nut just now," he said, laughing.

"Shut up, Toby, stop cock blocking!" she screamed, playfully swinging at him.

"Man, nobody is cock blocking your little fine ass. I'm gonna just walk ahead. Y'all love birds handle your business," Toby said as he increased his pace.

Tristen kissed Natalie on the neck and whispered in her ear, "I think you're it."

"What am I, Tristen? What is it?"

"Listen, I'm a virgin, but I'm still a man. So far from what I see, you're everything that a man could possibly want in a woman. I don't know exactly what our kiss just meant, but I felt something stir deep inside of me. I want you - not only sexually, but I want you with me for a lifetime," Tristen said. The liquor had not only loosened his tongue but it had made his conversation potent.

Natalie swayed at his every word, finding it hard to stand. She threw her arms around his neck, this time kissing him instead of the other way around. Those were the words that she wanted to hear, and although Tristen was a few years younger than she was, Natalie was sure that he was the man that she wanted to be with. "Tristen, I don't want you to do anything until you're absolutely ready. Do I want you to make love to me? Yes, but I am willing to wait until you're sure. I know how important it is for you to maintain your celibacy until you're sure or you're married, so if I have to wait, then we'll be celibate together," Natalie said. She was too old to fall in love so quickly, but in the short time that she'd known Tristen Graham, he'd shown her that her body wasn't merely a man's playground. She knew that she had a nice body, but Tristen didn't seem to be too interested in her physical appearance, only in her as a person, and she liked that. They strolled leisurely toward Billionaire's Row, lost in a sea of tranquility and newfound romance.

By the time they made it back to the condo, Natalie was convinced that Tristen was the only man for her. "Tristen, do you mind if I sleep here tonight? I will leave early in the morning so that I can make it to work on time, if that's okay?" she asked.

"Yeah, that's fine. You can take my third room. Just lock the door on your way out in the morning."

Natalie nodded in defeat, she hadn't planned on trying to seduce Tristen, but she hadn't planned on sleeping in another room either.

"Yo, Triz, you think I can use your car tomorrow? I want to try and find a job as soon as possible," Toby asked.

"Yeah, that's cool, if Natalie doesn't mind giving me a ride to work."

"I don't mind, but I really need to take a shower and lie down though. Do you have a towel?"

Tristen pointed to the linen closet. If he and Natalie were going to grow close in their relationship, then she would have to learn to make herself at home. She retrieved a towel and moments later Tristen heard the shower spring to life. Toby sat staring at his cousin in disbelief. For the life of him, he couldn't understand Tristen's fascination with remaining a virgin. Natalie was virtually throwing herself at him and he was treating her like one of the guys. He'd watched her sashay into the bathroom with her beyond tight Apple Bottom jeans.

Her ass was so round and plump that her cheeks sat on the top of her thighs. Toby laughed to himself, thinking of Natalie's bottom. From the side, it looked like and upside down question mark, but from the back it was a perfect upside down heart. *That's it*, he thought, *that's the word: perfect.*

"Yo," he whispered to Tristen. His eyes darted side to side as if he were afraid that Natalie might hear him from the next room with the water running. Tristen didn't say anything to him, he simply nodded a "what's up" in his direction. "Yo, kid, fuck's wrong with you? I could dig that shit when we were youngsters, but we're grown now, son. If you don't want shorty, I'll pop that cherry, yo," Toby whispered.

"Believe it or not, my dude, life is about more than popping cherries. I like Natalie, but I like her as a person more. I want to breathe in her essence, I want to bathe in her radiance, and I want to make love to her when the time comes, Toby, not just fuck her. Anybody with a penis and a pair of balls can fuck, man. I just respect myself and women more than just using their body for quick personal pleasure. Have you seen her?" Tristen asked.

"Hell yeah, that's why I say you're tripping!"

"No, Toby, have you *seen* her? Have you actually looked at her? Look past the physical and dig deep. She's gorgeous inside and out. There is a pain there that makes her the person that she is. When I look at her, I don't see her body, I don't see her face. It's like I only see her aura. When I'm around her, my soul dances, bro.

I mean, if this feeling is anything like being high, I understand why people do drugs," Tristen said.

"Damn, nigga, you haven't even known shorty that long. You sound like you're in love and shit."

"I just might be. But I'm confused, man."

"Confused about what? If there's one thing I know, it's that life is too short to not tell people how you feel," Toby said.

"I like her so much that I'm afraid to fail her as a man. I'm afraid that I may not be all that she needs, but at the same time, I feel an overwhelming need to take care of her. I'm tired of talking about it. I'm going to bed, Toby. Make sure you put gas in my car, dawg," Tristen said, tossing Toby his car keys.

Tristen walked into his room and undressed slowly. He loved having Toby around because they could talk about anything. When they were juniors in high school, Toby contracted syphilis while dating the school skeezer. April Hill had been around the school twice and back again and Tristen had warned him to stay away from her. Toby, true to form, couldn't be deterred. He wanted her and all that she had to offer. So on the night of their junior prom, Toby and April consummated their relationship. April received another notch in her skank belt and Toby received a burning, pus-discharging penis. It was Tristen who Toby had come to, begging him not to tell Ruth and Chester. He needed Tristen's help because, as he'd put it, "You're the smartest person I know. You know everything about everything."

Tristen had honored his cousin's wishes by not revealing his ailment and he had gone with him to the free clinic in Harlem so that there was no chance of their parents finding out. He'd even gone into the room while they tested him, at his cousin's behest. The nurse had taken a twelve inch Q-tip and inserted it into the tip of Toby's penis. He wriggled and winced in pain as she swabbed the inside of his shaft, withdrew it to smear the greenish-yellow goo onto a small glass plate, and slid it underneath a microscope. They were made to wait in the lobby, and moments later, Toby and Tristen were ushered into a counselor's office, where Toby was given amoxicillin. They were both lectured about the civil and moral responsibility of abstinence and given a brown paper bag full of condoms. As a condition of not telling their parents of their experimentation with unprotected sex, a teenager was required to watch a gory film, complete with pus-filled blisters and leaking anal cavities. By the time they'd left the clinic, they were both embarrassed and nauseous. That small but significant time in their life hadn't stopped Toby at all. As a matter of fact, it had served to make him more promiscuous, knowing that he was a shot and a few pills away from treatment. It had served to totally turn Tristen off to the prospect of sex until he could find a woman with whom he could honestly share, if not his whole life, at least a true love.

Thinking back on that time in his life, Tristen chuckled as he stepped into the shower. He washed slowly and felt his manhood stiffen. Tristen let his hand glide over his rigid body and closed his eyes, trying desperately to distance himself from the feeling growing in his loins. He cursed himself for the thoughts sliding through his mind. He wasn't sure whether he was just that attracted to Natalie or if the Patron had a hold on his senses. He reached for the remote and switched the water to cold. He felt his hard-on subside as the ice cold water cascaded across his low cropped hair and down his back. He shuddered as he stepped from the shower and reached for his towel. Tristen walked into his dark room and pulled back the covers. He snuggled deep underneath the goose down comforter and tried to relax. He'd just dozed off when a light tap on his door jarred him awake.

"Tristen?" Natalie whispered.

"Yeah."

"Are you asleep?" she said sweetly.

"Not really, I was just dozing. What's up?"

"Can I sleep with you?"

"Depends on what you mean by sleep with me."

"I mean, can I cuddle with you, will you hold me until I fall asleep? I won't try to fuck you, I promise. I just want to feel your hands on me, I want to feel your lips on mine, and I want to listen to your heartbeat until it puts me to sleep," Natalie said.

"No problem. C'mon, climb in," he said.

Natalie stood at the foot of Tristen's bed and dropped her towel. The silhouette of her body against the night light in the bathroom cast an angelic glow over Natalie's majestic curves. She climbed underneath the covers with Tristen and snuggled against his hardness.

She felt it throb against her firm buttocks and then she felt Tristen's strong hands probing her thighs. His long thick finger slid inside of her and she felt her insides stir.

"Tristen, please don't tease me, babe," she said, but Tristen had already drifted off into deep slumber.

Chapter 14

Natalie tossed and turned majority of the night, searching for that comfortable spot, but she never found it. She'd eased from underneath Tristen's firm grasp and sat on the edge of the bed. She had heard majority of the conversation between Tristen and Toby and it had warmed her heart. Tristen was a special breed of man, but silently she wondered if she was good enough for him. If Tristen really felt about her the way that he said he did, eventually she would have to tell him about her...*all of her*.

When Natalie was a young girl of only eleven years old, she'd been awakened by her twin brother Nigel yelling at the top of his lungs for her to wake up and get out of their room. They shared a small, rundown, wood-frame, two story house with their mother Felicia and her on again/off again boyfriend Rudy. She had sat up in her bed and rubbed the sleep matter from her eyes. The strong stench of something burning filled Natalie's nostrils and then she opened her eyes. She could barely make out Nigel's silhouette through the thick smoke. What she could see was the bright orange flame that glowed beyond their bedroom door through the smoke.

"Nat, get up, we have to go!" Nigel screamed. He took her by the hand and led her to their bedroom window. Nigel opened the window and they stepped out onto the wooden eave that hung over their front door. "Take a deep breath, Nat, and on the count of three we're going to jump. Make sure you bend your knees. Are you ready? One…two…three."

They jumped and hit the ground hard. Natalie had bent her knees as Nigel instructed, but she'd bent them too much. Her knees crashed into her chest as she made contact with the ground and she felt the wind leave her fragile body. She lay on the ground writhing in pain, trying her hardest to catch her breath. She managed to stand just in time to see the entire top floor engulfed in flames. Neighbors had begun to gather on the sparse lawn in front of their house.

"Nigel, where's Mama!" she screamed. "Nigel, where's Mama!" she screamed again, shaking her brother's arm.

But Nigel didn't answer. He watched the flames consume the house. Orange embers leapt from the house and faded into the night sky. In the distance, Natalie heard the wail of sirens drawing near. Again she turned to Nigel and pleaded, "Nigel, please tell me where Mama is."

"She's gone and Rudy is gone too," he said. His eyes were still trained on the blaze when the fire trucks and paramedics arrived.

"What do you mean gone, Nigel? Did Mama and Rudy go out?" Natalie asked.

Nigel took her hand and walked away from the crowd. Something was wrong, Natalie could feel it in her gut. She knew that her twin brother had problems and his mentality scared her. He wasn't above hurting animals and she often joked with him that it wouldn't be long before he moved on to bigger prey like humans. With dazed eyes and a slight smirk on his face, he stood staring at Natalie.

"I did it, Nat, I set them on fire," he admitted.

Natalie let out a shriek of horror. Inside, she knew that this day would come, but she wasn't prepared for it. She dropped to her knees and looked up at Nigel. "Why, twin, why would you do that? What are we supposed to do now?" Natalie cried.

"While you were asleep, I went downstairs to get a glass of water and Mama and Rudy were watching TV. I walked into the kitchen and all of the Cookie Crisp was gone. I just asked Mama what we were supposed to eat for breakfast before we went to school and she just laughed at me. She laughed right in my face, Nat. Then I saw the bowl. Rudy had that big ol' bowl that mama used to use to mix the cake batter. Remember how we used to lick the cake bowl? Anyway, I just asked Rudy why he ate all of our cereal, and you know what he said, Nat? He said, 'Fuck you, little punk-ass nigga! When you get a job and buy some damn cereal, then you can call some shots.' I said, 'You don't even work; my Mama bought that cereal.' He got maaaaaad, then he stood up and slapped me, and Mama just sat there laughing. So I killed them. I bet they're not laughing now," he said reflectively.

The twins embraced one another. Natalie vowed to Nigel that she would never divulge the terrible secret, a secret that only they shared. No, Nigel and Natalie shared something far more than their deadly secret. The neighbors never learned the truth. They rallied around the orphaned children and swore to care for them - that is, until the state came to take them away. The Texas Department of Families and Protective Services came to usher them away quickly, and with no known relatives, they were placed in foster care. Foster family after family would come to adopt the twins, but they made sure that they would never be separated. They would both act out until the families had no choice but to bring the children back. That was before the Kleins came into their lives.

David and Maggie Klein had come into the orphanage looking for not only one child, but preferably twins - young black twins. In an open meeting with their caseworker, the middle-aged white couple had professed their love for children and explained that they had money, property, and love, but no one to give it to. The twins, as they explained, would be beneficiaries to all that they had to offer. By the time the Kleins were finished with their pitch, not only were the twins convinced, but the state of Texas was also.

The Kleins were true to their word. They had multiple properties, cars, and plenty of money. The children were afforded the best of everything and they were finally happy. They played and frolicked on one hundred acres of the greenest farmland that the outskirts of Dallas had to offer. Never before had Natalie or Nigel, for that matter, seen so many toys. Anything that they thought of was available; all they needed to do was ask.

Yes, life with the Kleins had been all sunshine and meadows until the adoption was finalized. After the finalization, things seemed to take a downward spiral.

Natalie and Nigel were twelve years old when it began. On more than one occasion, the twins would come in from school to find their parents milling about the house naked, as if it were some type of natural thing. They'd walked into the house once to find the Kleins in a sexual embrace and had been frozen with shock at the sight that lay before them. David Klein had his wife on the arm of the couch with her legs thrown across his shoulders. He thrust in and out of her vigorously, careful to keep one of his massive hands cupped around Maggie's throat. Maggie allowed guttural, ecstasy-filled sounds to escape her lips. Her head was tilted back with her eyes closed. She tried desperately to steady herself on the soft couch cushions as David pounded her relentlessly. Nigel and Natalie both stood in dazed terror at the sadistic spectacle taking place in front of them.

David Klein had looked up and seen his young onlookers gawking, but he never broke stride. He simply kept stroking with a lascivious grin plastered across his face. "Seems as though we have an audience, Maggie," he said.

Neither one of the children spoke or dared move.

"Natalie, do you and your brother know what we're doing?" Maggie asked between moans.

Natalie shook her head sheepishly. David pulled his phallus from Maggie's wet, gaping hole and started toward Natalie. All the while, his rigid manhood swayed and flapped clumsily from side to side. Nigel stepped in front of him to impede his progress, but David simply pushed him to the ground. His eyes were trained on Natalie, his budding prize, whose body had begun to sprout and blossom.

"Don't touch my sister or I will kill you!" Nigel screamed.

But David ignored him and kept moving toward Natalie. "Your mother asked you a question, Natalie," David said.

Natalie wasn't sure what to say. Her young mind raced and she felt lightheaded, unsure of what her response should be. She only managed a weak "no" in her fragile voice.

"This is called making love. It's what two people do when they love each other," David said as he inched closer to her. His erect penis grazed the fabric of her blouse and she felt her knees go weak. David was so close to her that she could feel his manhood pressing against her stomach, but she was afraid to move.

"Nigel, Nigel, come to me!" Maggie beckoned, but he didn't move. No, Nigel remained deathly still with his eyes focused on Mr. Klein, waiting for the perfect opportunity.

"Do you love me, Natalie?" David asked.

Natalie couldn't speak. She searched for an answer, but her answer never came. Her slender but curvy twelve-year-old frame trembled from fear. Natalie's eyes were affixed to the floor, afraid to meet David's gaze.

He took her head into his hands and lifted her face so that he could see her eyes. He took her hand and forced it to his erectness. "You like that?" he asked, still looking into her eyes, but there was nothing there. Her face was devoid of any distinguishable feeling, save for the tears that rolled freely down her cheeks.

"Mr. Klein, please!" she begged.

"No, not Mr. Klein, pretty girl. I want you to call me Daddy. Can you do that? Can you call me Daddy?" he asked, using Natalie's hand to masturbate his penis.

Maggie was just as hedonistic and sadistic as her husband, if not more so, because as her husband molested the young girl, she cooed and played with her clitoris as if she were turned on by seeing her man violate the young girl's innocence.

Natalie could no longer take it. She dug her nails into the skin of David's exposed member. She dug and clawed until she felt the skin rip and blood ran freely between her fingers. A shrill, screeching scream pierced the tranquility of the spacious farmhouse. David slapped Natalie violently, sending her soaring across the room. He dropped to his knees in agonizing pain, gasping for breath, and Nigel pounced. He struck David across his temple with a candle holder that sat on the nearby end table. Blood poured from his temple, staining the hardwood floor as he lay in a prone position, somewhere between darkness and reality. Maggie screamed in horror and lunged at Nigel, clawing and scratching at him until she caught just the right amount of his shirt. Maggie held him close, close enough so that he could smell the stench of sex permeating from between her legs.

David struggled to his feet, groaning as he attempted to steady himself. "You little bitch!" he screamed. David snatched Natalie and ripped the blouse from her body. "That's it, I'm tired of being nice to these little cretins. To the basement they go," David had said.

That's exactly where they'd stayed for what Natalie came to understand later was somewhere near four months.

Natalie shifted on the edge of the bed uncomfortably and Tristen sat up in bed. "Is everything okay, Natalie?" he asked.

"No, Tristen, it's not, but I'm afraid. I'm afraid that if I share with you what's really wrong with me, you won't want to be my friend, let alone still consider being my man."

"Why don't you let me be the judge of that? I'm a lot more understanding than people give me credit for. It's not like you've killed anybody."

Chapter 15

Esco paced the floor in the hotel suite that he and Yummi had been residing in for the past few weeks. He was there alone with too much time to think and his mind was playing tricks on him. Yummi had been incredible since they'd arrived in Dallas. She showered him with gifts and anything that he wanted was readily at his disposal. She'd shown him around the city, taking him to the many different gambling dens in town. She'd supplied the money for him to gamble and stood by his side as he turned hundreds into thousands.

Esco still hadn't been totally honest with her concerning his intentions in Dallas. He'd led her to believe that he was in Dallas in search of the man that had molested his daughter. He'd hatched a plan that would most certainly work if she was willing to help. It was simple. Yummi was gorgeous and Toby was a virile youngster with far too much testosterone. One look at the beautiful Oriental and Toby would lose his mind. He would have her use what she knew best to lull him into a false sense of security and then Esco would attack. He'd murder Toby and leave Yummi to take the fall. He smiled mischievously at his perfect plan.

Esco walked to the window and looked out onto the busy Downtown Dallas street. The gunmetal grey clouds sagged heavily, pushing grape-sized rain droplets down onto the ground below. Heavy rain beat across the window like the steady tap of a drummer's snare. In the distance, lightning sparked and Esco found himself silently counting until he heard the boom of faint thunder. The sharp crackle of lightning popped again, but this time rolling thunder came much faster, only two seconds lapsed. *Two miles away*, he thought.

Yummi left Parkland Memorial Hospital with a heavy heart. She'd gone to the hospital at the same time every day since arriving in Dallas. Every day was the same routine. She would leave the hotel and take the short fifteen minute drive. She'd stop inside of the coffee/gift shop and get Candy a dozen roses, a fresh bear claw, and a hot cup of coffee with three creamers and two sugars. Today was different though. She'd arrived at her usual time only to find Candy's room empty. Apparently, not even an hour before Yummi had come, Candy took her last breath. The news hit her hard, not because they had been super close, but because she saw herself in Candy. That could have just as easily been her who'd died.

Over the course of the few weeks that she'd been able to spend with Candy, they'd had extensive talks about everything from past experiences to dreams deferred. By her own admission, Candy had said that it was her own fault that she'd caught the virus. She said that her mouth had always gotten her into trouble with everyone, from pimps and johns alike. On their last day together, as Candy and Yummi talked, Candy began to cry. She had shrunk to a sparse ninety-seven pounds and her hair had started to fall out in large clumps, leaving her looking a lot like a scientific experiment gone wrong. Crusty matter and dried tears mixed with her new tears to form a muddy mix that streaked her cheeks. Her eyes were lifeless, and where they had once held a beautiful pecan brown hue, they were now a glazed-over milky greyish color. She'd gone blind as the AIDS virus had spread.

Yummi had put on latex gloves and grabbed a nearby washcloth and wet it with hot water. She wiped the crust from Candy's eyes gently. The warm water seemed to soothe her weary spirit and she exhaled a great sigh of relief. "Why are you crying, Candy?" Yummi asked.

"I guess because I am conflicted, Yummi, and I don't know what to do. On one hand, I'm sad because I'm blind, but on the other hand, I'm grateful that I'm not able to see what I've become. I don't want to die, you know? I mean, I don't have any children, I've never been married, and I've never known true love, but at the same time, I'm ready to die because I'm tired of suffering. The world is better off without me anyway."

"Candy, don't talk like that. You're a wonderful person, and - " Yummi started.

But before she could finish her sentence, Candy cut her off. "Girl, please, I've been in the streets since I was thirteen years old. Besides you right now, nobody has ever given two shits about me and I've accepted that.

I've always tried to be extra careful. Even though I was turning tricks, I still wanted to maintain some type of dignity. I know you remember how anal I was about Yellow Shoes keeping us supplied with condoms? That was because AIDS was always my biggest fear while I was out running the streets. I've always, for as long as I can remember, let men rule me. If they beat me, I didn't care. If they cheated on me, I didn't care. If they degraded me, so what, because I was searching for something that the men were obviously incapable of giving, and that's love."

"Candy, you've never been in love? Not even once?" Yummi asked.

"Nope, not once. I think that when you actually find love, you know it. From the pit of your stomach to the tip of your fingers, you know it. I always imagined that when two people's souls connect, there's a surge of positive energy and at that point in time nothing else matters. I think God pairs us at birth, like it's preordained by Him who your perfect mate is, but it's left up to us to navigate our way through this wilderness to find that person. Does that make sense?"

"It makes perfect sense, my love," Yummi said softly.

"Yummi, will you make me a promise?"

"Yes, of course, just name it," she said.

"Promise me that you will never let a man use you for his own selfish reasons. You deserve a wonderful life filled with joy and happiness. Promise me!"

Yummi didn't speak; she simply nodded. Her words had caught in her throat and she choked back tears.

Although the virus had ravaged her body and had taken her looks, Candy was a beautiful woman on the inside. Yummi rose to her feet, leaned over Candy's body, and kissed her on her forehead. "I promise, Candy. I will see you tomorrow for another one of our amazing talks," she'd said, but tomorrow would never come.

Yummi sat in the rental car and the weight of the world seemed to slam down onto her shoulders. Violent sobs racked her body as she cried. She cried for Candy, she cried for herself, and she cried for all of the girls that had been caught up in the life just like them. She didn't want to die like Candy, alone with not so much as an aunt to claim her body. Left to their own devices, the state of Texas would have just had her body cremated to save the space and expense of burying her. They saw her as indigent, only one step above being homeless, and when Yummi had asked the doctor what they planned to do with Candy's body, he'd replied sarcastically that he had no clue. He said that the hospital had done enough charity work and that Candy had done the world a huge favor with her death. With no next of kin, Yummi had to practically beg the hospital to hold Candy's body until she could make funeral arrangements. She wanted to at least give Candy that bit of dignity. Yummi was determined to give her a wig, some makeup, and a pretty dress for her home going service. Yes indeed, that was the plan for her old friend.

The rain had begun to fall just as she'd made it to the car. Now the raindrops beat a rhythmic tap dance on the roof of her rental. The clouds rolled and swirled ominously as Yummi drove toward downtown Dallas. The nearer she got to the hotel, the darker the clouds got and the heavier it rained. By the time she made it to the parking garage, she could barely see two feet in front of her. *Just my fucking luck,* she thought as she attempted to pull into the garage. They'd closed the gate and above the gate, attached to the building in bright neon green, it said, NO VACANCIES. Yummi cursed under her breath. She would have to park on the street and feed the parking meter.

She pulled into curbside parking and fumbled around in her purse, searching for a few quarters, at least enough to pay it up until the rain stopped. Yummi slid over into the passenger's seat and took a deep breath. She hated the feeling of being soaking wet, let alone being soaking wet and walking into a freezing hotel lobby. Again she cursed, this time out loud. "Shit!" she huffed as she opened the door and climbed out into the monsoon-type rain.

Yummi tucked her shoulders as if trying to retreat inside of herself and jammed three quarters into the meter quickly. She noticed that the raindrops were no longer pelting her head. She could see rain falling all around her, but she wasn't affected by it. Yummi blinked the last of the raindrops from her long eyelashes and that's when she saw him, her knight in shining armor standing behind her, bravely withstanding the downpour as he shielded her from the rain with his umbrella. She stared at him for a long while until his bright smile and witty sense of humor snapped her back to reality.

"Okay now, beautiful one, any day now. I'm already in disbelief that I'm risking pneumonia for a woman that I don't even know," he said sweetly.

"Well, you're a sweetheart, thank you so much. I hate getting wet - well, this kind of wet anyway," she said flirtatiously.

As they walked to the front entrance of the hotel, they exchanged flirty glances. "Well Miss I-hate-to-get-wet, this is where I get off," he said, and then added, "By the way, do you have a boyfriend, a man, a husband?"

"No, none of those. I mean, I have a friend, but it's nothing serious," Yummi said.

"Cool, so if I give you my number, will you use it? Maybe we can grab some lunch or something."

"That sounds good to me," Yummi said excitedly.

"Don't just tell me that, because if you don't call, I will be heartbroken," he said, putting on his best pouty face.

"One thing about me, sweetie, I never lie. I always say what I mean and mean what I say, and besides, you're a cutie so I'll make sure I call," Yummi said.

He scribbled his name and number on a piece of paper and handed it to her. He made sure to let his hand linger just a little bit to feel her soft skin. Yummi looked down at the paper and then touched his cheek gently before they parted ways. Once she was safely inside and out of the rain, she looked at the paper again. It read: TOBY GRAHAM 973-555-1050.

When Yummi walked into the lavish hotel room, Esco had the television's volume up full blast watching classic episodes of *Gilligan's Island*. He was in his boxer shorts, laid back on the couch eating from a large bag of Ruffle potato chips. He had one foot on the coffee table and the other on the couch. Potato chip crumbs had fallen and were trapped in the matted hair on his chest. He'd been smoking in the suite too, even though Yummi had asked him to use the balcony if he wanted to smoke. He'd used her new *Us Weekly* magazine to stamp out his cigarette butts.

Yummi looked at Esco with disgust in her eyes. He still hadn't looked up from the TV to acknowledge her presence. She turned on her heels and walked toward the bathroom to remove her wet clothes. "Ugh, I'm so glad that I didn't sleep with him!" she said to no one in particular.

When she'd first met Esco, she'd gotten the impression that he was sweet and about his business, but he was a user, just like the rest of the men that she'd known in her lifetime. She knew that he thought she liked him because she spent money on him, but truth of the matter was that she'd hoped that he would get the picture. She'd spent enough money on his gambling habit for him to make enough money to be on his own.

He'd done just the opposite. Esco had implanted himself into her life and refused to leave. Yummi had even offered to get him his own hotel room closer to south or west Dallas where the gambling shacks were more plentiful, but he hadn't taken the bait. Now she felt trapped, and with Mr. Umbrella, Toby Graham's number in her pocket, she needed Esco to get lost now more than ever. She smiled to herself, for as much as his deep baritone voice had startled her and made her nervous from the onset of their meeting, his soft eyes and kind demeanor more than made up for it.

She started the hot shower and closed the door so that the steam would build more quickly. Yummi peeled out of the wet, soggy clothes and stepped into the shower. She let the steamy water cascade over her jet black mane and then held her face to the stream of semi-scalding hot water. Moments later she heard the creak of the bathroom door opening. She held the shower curtain close to her body and stuck her head in the space between the shower wall and the curtain. Esco stood leaning against the sink, still munching on his chips.

"May I help you, Esco? I'll be out in a minute," she said.

Esco only smirked at Yummi. With no warning, he turned his back to her and began urinating in the toilet – well, not actually *in* the toilet. His hot piss splashed onto the toilet seat and then trickled down the toilet bowl. His dark, apple juice-colored urine held a sickly stench and the steamy bathroom only compounded the situation. Yummi shook her head at his repulsive behavior. It was as if he hadn't even aimed for the toilet. Without washing his hands or flushing the toilet, Esco turned back to Yummi, still munching on his chips. "I need your help with that little situation that I told you about."

"Okay, so what am I supposed to do?" Yummi asked incredulously.

"I need you to get next to the little nigga and put that pussy on him real good to the point where you put his ass to sleep, then I'll handle the rest."

"So just because I used to be a whore, it makes it alright for you to come at me like this?" she asked.

"Come at you like what? I'm asking for your help."

"This is the deal, Esco, take it or leave it. I'll help you take care of your little problem, but only if you move out of the room and get your own spot," Yummi said firmly. She knew that she had him where she wanted him and if he didn't agree to move out, she'd leave. All she needed to do was wait until Esco walked down to the corner store across the street from the courthouse to get cigarettes. He usually stayed there far too long, probably because the cashier there was young and pretty.

"Damn, it's like that?" Esco asked.

"Yeah, it's just like that. So what's it going to be?"

"Okay, ma, you win. I'll pack my shit and get out of your hair. Just be ready to handle business when I give you the word," Esco said.

Chapter 16

Tristen sat on the phone listening intently to his mother, who felt the need to put his father on speaker phone. "Tristen, tell your father what you just told me," his mother said.

"Hello, Dad, I was just telling Mom that for a few months now, basically since I started working for CrossTech, I've been going through some real tough times. The guys that I work with are really racist to the point that it makes me want to quit," he said.

"Racism? What's going on?"

"I don't know what their deal is with me. I do my job very well, but there's always a statement here or a gesture there that lets me know what they think of me. Like case in point, I walked into my office one day only to find coupons thrown across my desk. Now, I like to save money as much as the next guy, but the coupons were only for three items: grape soda, chicken, and watermelon. When I saw the guys responsible for it, I was angry but I held my composure and politely asked them to not enter my office without my permission," Tristen said.

"Yeah, so what did they say?"

"They just laughed. The older one, Frank, actually had the nerve to tell me to lighten up, like it was some sort of joke or something. I just walked away." He had a sad, monotone quietness to his voice and both his mother and father picked up on it. He wanted to go home, but he was a grown man now. The days of clinging to his mother's apron strings were over. But Tristen didn't know how to handle the constant harassment and humiliation.

"Oh hell no! Have you gone to HR, son?" Chester asked.

"Yes sir, I have, and they mentioned it to them and did a little investigation, but that only seemed to make the situation worse. A couple of days after I reported them, I walked out of my front door on my way to work to find the remnants of a small wooden cross. It had been burned to a crisp in the hallway in front of my apartment. There have been other instances where they've made off-color remarks and I just let it go. It's to the point where I just want to quit and come home," Tristen said sadly.

"Son, you know quitting is not an option for Graham men," Chester said.

"So what am I supposed to do, Dad?"

"Sometimes the only way men learn is by receiving a nice ass whipping. I don't condone violence, but I'm also military so we do things our own way. Do I need to load up with weapons and come to Texas?" Chester asked.

"No, Dad, what would that prove? Besides, I'm not going to have you put your career in jeopardy and risk going to prison because of a few racist parasites."

"That's my boy!" Chester said and then added, "So what are we going to do about it?"

"I don't know, I haven't figured that part out yet."

Ruth Graham had listened to both her son and her husband. She respected her husband above all else and she loved her son infinitely, but there were things that Tristen needed to know, and for whatever reason, Chester wasn't telling him. Maybe he wanted to protect their son, but she knew that he knew. "Tristen, they don't like you because you're the white man's biggest threat. You're a young black male with obvious intelligence and it scares them. It terrifies them because you're smarter than them and your potential is limitless. So there will be no ass whipping or weapons involved. No, you remain intelligent because I'm going to tell you something. If you go out like they expect you to, which is violently and ignorantly, Tristen, you've allowed them to win. Use what God has been gracious enough to bless you with to see you through. You're blessed and gifted, Tristen, and when you're protected by Him, no man can stand against you," Ruth said.

Tristen wanted to believe that; he *needed* to believe that. He would let it go for now, but he wasn't exactly sure how much more he could take. There was more pressing business to deal with presently though. He'd been seeing Natalie for months, getting to know her, but she still hadn't opened up about why she had been sitting on the side of the bed crying that one night.

Natalie was on her way to his apartment now with dinner from her favorite Chinese restaurant. She was mushy and Tristen liked it. She'd made a big deal about it being their three month anniversary, and although Tristen didn't even know that were an official couple, he still obliged her. He'd even offered to take her out to a nice restaurant, but Natalie had insisted that she only wanted to stay in, eat Chinese food, watch a movie, and cuddle. Since she'd been gone, he'd gotten an opportunity to kick back with *The 48 Laws of Power*.

"Law 9: Win Through Your Actions, Never Through Argument:

Any momentary triumph you think you have gained through argument is really a Pyrrhic victory: The resentment and ill will you stir up is stronger and lasts longer than any momentary change of opinion. It is much more powerful to get others to agree with you through your actions, without saying a word. Demonstrate, do not explicate."

It seemed as though Robert Greene was talking directly to him and his dilemma. He hadn't told his father and mother, but there had also been threats of bodily harm. On one occasion, they'd invited him to the gym for a game of basketball and he'd reluctantly agreed in the hopes of burying the hatchet. Everything seemed to be going fairly well until it was time to pick teams. They'd fussed and fought over him, even after he'd assured them that he didn't know how to play basketball very well.

Sean Westbury had laughed and said, "All niggers know how to play ball."

He wanted to smack the fire from Sean Westbury, but he'd let him make it. The funny part about the whole situation was that Tristen wasn't a hard man and he knew that, but Sean Westbury was soft as wet toilet paper. It was no secret that he liked men. He was a closeted homosexual and Tristen found that hard to respect - not the part about being a homosexual, but the closeted part. He'd always been taught that you should never do anything that you were ashamed of, and if he liked men, then he should own that truth.

They'd started the game, and surprisingly enough to Tristen, the game was going smoothly until Frank passed him the ball and he went in for a layup. He got airborne like Michael Jordan in his prime; his form was superb and his technique was flawless. David Ganzelle couldn't have timed it any better. He went up under Tristen, taking his legs from under him in mid-air. Tristen came down hard, slamming his head and back against the hardwood of the basketball court. He lay prone in agonizing pain until anger overtook the pain and he sprang to his feet.

"What's your deal, bro?" Tristen asked heatedly.

"I'm not your bro, bro," David said sarcastically.

Tristen was livid. He wanted to punch David, punch any one of them, but he held his composure. Things had started to really get out of hand. He couldn't lash out for fear of losing his job, and to a certain extent, he felt like a coward. He limped out of the gym with his tail tucked between his legs, angry and in pain.

He passed Mr. Wilkins on his way out of the gym. The elderly black man stood there, leaning on his mop with a look of sadness and empathy in his face. "You had enough yet, youngster?" Mr. Wilkins asked.

"Man, I'm going to end up hurting one of those dudes, Mr. W."

"Can I give you some advice, Tristen?" he asked.

"Of course, sir. Whatever you can share to help me get past this madness would be greatly appreciated."

"Walk with me, Tristen. These walls have ears," he said.

They walked and talked about random things until they made it outside to the courtyard. Mr. Wilkins looked around warily and then began to speak. "Tristen, I admire you, young man. You're smart and you're brimming with talent. They want to knock you off of your pivot and I see you faltering. I let them beat me, Tristen, literally, and I'm ashamed. I walk around here with my head low and my mouth shut because truth of the matter is, they don't want us here. These people have done everything in their power to make sure that there are no black people in this corporation. Shit, I'm just a janitor and they don't want me here."

"Mr. Wilkins, I just want to work, do a good job, and pay my bills."

"Youngblood, that's what we all want, but dig these blues. The white man wants you up under his thumb at all times. Any display of intelligence or aggression and they will shut you down every time," Mr. Wilkins said.

"So what are you saying? Am I supposed to walk around here like a good little black boy with my head down?"

"Hell naw! I'm saying if you're gonna make these sons-a-bitches pay, make 'em pay twice," Mr. Wilkins said, and then added, "You're like the black Messiah around this motherfucker, Tristen. It's not only me, you, and Natalie but the Mexicans and the Chinese, shit, even Raj. We're all treated like trash and none of us have ever had the courage to do anything about it. Just something to think about," he said.

Mr. Wilkins's words kept playing in his head as he read his book, waiting on Natalie. Tristen walked to the bookshelf and replaced the book. He paced the floor a bit, thinking of Toby, who'd taken a job at a local sandwich shop in downtown Dallas. Tristen was beyond proud of Toby because he was trying his hardest to turn his life around. He was almost never at home because he would literally beg his manager for overtime and she happily obliged. She'd remarked that she'd never had such a hard worker working for her before and that seemed to make Toby work harder. The feeling of being good at something was definitely a motivator for making a man dig his heels into his work deeply and give it his all.

Natalie used the key that Tristen had given her to let herself into the apartment. "Hey, honey bunny. I got you sweet and sour chicken and house fried rice. Is that okay?" she asked cheerfully.

"Honey bunny, huh? That's fine, love, I told you to surprise me, so whatever you got is fine."

"'Kay. Did you find a movie to order, babe?" Natalie asked.

"I actually found two. One of them is called *12 years a Slave* and the other one is called *Fruitvale Station*."

"Damn, I want to see both of them. I saw the advertisement for *Fruitvale Station* and it looks good as hell. You want to watch that one first?" she asked. She opened the container with Tristen's food and handed it to him.

He dug into the house fried rice. It was loaded with chicken, shrimp, and pork, and something struck him as odd about the rice. A different taste invaded his taste buds. "Why does this rice taste different? It's like they've added something."

"They put fresh crab meat in their house fried rice, baby, that's probably what you taste," Natalie said.

Tristen shrugged because whatever they'd put into it was welcomed by his palate. "Natalie, I really don't want to watch a movie; I want to talk to you."

"About what, love?" she asked. In reality, she knew exactly what he wanted to discuss. He'd opened up to her more than ever, and if she was going to have even the slightest chance with him, she would have to bare her soul. Her confession would either make or break them.

"I want to talk to you about why you were crying on the side of the bed that night."

"I wasn't crying, Tristen. I just couldn't sleep," she protested.

"I just want to know all of you, Natalie. I like where our relationship is headed, and if we're going to move forward, I want to do it without running into surprises.

You told me once that I probably couldn't handle your past. I want you to respect me enough to give me that option," Tristen said seriously.

Natalie took Tristen's face into her hands and stared intensely into his eyes. Her eyes spoke of a pain so deep that it threatened to rip her soul to shreds. She was terrified of losing Tristen to her horrible truth, but she was even more terrified of losing him for not sharing all of her. She kissed him deeply and Tristen could feel her lips trembling. As their tongues meshed and swirled about, Tristen tasted the salty moisture of Natalie's tears. She leaned back to look at his face once more, her eyes searching his eyes for a sign of reprieve, but it did not come. Natalie kicked off her shoes, scooted into the corner of the couch, and brought her knees to her chest. She had a rapt look in her eyes as though recounting troubled times from days past. She started at the beginning, narrating her history.

As Natalie talked, Tristen found a newfound respect for her. She had dedicated her life to protecting the secret that she and her brother shared. After Natalie had assaulted David Klein, the twins had been stripped naked and thrown into the basement. It was a damp and drab space with one small window. When the sun was high enough to allow sunlight in, it only shone in one direction. Nigel and Natalie thought for certain that they would die in that basement. The fear had set in and in every noise that they heard their anxiety heightened. In the minds of children treated in such a manner, it's no wonder they believed that the Kleins would eat them for certain.

"I think they are cannibals, Nigel." Natalie had whispered one day.

"I don't think so, Natalie. If they were cannibals, they would be trying to fatten us up to eat us. Every day it's the same thing, either peanut butter or ramen noodles."

Night after night they slept in that basement on old tattered blankets that they'd found in a box of raggedy linens. They lived like savages among the civil, oftentimes finding themselves squatting like natives as they ate their rations. One night as Natalie lay looking up through the small portal of a window, she turned to Nigel. "Nigel, do you love me?" she asked.

"Of course I love you, Nat, you're my twin, my other half. If I didn't love you, I couldn't love myself."

She turned her back to him and began to cry. "You know we're going to die here, right?" she asked through her tears.

"We're not going to die."

"Do you believe that, honestly?" she asked.

"I don't know what I believe. I just don't feel like we're going to die. Mommy used to tell us all the time that love conquered all, remember that? I remember she used to say as twins, we were all we had and that one day our love would save us. I didn't know then what she meant, but being in this situation, I have to believe that she was right."

"The Kleins said what they were doing was for people that loved each other. Maybe that's the only way we'll survive this madness, Nigel," Natalie said. Neither one of them knew what sex was, but if it meant a means to survive, then they would do it.

The first time they tried it, they both found it to be uncomfortably painful. After a while, though, they'd gotten used to it and the pain was no more. They didn't just have sex to have it; it was their medicine. They used it when one or both of them were depressed and felt that there was no tomorrow. Sex had become for them a beacon of hope and a way to express their love to one another. They didn't know that it was incest and to them they were doing nothing wrong. They were together, lost in a world where no one knew that they existed. The state of Texas had forgotten that Nigel and Natalie were left in the care of the Kleins, evidently, because as far as they could tell, no one ever came to check on their wellbeing.

One night as they sat eating their gruel, they heard the Kleins' voices outside of the basement window, laughing, giggling and in an extra jovial mood. Moments later they saw headlights and then heard the sound of the car's engine as it drove away and faded into the night. For the first time since they'd been held captive, the Kleins had left at night. Natalie had tried to keep count of the days and nights, but after a while she'd lost count. Their days had blended into nights and then back again until time was one big blur.

"Nigel, they're gone. We need to try to get out of here," Natalie said urgently.

Nigel sprang to his feet and began looking around the room for something to break the small window, but there was nothing. He took a milk crate that sat in the corner and pushed it to the wall just beneath the window. He stood on the milk crate and beat the window with his fist until it broke. Shards of glass tumbled to the ground at Natalie's feet. Nigel tried to pull himself up through the window but to no avail. "Natalie, help me and then I will pull you out," Nigel said.

Natalie stepped up to the milk crate and Nigel put his foot on her shoulder to push himself up. Natalie stood on the broken pieces of glass and winced underneath Nigel's weight as the glass cut into the soft soles of her feet. The jagged glass pieces still left in the sill of the window frame cut into Nigel's hands as he lifted himself to freedom. Once on the outside, he looked around carefully and then lay on his stomach, reached into the window, and pulled Natalie through the window. The soft flesh of her back along her spine ripped as a lone piece of serrated glass sliced into it. She moaned but she did not scream. Natalie could feel the cold trickle of blood oozing down the center of her back, but she didn't care. Nigel helped her to her feet and they began walking toward the wood line.

The night was extremely chilly and as they walked, Natalie felt herself getting woozy. She stumbled, but Nigel was there to catch her before she hit the ground. He held her close to himself so that they could feel one another's warmth. They walked for what seemed like hours over lush meadows and through the woods. Nocturnal creatures beckoned through the night air but the twins continued to move.

"I don't know how much longer I can walk, Nigel," Natalie whined.

"We have to keep moving, Natalie. It's cold as shit out here," he ordered.

The wind whipped and swirled menacingly around the preteens' naked bodies. Natalie shivered uncontrollably. She still felt light headed, but she continued moving. Nigel was almost dragging Natalie now, who was barely able to keep up.

"I can't run anymore, Nigel! I'm tired and my feet are hurting!" she screamed.

"Do you want to die, Natalie? Huh, do you?" he scolded.

"No!" she whimpered.

"Well then, we have to keep moving." Nigel was running on pure adrenaline. He'd convinced himself that the Kleins were right behind them, hunting them as if they were game-worthy prey.

Then he saw it: the dim lights of passing cars on a road not even fifty yards away. Nigel increased his pace, teaming toward the highway ahead. They reached the dark, two lane road with its sparse overhead street lights and began walking along the shoulder, careful to stay hidden in the shadows. The twins were cold, hungry, and disoriented. Neither one of them had any idea in which direction they were traveling, but they marched on.

Nigel looked back warily. Natalie was dragging her feet as if weighted with lead. "Lord, if you're there, please help my sister, please, God!" Nigel prayed loudly.

In the distance ahead of them, Nigel saw headlights barreling toward them. As the lights drew nearer, he took Natalie's hand and ran to the center of the road. He flailed his arms anxiously, trying to get the driver's attention. The eighteen wheeler's back tires screeched and squealed to a smoky stop not twenty feet from the frightened children. The lights all but blinded them both as they tried to shield their eyes from the sudden rush of illumination. The truck's air brakes clunked and hissed as the driver emerged with a startled look on his stern face.

He was a huge man with oversized features and a beard to match. He wore overalls, a plaid flannel jacket, and a baseball cap with an iron on patch that read "Mac" on it. As he neared the children, his features softened. They were both naked, bloody, and very dirty. It looked as though they had been badly beaten. "What are you kids doing out here? You're going to catch your death of cold out here. Get in the truck and warm up," he said.

Natalie cowered behind Nigel, trying to disappear into nonexistence. *He looks more like a lumberjack than a truck driver*, Natalie thought.

Nigel shuffled past the man with Natalie in tow. They climbed into the truck and looked around nervously. An assortment of rainbow-colored lights lit up the dashboard. The vibration of the large metallic monster matched the hum of the truck's engine, but they welcomed the heat. The truck driver climbed into the rig and cranked the heat up to the maximum. He reached into the sleep cab behind his seat and retrieved two smoked grey wool blankets and handed them to the children. "

What happened to you kids?" he asked.

But neither of them spoke. They looked straight ahead as if in some sort of dazed confusion.

"Well, this is a hell of a way to spend Christmas Eve," he huffed.

Natalie looked at the man. He had to be mistaken because the Kleins had thrown them into the basement a week before Halloween. She and Nigel had been so excited about going trick or treating in the nearby neighborhood where most of their classmates lived. There was no way they had been locked away for more than two months. She looked away from the liar; he had to be lying. Natalie saw a sign that read "DALLAS 9 Miles". The closer they got to the city limits, the more festive the decorations became. It really was Christmas Eve!

The truck driver pulled along the street in front of the police station and instructed the kids to get out. He wasn't exactly sure what they'd been through, but he knew that they needed help. He stood between them with a hand on each of their shoulders. He had six children of his own and his heart went out to the twins. Children needed nourishment and guidance, not neglect and abuse, and he wanted them to know that they weren't alone.

They entered the police station and the truck driver went into daddy mode. "Excuse me, I need some help over here, excuse me!" he screamed.

An elderly policewoman that looked more like she should be knitting quilts and baking cookies than behind the desk at a police station waved for them to come over. "How may I help you, darling?" she asked.

"I found these here kids walking on the road butt-ass naked, bruised up and whatnot. They won't tell me what's wrong, but something ain't right," he said.

"And you are?"

"I'm Wilbur Tubbs. I drive for Swift Freight and I was making a run when I found these babies!" he said heatedly.

"Do you mind if I have a detective take your statement and then we'll let you get back to your job."

"With all due respect, ma'am, fuck my job! I have six kids at home that I would die for and I'm not going to be able to sleep until I know these kids are okay. If it's some sick bastards out there preying on kids, I wanna know!" Mr. Tubbs said.

Officer Granny gestured to a detective who quickly took Wilbur Tubbs into a room, and neither Nigel nor Natalie ever saw him again.

She escorted the children into another room where two detectives waited. Nigel and Natalie both recounted their harrowing tale from beginning to end, making sure to not leave anything out - that is, except the part where Nigel set fire to their house, subsequently murdering their mother and Rudy. They even told the detectives how they'd *did it* to stay warm and to stay happy in the face of their adversity, because they loved each other. The detectives let them talk freely.

It wasn't until they were finished and fell silent that one of the detectives spoke, "Nigel, Natalie, do you think that you two making love is wrong?" he asked.

Both twins shook their heads no in unison.

"Well, it is. You kids shouldn't be doing that," he said.

"But Mrs. Klein said two people do it when they love each other," Nigel said.

"Yes, when a husband and wife love each other, not a brother and sister. She only told you guys that because she and her husband were sick individuals. We'll talk about that later though. Do either of you know the Klein's address?" he asked.

"I can show you where the house is. I watched the way Mr. Tubbs brought us here," Natalie said.

"Well, I memorized the address!" Nigel said proudly.

"The address will be just fine. We don't want you kids in any more danger, plus the temperature is still dropping," the detective said.

Officer Granny came into the room and brought both kids a set of clean clothes. "I know this is a terrible way to spend Christmas, but at least you're both safe and together. After you both change we'll get something to eat. How does that sound?" she asked.

They both nodded yes as the two detectives exited the room. Officer Granny stood staring at the kids. Natalie's feet were dirty and bloody. Dirt had woven its way into her matted, kinky hair and mud was caked underneath her fingernails. Her entire body was smudged with blood and mud. Officer Granny examined her carefully and noticed a foot long laceration on her back. The blood around the wound had begun to coagulate and crust over. The elderly officer could only shake her head. There was no way that these children deserved what they had been through. Nigel was the exact same way, except his wounds were in his small hands. She had to coax him into opening his hands. Nigel's hands were balled into fists so tight that the blood had begun to flow and dripped slowly to the linoleum tile below. Yes indeed, they were twins in every sense of the word, right down to the sadness and trepidation in their eyes.

Chapter 17

Tristen couldn't believe his ears. His mind swirled, his heart hurt, and he felt dizzy with anger. Natalie had bared her soul to him and as she talked to him, it was as if a weight had been lifted from her shoulders. She'd allowed Tristen into the deepest recesses of her being and exposed secrets that had lain dormant since she could remember. He wanted to protect her, be the rock in her life that no man had been outside of Nigel.

"I hope you don't think I'm a bad person, Tristen," Natalie said.

"No, actually I think you're a wonderfully loyal person. We all make mistakes, babe, and you're no different. The relationship that you and Nigel have is special and I can't judge you, baby, because you did what you thought was necessary to survive."

"Tristen, you have no idea how hearing you say those words makes me feel. You know, besides Nigel, you're the only one that knows my history."

"And I appreciate you sharing something so deep and personal with me. I just have one question though," Tristen said.

"What's that?"

"What ever happened to the Kleins?"

"Well, after we gave the police the address, they went to the farm to arrest them. When we went to court, it came out that they were coming from a Christmas party. They had us in the basement of their home and they were out partying. The DA did a fantastic job though, and come to find out we weren't the first," she said.

"They'd done it before?" Tristen asked.

"Yes, three times before, and one of the girls still hasn't been found. To think back on how they turned on each other during trial is funny. They both claimed that they did it for the other person, but the judge gave them both life sentences."

"So they are locked up tight right now then, huh?" Tristen mused.

Natalie covered her mouth to stifle her giggle. Justice was amazing and the Kleins had gotten their just desserts. "Actually, Maggie died of a heart attack shortly after she was sentenced so she never really got a chance to start serving her sentence. Then about a month before our sixteenth birthday, Officer Paloma - that's the old lady that I was telling you about - she came to the foster home and sat Nigel and me down. She read a newspaper article to us that stated that after repeated rapes in prison, David Klein had slit his own wrists. They brutalized him from what the paper said. It's funny because they tortured us, but when it happened to him he couldn't take it and went out like a punk."

"Shit, I'd kill myself too if I was getting my asshole reamed out every night."

They both laughed at the notion. Natalie couldn't believe how understanding Tristen was. He was a Godsend and she was glad that there were no more skeletons in her closet. "Nigel and I got a special kind of justice though. We took the Klein's last name after they adopted us, so when they were both dead, we received letters on our eighteenth birthday stating that we would each receive $125,000 apiece from Maggie's $250,000 life insurance policy. David had the same policy, but because he killed himself, they wouldn't pay out. As soon as those checks cleared and were in the bank, we went right down to the courthouse and changed our last name back to Sinclair," she said triumphantly.

"Wow, that's good, big baller!" Tristen joked.

"I want to take you somewhere tomorrow, if you don't mind," she said.

"Where?"

"It's a surprise. Are you down?" Natalie asked.

"I'll go anywhere that you want to take me, baby girl."

Tristen stirred in bed; the smell of bacon and coffee invaded his nostrils. He sat up in bed and sniffed the air. Just as he'd thought, the strong scent of freshly brewed coffee wafted through the air. He stood and walked to his dresser and removed a pair of basketball shorts and a T-shirt. He tried futilely to suppress his early morning hard-on, but nothing helped. Tristen heard the sound of cheerful laughter coming from beyond the bedroom. He walked into the dining room to see Natalie standing over the stove cooking and Toby sitting at the dining room table sipping a cup of coffee.

"Well good morning, sleepy head, glad you decided to join us," Natalie said cheerfully.

"Yeah, G, Natalie got the bacon, eggs, grits, and biscuits going up in here. She wouldn't even let me get a plate, talking about the King eats first!" Toby said.

Tristen smiled. He cupped Toby's shoulder and said, "Yeah, Chief, the squires and court jesters eat last, yo."

They all laughed. "Yo, but, on the serious side, I met somebody and she seems really nice," Toby said.

"Damn, dude, that was fast! You didn't waste any time," Tristen said.

"It's a long story, but we've been talking on the phone and I really dig her. She's from here but she was living in Newark. Her name is Yummi."

"Yummy? What kind of name is that? Is she a stripper or something?" Tristen asked curiously.

Toby's raucous laughter filled the lavish apartment, bouncing from wall to wall, coming to rest in the drums of Natalie and Tristen's ears. "Noooooooo, man, she's Chinese and her name is Yo Mi, but she pronounces it Yummi," Toby said.

"Chinese? Oh, you got something against a strong black woman?" Natalie asked.

"Hell to the naw, Nat, I actually love *all* women. She could be pink with lime green polka dots and if she's attractive, then I'm all over it. We just happened to meet and were attracted to one another."

"Uh huh," Natalie huffed as she turned around to tend to her eggs.

"Why does it have to be about color, Natalie? I don't see that shit," Toby said.

"Why are you cursing on God's day? And it's not about color; I'm just playing with your sensitive butt."

"I just want the chance to have what you and Tristen have, that's all," Toby said.

"What exactly do Tristen and I have?" she said, putting their plates in front of them.

"Come on, ma, a blind man can see y'all in love. All of this official shit is bogus. Oh, it ain't official until it's on Facebook!" Toby said sarcastically.

Natalie started to speak; she was going to check Toby and put him in his place.

Tristen stopped her. "Hold on, baby, I got this. Toby, when have you ever seen me put my business on Facebook? Listen, Natalie knows that I love her and that's all that matters to me. Our love is organic; it's natural, you know? We're building slowly and I don't think we need titles,. She's mine and I'm hers. That's it, that's all," Tristen said.

"That's what I mean." Toby stood, walked over to Natalie, and put his arms around her. He was still chewing when he started talking. "I didn't mean any harm. I just meant I want something solid and long-lasting, and the way this lady talks, she's ready for the same," he said, wiping biscuit crumbs from his mouth.

"I understand. Now go finish eating so that we can go!" she ordered.

Tristen and Toby both said, "Where are we going?"

"Just put on some clothes, something nice; it's a surprise. I'll be back to get you both at eleven o'clock, so be ready."

A couple of hours later they were pulling into the parking lot of New El Bethel Baptist Church. It wasn't a small church, but it wasn't large by any stretch of the imagination either. Sunday worshippers filed into the church in droves. A spectrum of colors from pastels to earth tones filled the parking lot as people made their way inside to hear the word of God. Old women that looked as though they'd been members of the church since it was built congregated near the front door in pinks and yellows and lavenders, scolding playful children who were not quite ready to go inside. The elder's hats were an ostentatious affair, boasting wide brims and broad feathers.

"If I'd have known that we were coming to church, I would have worn a suit," Tristen said.

"The Bible said come as you are, man, so we're straight!" Toby said, trying his best to smooth the wrinkles in his Sean John shirt and jeans.

The trio exchanged pleasantries with the old women at the front door and then went inside to take their seats. They walked into the church to the sounds of the choir singing. Their melodic mixture of sopranos, altos, and tenors filled the midsized church with happiness and hope.

"I'm just a nobody, tryna tell everybody about somebody who can saaaaaaave anybody.

I'm just a nobody, tryna tell everybody about somebody who can save anybody.

And he said, I'm on the streets day and night, that's my life.

That's my home, ain't got nowhere else I could go.

So I just walk the streets telling people about Jesus, from corner to corner, door to door

But they all make fun of me and say I'm just a nobody..."

As the choir finished the selection, words of praise could be heard from the young and old alike. "Hallelujah, praise the Lord, thank you Jesus," sang that song" along with cheerful and praise-filled clapping echoed throughout the worship hall.

The Reverend stood and looked out over the congregation. His eyes came to rest on Natalie, Tristen, and Toby and he smiled. "Good morning, everybody," he said.

"Morning, Reverend," the congregation said.

The young, handsome preacher stood regally. There was an aura of peace surrounding him and he glowed with the brightness of a man that had been touched by

God. He had, as the saying went, been bathed in the blood of the lamb. His smile was contagious, almost infectious, and his parishioners felt it. He raised his hands to quiet them as he began to speak.

"God is good all the time," he said.

As if on cue, his audience responded, "All the time, God is good!"

"I'm not perfect by a long shot. I've done things that I'm not proud of, but my God is a forgiving God." He said. "If you would this morning, good people, I would like for you to turn your bibles to Luke 22 verse 47 and 48. I want to talk to you this morning about loyalty. 47 reads, 'And while he was still speaking, behold, a multitude; and he who was called Judas, one of the twelve, went before them and drew near to Jesus to kiss him'. Verse 48 says, 'But Jesus said to him, Judas, are you betraying the Son of Man with a kiss?' We talk all the time about love and loyalty, but this is a prime example of loyalty gone wrong. We wanna believe that the people we hold in the highest regards see us in the same light," he said.

The church had gotten a little hotter and a little quieter. The preacher reached into his pocket and removed a handkerchief and wiped his sweaty brow. "If you want loyalty, bring it to Jesus. If you want somebody who's going to be in your corner, not talk behind your back and hold you down, bring it to Jesus. He's the only person I know that's always loyal, always on point, and always on time!" he shouted. He'd begun to do a little dance, skipping across the stage and jumping up and down, filled with the Holy Spirit. His delivery was syncopated and rhythmic as he began to speak again. "Judas betrayed Jesus with a kiss for thirty pieces of silver and he was one of twelve disciples! He sat at the table and broke bread with Jesus and drank his wine, huh, and still betrayed Jesus. He swore allegiance and denied all wrong, but still he betrayed Jesus. Even old Peter had the nerve to deny Jesus. He swore his love for Jesus but Jesus knew the real deal. He said, 'Peter, before the rooster crows, you'll deny me three times.' If Judas and Peter had learned the truth from Jesus and still were disloyal, how do you think the common man can be loyal to the common man? Hallelujah?" he said. Sweat was pouring from him profusely. He removed his suit coat and continued his sermon.

Tristen, Natalie, and Toby sat mesmerized by the oration, each lost in his and her own thoughts. After he'd finished preaching and church was over, the reverend walked up to the trio. He hugged Natalie and she introduced them.

"Tristen, Toby, this is my twin brother Nigel."

Then it dawned on Tristen why he looked so familiar. Nigel extended his hand and Tristen shook it eagerly. "I'm glad to meet you, man. You have an amazing sister. I was looking at you like wow, he looks familiar," Tristen said.

"Thank you, Tristen, I've heard a lot about you. As a matter of fact, every time I talk to Natalie she brings your name up, so I'm assuming since you're still around, you must be doing something right," Nigel said.

"Oh Nigel, stop it!" Natalie said, and then added, "I really enjoyed your sermon today. There are some disloyal people out here."

"Why don't you all walk with me? Let's talk," Nigel said.

They walked toward Natalie's car, listening to Nigel expound on his beliefs a little further. "Tristen, I want to thank you for being a part of my sister's life. I'm sure she's told you a little bit about our past. We've never had anybody, but I found solace in Christ. Natalie, on the other hand, only has me, and as much as I've tried to bring her to the Lord, the truth is, she's grown and I can't make her do anything."

"It's my pleasure, honestly. That's why I could relate to your sermon. Your sister is immensely loyal and I only hope to return such loyalty."

"Let me tell you something, Tristen. People get the wrong understanding of the Bible; they take it too literally. They see 'turn the other cheek' and they see it as weakness. They see 'vengeance is mine sayeth the Lord' and they think it's all on God. Understand that faith without works is dead, Tristen, and as much as we would like to believe that God is going to do it all, that's just not true. I'll pose a question to you, young brother. Let's say that you're extremely talented, but you're extremely misinformed about how God works. In your mind, you believe that God blessed you with the talent, so whatever is for you God will send your way, right? Wrong! In reality, God blesses you with talents and gifts, but you have to put yourself in position to use those gifts. Vengeance is never a good idea for an uneducated man, but I will tell you a secret that many people overlook about the Bible. In the good book, people got killed just about every day, and if you know anything about the Bible, people used to do it in the name of God. God is not going to send down a magical lightning bolt to smite your enemies. He will, however, allow you to get even so to speak through divine situations," Nigel explained.

"What do you mean through divine situations?" Tristen asked.

"I mean that a lot of times when things happen to people that have violated people that are protected by God, bad things tend to happen to them, sometimes out of the blue. Most of the time you don't have to touch them because God has your back. At other times, though, it may be necessary to get your hands dirty," Nigel said, winking his eye at Tristen.

Toby walked away from the conversation toward the edge of the road and lit a cigarette. He smoked, but he didn't want to pollute anyone else's lungs. He inhaled deeply and let the thick white smoke trickle from his nose and mouth.

A soft, familiar voice startled him and he jumped. "I'm sorry for scaring you, baby. I see you decided to come and give the Lord some of your time," the woman's voice said.

Toby turned to see the old lady from the plane that had called herself Mother. Mattie Daniels stood a whole 5'1" tall with bluish-grey hair and a beautiful disposition. Her voice was as soothing as light rain on a tin roof. She was classic church mother chic, with her soft, butter yellow dress and wide-brimmed hat to match.

She hugged Toby affectionately. "How have you been, baby? How's your transition been to the Dallas life?" she asked.

"I'm fine, Mother Mattie. My transition has been okay, I guess. I found a little job at a sandwich shop in downtown Dallas, so I'm working. And actually, I'm here with my cousin and his friend. The reverend that just spoke is her brother," he said.

"Reverend Sinclair? Lord ha'mercy, you're a friend of Natalie's? She's just as sweet as sugar," Mother Mattie said, and then added, "Let's go and say hello, sweetie."

"Ahhh, Mother, I see you've met Toby. He's one of Natalie's friends," Nigel said.

"Hey, Reverend. Yes, I actually met this young man on a plane coming from New Jersey. He has a lot of questions. I really want you to try and convince him to join our mentoring program. Toby, did you know that Reverend Sinclair is the youngest that this church has ever had? This boy is touched by God's hands; you could learn a lot from him. Now I'm gonna leave y'all babies to talk. I'm praising Jesus that he brought you all to us this morning. I'm going home. I got me some greens with ham hocks cooking and my butter beans been on low in the crock pot since last night, so I'll talk to y'all later," she said.

They all exchanged hugs with Mother Mattie and bid her farewell. Nigel Sinclair smiled brightly as he waved to Mother Mattie. She'd welcomed him into New El Bethel Baptist Church with open arms and had been instrumental in the retiring Pastor's decision to name him as his successor. "Tristen, Natalie has told me about your troubles with the men on your job and I've prayed heavily on it. I can tell you this: God gave you something special. You're what most people call a beautiful mind, but in order to maintain that mind, you will need to understand that self-preservation is key," Nigel said.

"I understand that, but I'm nobody's gangster and I'm not a hard man. I'm just a simple guy that wants to work and live my life. I didn't sign up for this extra mess and it seems as though these guys are doing everything in their power to make my life a living hell. I've been to HR, I've even called a lawyer that abruptly told me that I hadn't been there long enough to have a case. So it's like I'm stuck. I can either work there and keep dealing with it or quit."

"What keeps you there? I mean, with your brain, you can go anywhere and be an asset," Natalie asked.

"It's kind of like Nigel said, I guess. I'm on the fine line between loyalty and stupidity!"

"Nobody is perfect, my friend. I've had to, for the lack of a better term, step outside of myself and deal with those racist dudes. I had to call my mind back though because I'm a man of God. I'm still an infant in this thing called Christianity, so I make no apologies for being who I am," Nigel said.

"What are you telling me, man?"

"I'm telling you to handle it the best way that you know how. My sister is the happiest that I have ever seen her and I don't want to see her lose that light. I like you and I want you to take care of her. If and only if you find yourself in a position that you find that you just cannot handle, I want you to call me and I will handle it my way - God's way!" Nigel promised. He kissed Natalie on the cheek and shook Toby's and Tristen's hands. He held Tristen's hand and stared into his eyes as if searching for something.

For a split second, Tristen was intimidated until it dawned on him that Nigel wasn't trying to size him up, but rather, the look in his eyes was a look of shame and sadness. He knew that if Natalie felt about Tristen the way that she'd said, then she had undoubtedly told him of their incestuous indiscretion. Tristen took his second hand and let it rest on top of their handshake. His smile was warm and inviting as if to tell Nigel silently that he understood and that there was no judgment coming from him. Tristen would defend his honor and his woman with the last drop of his blood if necessary.

Chapter 18

David Ganzelle, Brennen Goldstein, Sean Westbury, Frances Trimble, and Caleb Weeks sat in the third floor conference room of CrossTech. It was after hours and every employee there had gone home for the night - or so they thought. The large panoramic window cast an unnatural and creepy reflection on the clandestine meeting.

"We've got to do something about that coon!" David Ganzelle shouted.

"Lower your fucking voice, David! It's only us here, but your big mouth is going to wake the dead. I don't see what the big deal is. The kid just started, for Christ's sake," Caleb whispered.

Frank Trimble's southern drawl drowned out the hushed argument of the two men before it even got started. "The bottom line is, Tristen Graham is positioning himself to take over this company."

"Take over the company? How the hell do you figure that?" Sean asked.

"Black folks are like roaches. Once he's in, he'll bring his cousins, his aunts, his sisters and their forty kids. Have you ever heard the term there goes the neighborhood? Well, if we don't do something to stop him, that's going to be CrossTech: blacks everywhere!" Frank barked.

"You guys are worrying about the wrong shit. That black bitch Natalie is the problem. You know she's pulling his strings, running her nigger mouth with her fucking pillow talk," Brennen said.

Everyone in the room knew that his tirade was more about jealousy than worry about position in the company. He was obsessed with Natalie and each of them knew it. He wasn't in love with her, he wasn't pining for her, he didn't really give a damn about Natalie; he just didn't want anyone else to have her.

"You Yankee boys don't know how to deal with uppity niggers, but I do. In Alabama, we string 'em up when they get beside themselves," Frank said.

"Wait one goddamn minute, Frank, I'm nobody's killer. I don't even know why we're so concerned with one man, and a young-ass boy at that," Sean said.

Without saying a word, Caleb produced a manila folder. It was Tristen's mock-ups of the NR 613. "If we allow Tristen to bring the finished product of this invention to Hayden, he will hand Tristen this company on a silver platter. This little piece of shit will make Hayden Cross a billionaire and Hayden will bow at his feet. Where will that leave us?" Caleb asked.

"If the company gets paid, we all get paid," Sean said.

Caleb snatched Sean up by his collar. His disdain for this perverted little employee was apparent and his lack of knowledge was frustrating. "When have you ever made this company billions? No, scratch that, when have you ever made it millions?" Caleb barked.

Sean quickly broke Caleb's grasp. "Never!" he exclaimed.

"Yet we still keep you around, right? So what makes you think that Hayden won't all but hand Tristen this company for a billion dollars? We're not talking simple logistics; we're talking defense contracts, the shit that spy movies are made from. There is no way that Hayden Cross would ever jeopardize losing Tristen, so we have to do this on our own."

"If that's the case, why don't we just kill him and take the technology?" David Ganzelle sniffed.

He'd meant it jokingly, but the men in the room had begun to mumble as if they were actually considering it - all of them, that is, except Brennen. His mind was still on Natalie Sinclair. He would make both her and Tristen pay. She would pay because of her disloyalty and Tristen would pay because he was…black.

Chapter 19

Natalie sat with her back against the couch, nestled deep into the cushions with her feet resting comfortably on Tristen's lap. He massaged her feet gently while they watched *Law and Order: Special Victims Unit*. With every touch of his hand, she felt her insides quiver. She'd never met a man that was able to express himself so well. When he'd told Nigel that he was nobody's gangster, she'd found a new respect for him. They'd dropped Toby off at the sandwich shop after church, gone to Two Podna's Bar-B-Q for dinner, and had really gotten a chance to know one another. He'd promised to always take care of her and be in her corner and she'd done the same. She searched her soul for the reasons why she was so madly in love with this young man, but love needed no explanation.

Tristen moved Natalie's feet and kneeled in front of her. He positioned himself between her legs and lay his head on her breasts. Their breathing meshed and as she inhaled, he exhaled, leaving no space for intrusion.

"You feel that, Tristen? Our bodies are in rhythm; they're in perfect sync," she said.

But he did not answer. He lay listening to her heartbeat, the very core of her. Before long, Natalie felt wetness reach her skin through her blouse. She lifted Tristen's head, but he averted his eyes.

"Are you crying, baby? What's wrong?" she asked.

It was something about the caring tone in which she spoke that put Tristen at ease. "I'm sorry Natalie. You must think I'm a big punk for crying," he sniffled.

"Not at all. Real men cry, my love. It's the man-child that thinks that he's a man who refuses to cleanse himself with tears. If you need to cry, let it out."

"I'm tired of being the nice guy all of the time. I listened to what your brother had to say today and it made a lot of sense, but at the same time, I feel like I need to let them feel me. I hate feeling like I have to be the voice of reason all the time. It makes me feel like I'm going to snap one of these days!" Tristen cried.

"Babe, listen to me. Although I would never encourage you to do anything negative, I will say this. You are a man, a very intelligent man, mind you, and no one can take that away from you. Whatever you decide to do though, I am behind you one hundred percent."

"You know what else brings tears to my eyes? The fact that I love you more than I've ever loved any woman besides my mother. I've had girlfriends, of course, but it's never been like this, and if something happened to you, I don't know what I would do," Tristen said.

"Nothing is going to happen to me, babe, promise."

Tristen stood and pulled Natalie to her feet. He took her arms and put them around his neck and gripped her waist tightly. He kissed her as he might never see her again and then just as quickly he let her go. He stepped back and removed his shirt and turned on his heels, headed for the bathroom. He stopped in the doorway between his bedroom and bathroom and turned back to look at Natalie.

"Are you coming?" he asked as he dropped his pants and boxers.

Natalie stood up excitedly. She didn't know where it would lead to, but her loins twitched with anticipation. She watched Tristen's sinewy but muscular frame disappear into the bathroom and moments later, she heard the soft hum of the shower head spring to life. She slithered out of her skirt and unbuttoned her blouse slowly. She walked seductively toward the bathroom, unclasping her bra along the way. She wiggled out of her panties just as she made it to the entrance of the bathroom.

Tristen stood at the back of the steamy shower. His fully erect penis sliced through the thick steam like a serrated-edged knife. He beckoned to Natalie from beyond the mist and she went to him, open and ready for him to take her. He embraced her and she could feel his hard penis pressing against the softness of her wet skin.

"I want to do this, baby, I want to make love to you, but I need to know that it's me and only me," he said.

Natalie nodded yes as she kissed him savagely. She reached for the soap and lathered her hands. Natalie let her hands glide over Tristen's chiseled chest and down to his manhood. It throbbed and pulsated between her fingers as she stroked it softly. Tristen cupped Natalie's butt with both hands and lifted her and carried her to his bed. He laid her on the bed gently and kissed her breasts softly.

"Natalie, I have a confession to make," Tristen said.

"What's on your mind, baby? You can tell me anything."

"I feel like a fool because I have absolutely no idea what I'm doing and it's embarrassing," he said, chuckling slightly.

Natalie laughed with Tristen. They lay there wrapped in one another's arms until she started to rub his penis again. "Don't worry about anything, baby, I got you. Just lay back and relax and let me take care of your body."

Tristen laid back like Natalie asked, but he pulled her to him. "It's not all about me, baby. I want you to teach me what turns you on, I want you to teach me how to please you," Tristen said huskily.

Natalie simply smiled. She kissed him passionately, letting her soft lips linger on Tristen's trembling lips. She kissed his neck and then his chest, circling his nipples with her tongue. Natalie let a trail of warm kisses travel from Tristen's chest to his navel and he trembled from pleasure. His entire body tingled as she circled the tip of his penis softly with the tip of her tongue. Tristen tried to remain calm, but it was useless. He felt pressure rising from deep inside, building, stretching his manhood until it throbbed painfully. Natalie took him into her mouth gently. She tried hard to take his full length into her mouth, but she gagged from the thickness. She licked the shaft of his erectness, swirling her tongue periodically around the head while she played with his swollen balls. They were tight, heavy and full. She reached beneath herself to feel her own wetness. She played in her moistness before bringing her fingers to Tristen's lips. He licked them eagerly, sucking the juices from her slender fingers. She couldn't believe how wet she was, how utterly turned on she was from their oral escapade. She pulled Tristen's hardness from her mouth with a wet plop and stood over him. She bent and kissed him, then disappeared into the bathroom.

Natalie returned moments later with a towel draped across her shoulder. Even in the darkness, she could see Tristen watching her every move. She walked to the stereo mounted in his bedroom wall. The Quiet Storm on K104 was playing Natalie's favorite song. Whenever she heard "A Couple of Forevers" it always made her daydream and fantasize about Tristen, and now they were taking their first steps toward forever.

"I see it clear, my heart is here, we got each other, let's take it from there

And if I could I'd love you a forever at a time

Oh, oh, oh

What we've been through no one else knows, 'cause all that matters is how far this goes

And it will go until it starts again oh, oh

Me and you are built like armor, nothing can stop love from loving on us

And I'm not asking for much, just a couple of forevers

A couple of forevers, I'm the only one, you're the only one

Together 'til never I'm talking my forever

Just a couple of forevers."

Natalie used the towel to pat her wetness. She was entirely too wet, and besides, she would need the towel. Natalie had that wet-wet. She was a squirter, and if Tristen worked the middle like she thought he would, then she would indeed flow like an open faucet. She lay next to Tristen and kissed him on the cheek.

"Are you ready for class, baby?" she whispered. Tristen nodded coyly. She pulled him on top of her and whispered in his ear again, "Love making is about patience and sensuality, baby. Kiss my body softly, pay extra attention to my earlobes, my nipples, and my inner thighs. Those are my secret spots."

Tristen was a good student. He kissed her neck, then her chin, and then he mimicked the licking motions that she'd made to his chest. He circled her nipples with his tongue, pausing to suck them gently. He let his tongue trail down to her navel and then spread her thighs. Tristen expertly kissed and licked her inner thighs. He went so far as to leave his hot wet kisses on her knees, shins, and ankles. He sat back on his haunches and took Natalie's foot in his hand and massaged it sensually. He then placed her perfectly manicured toe in his mouth and kissed it while playing with her clitoris with his thumb.

"Wait," she said, nearly out of breath. Natalie took the towel that she had and placed it beneath her.

After the towel was spread, she pulled Tristen to her and kissed him deeply again. Their tongues locked and swirled about in one another's mouths, sending jolts of electricity and pent-up sexual tension-filled sparks flying between them.

"I want you to kiss and lick my clit as soft as you can," she said, guiding his head to her pussy. She used one hand to guide his chin, and with the other hand, she used her index finger and middle finger to expose her erect clitoris. The tip of his tongue touched her love button and she shuddered. He started sucking it slowly, churning his tongue around her clit, darting his tongue in and out of her with sexual expertise.

"Oh...my...God...Tristen...you   lied!" She stuttered. She felt her eruption building, but she wanted to hold it. "Stick one of your fingers in and move it like you're telling someone to come here!" she instructed.

Tristen did as he was told, all the while, still paying close attention to her clit, and then it happened. A rush of wetness, squirt after squirt of succulent sweetness, sprayed Tristen across the chin. Yet he kept licking and slurping, bobbing and sucking her clit until it happened again and again. Wave after euphoric and orgasmic wave racked her petite frame until she could no longer take it. She forced his face away from her lower region and rolled to the other side of the bed.

"Oh my God, baby, that was unbelievable! I thought you said you never did this before," she said, panting heavily.

"I haven't. Did I do well?" Tristen asked.

"You did fantastic! Lay down, baby."

Once Tristen was lying down, she positioned herself over him and guided him inside of her. Tristen gasped at the feeling. There were so many thoughts running through his head, the most important of which was the fact that he was glad that he'd waited and he was experiencing this with Natalie. She gyrated her hips, absorbing the thickness that was buried deep inside of her. Natalie guided Tristen's hands to her breasts. She arched her back and bore down on his stiffness. Electrified ripples of ecstasy poured through her body as she wiggled and rotated her hips. She rolled off of Tristen with weak and shaky knees. Natalie got on all fours and buried her head in the goose feather filled pillow beneath her.

"Go deep, baby, stir this pussy like coffee," she said seductively.

Tristen mounted Natalie slowly and thrust the length of himself into her. She gasped and shook violently trying to get away, but Tristen pulled her back to him, unwilling to pull out of the most glorious feeling that he'd ever felt.

"Harder!" she screamed, and Tristen obliged. "Oh God, stir it, Tristen, stir this pussy like coffee!" she cried again, and Tristen obliged until he felt the hot, sticky mist of Natalie's fluids. She collapsed unto the bed, unable to move.

Tristen put his hand on the small of her back. "Are you okay, baby?" he asked.

"I'm more than fine, Tristen. Okay, last lesson. I want you to put my legs on your shoulders and dig deep. Go fast, then slow, and make sure you're grinding hard, baby."

"Got it: fast, slow, deep, grind!" he repeated.

Tristen took Natalie's legs and threw them over his shoulders. He positioned himself over her and let his man muscle slide as deep as it would go, up to the hilt. He followed her instructions to a tee. She bucked and thrashed and she clawed at his back as he hammered away at her insides. Natalie pulled him close and kissed him passionately, but something was wrong, something had to be wrong, because Natalie was crying. Tristen tried to withdraw himself, but she only grabbed him by his butt cheeks and buried him deep within her again.

"Don't stop, Tristen, faster, oh my fucking God, harder! Damn, this is some good dick!" she screamed.

"Why are you crying then?"

"Because it's good, baby, damn!" Natalie said.

Tristen couldn't believe his ears. Toby had told him, *"If your dick game is proper, son, they will shed tears for the pipe."* Tristen hadn't taken it literally. He felt empowered; he felt like beating on his chest, proclaiming victory over all things Natalie. "I love you, Natalie, I love you so mu-" he started, but before he could finish, he felt Natalie's walls contract and he came, and so did she. He rolled off of her and stared into her eyes. "I'm sorry that I came, baby," he said apologetically, dropping his head.

"Are you kidding me? That was fantastic, Tristen! Two hours and some change? Shit, that's freaking wonderful. Boyyyy, I'm glad you're mine, because that, my friend," she said, pointing to his penis, "is the kind of dick that will make a basic bitch lose her ever loving mind!" she said jokingly. She kissed him again. *That was yummy, maybe he'll give me some more before I leave in the morning to go home to shower and change for work,* she thought.

Chapter 20

Brennen Goldstein sat parked outside of Billionaire's Row, fuming. He'd come into the lobby at the same time that Tristen and Natalie had entered the elevator. He'd ducked behind one of the massive decorative columns to avoid being seen by the couple. They were walking hand in hand as if they were in love and it had made his blood pressure soar. He couldn't understand the hold that Natalie had over him, but he didn't like it. After hours of waiting, she'd finally come out of the building and started driving toward her small apartment in lower Turtle Creek. He watched her disappear into her building and then he followed close behind under cover of darkness. Although the building was nice, it was far too dark. It gave him the creeps and reminded him of a bad episode of *Law and Order: SVU*. The overhead lights in the hallway flickered on and off as Brennen made his way toward Natalie's apartment.

Natalie walked out of her apartment to find Brennen leaning against the wall in the hallway just outside of her apartment. "It's kind of early for work, isn't it?" Brennen asked. It was still dark outside, just before dawn, and Natalie liked to get an early start. Brennen knew this, so Natalie was irritated by his offhand remark.

"What are you doing here, Brennen? I thought that I asked you not to come to my place anymore?"

"Why? Because your little nigglet boyfriend will get mad? Well fuck him and fuck you too!" he said.

Natalie could smell the remnants of liquor on his breath, probably from pulling an all-night drinking binge again. "I'm not going to argue with you, Brennen, it's too early for this shit."

"I'll make a deal with you. Give me some and I won't kill you," he said, producing a large butcher's knife.

Natalie had faced worse demons than the one standing in her hallway, but there was something about the look in Brennen's eyes that scared her. She didn't understand his obsession with her, but after the night that she'd had with Tristen, there was no way that she was sleeping with Brennen Goldstein. She attempted to push past him to make it to the elevator, but he blocked her path and raised his knife. "I'm not fucking playing with you! You're going to give me some pussy and suck my dick with those big juicy lips or I'm going to cut your tar baby head off!" he slurred.

"Brennen, I don't know what's wrong with you; your ass must be drunk or something. But I'm not doing shit with you!" she barked.

Brennen punched her with such force that she felt dizzy. Searing pain ripped through her face and she could feel the blood oozing slowly. She reached for the doorknob, trying to get inside of her apartment to safety, but as soon as she turned the knob, Brennen shoved her hard and she went crashing to the floor inside of her home. He dropped down on top of her and wrapped his hands around her neck. He choked her and Natalie felt herself going numb. She felt lightheaded. *Maybe if I play dead, he'll leave me alone*, she thought. That thought was quickly replaced with dread as Brennen's fist smashed into her cheek. Natalie tried to fight back, but she had no strength.

"You're going to die today. You should have just been with me," he said.

With every word that he spoke, he landed another punch and Natalie laughed. Although she was in excruciating pain, she laughed. He slapped her again and Natalie laughed again. The more she laughed, the angrier Brennen became.

"What's so goddamned funny, bitch?" he asked curiously.

Natalie did not answer. She stared at him through swollen eyes and he struck her again. This time Natalie coughed up blood and spit into Brennen's face. "Do you know why I'm not talking to you? Because I don't talk to dead men. Nigel is going to rip you to shreds when I tell him what you've done." Natalie laughed.

"Who said you'll get a chance to tell your coon brother anything?" he sneered as he slid the butcher's knife into her rib cage.

Tristen was antsy. He paced back and forth across the plush shag carpet in his condo. It was a quarter to nine and Natalie still hadn't returned. He heard the sound of keys jingling from beyond the door. Tristen rushed to it and snatched it open. Toby stood there dumbfounded, fumbling through his keys to find the right one.

"Damn, Triz, you scared the shit out of me, Cuzzo," Toby said.

"Sorry, my dude, I thought you were Natalie. She should've been here to get me by now."

"Maybe she forgot about you and went straight to work," Toby said.

"Yeah, maybe," Tristen said reflectively, but truth was, that wasn't like Natalie. She was always at Tristen's by eight-thirty with coffee and pastries in hand. Tristen dialed Natalie's cell and then her desk at work, and when she didn't answer either phone, he got worried. "Toby, I'm going to catch you later. I need to run to Natalie's. Something is wrong, I can feel it," Tristen said.

"You need me to come with you?" Toby offered.

"No, it may be nothing at all. I'll call you and let you know what's up," Tristen said, exiting his condo.

He made it to Natalie's in less than ten minutes, thankful that he'd caught all green lights on the way over. He stood at the elevator, frantically pushing the button, but the elevator never came. Tristen pushed the door open leading to the stairs and climbed them two at a time until he reached the second floor. He bent over, winded, trying to catch his breath. He hated Natalie's building, not only because it was too dark, but because the elevator was notoriously slow. He walked down the hallway, apprehensive of what lay ahead.

Tristen made it to Natalie's apartment and gasped in horror. Her door was wide open and there was a trail of blood leading somewhere into the darkness of the hall. Tristen peeked inside of the apartment and saw a puddle of blood staining Natalie's cream-colored Berber carpet, but there was no Natalie. He turned on his heels and headed toward the hall to follow the trail of blood. He wanted to run, but he was afraid of what he might find. Was she dead? Was she hurt? Had she hurt somebody? He couldn't shake the eerie feeling of dread that filled his body. Fear consumed him and grief overtook him as the thought of what might have become of Natalie seized his mind. Tristen began to weep softly and then he saw her.

Natalie lay motionless, half inside of the elevator and half inside the hallway. She was lying on her stomach with her head twisted in an awkward position as if she were trying to look back and above her at the same time. The elevator doors dinged and slammed against her damaged body repeatedly. The eggshell white business suit that she wore had turned a deep crimson along her left side.

"No, no, no, baby!" Tristen cried as he turned her over. He felt the subtle heave of her shallow breathing. His Natalie was still alive. "Who did this, baby? Natalie, can you hear me? Who did this to you, baby?" Tristen asked frenetically.

Natalie lifted her arm weakly, fighting to make a fist. She extended her index finger and pointed to the mirror behind Tristen. In her own blood she had smeared BG onto the reflective glass.

"Brennen Goldstein did this shit?" Tristen asked.

Natalie opened her eyes just long enough to make eye contact with Tristen before she slipped into unconsciousness.

Chapter 21

Esco sat in his dank motel room listening to the crackhead Lorna from next door trying to lie her way up on another five dollar hit. "Esco, I'm just trying to get five more dollars so I can catch the bus to see my momma," she said through missing teeth.

"And what are you going to do for me if I give you my five dollars?" Esco asked.

Lorna put her hands on her frail hips and cocked her head to one side, much like a curious puppy might. "Whatever you want me to do, daddy," she said, trying to sound seductive.

"Suck this hot meat; I'll give you five dollars. What's up?" he said as he dropped his boxers and leaned back in his chair.

Lorna took Esco's flaccid penis into her hands and stroked it a few times. "When are you gonna gimme some of this dick, Esco?"

"When RuPaul makes President of the USA. Shut up and put something in your mouth, bitch! I ain't fucking with your dirty leg ass like that, ma." Esco closed his eyes and tried to imagine that Lorna's lips belonged to his ex-wife. She bobbed and slurped on Esco's little five inch penis until she felt his testicles tighten and swell, then she stopped. "What the fuck are you stopping for, shorty? I'm about to cum. Kick that shit, yo!" Esco spat.

"What if I told you that I got some information that's worth more than five dollars? What would you say?"

"I'd say stop bullshittin' and finish blowing this meat whistle, then we can talk about it."

Lorna dropped her head back into Esco's lap and continued slurping away. Moments later, he shot his hot load into Lorna's mouth. She swallowed it, licked her lips, and rubbed her stomach as if she'd just finished a hefty meal. "Now what info could you possibly have for me?"

"Remember the picture of that boy you showed me? Well, I found him," she said proudly.

"What? Where?"

"Downtown. I went to pay some old tickets and went into the sandwich shop across the street from the courthouse and he works there. I wasn't sure if it was him until I saw his name tag. It said Toby. Ain't that what you said his name was? Toby or ToTo or something?" she asked.

Esco didn't say a word. He just walked to a nearby table and retrieved a crumpled twenty dollar bill. As soon as he handed her the money, she scurried out of the motel room like a frightened mouse. Lorna walked out into the parking lot of the rundown motel and yelled for Mook, a young crack dealer that worked the Snooty Fox

Motel. Esco stood in the doorway and shook his head. *Guess that bitch forgot about seeing her momma*, he thought. Dope smokers were all the same. They would say and do anything necessary to get that next hit. Esco had been around crackheads his whole life. The information that Lorna had given him was worth far more than he'd paid her. He closed the door, sat on the edge of the bed, and dialed Yummi's number.

"Hey, what's up?" she said.

"Yo, I found that little bitch-ass nigga I was telling you about."

"Okay, so again, what's up?" Yummi asked impatiently.

"Listen, all you have to do is get him alone and then call me. I'll take care of the rest."

"Where do I find him, Esco?"

"He works at a little sandwich shop across the street from the courthouse downtown. His name is Toby," he said.

Yummi felt the blood drain from her body. He couldn't be talking about *her* Toby. They knew each other intimately. They had given each other pleasure beyond the physical and she'd fallen for him hard. She'd never known real love until she met Toby. The things that they'd shared surpassed conventional love and sex. They'd shared their hopes, dreams and fears.

"Yo, ma, you there?" Esco said.

"Yeah, I'm here."

"You good? You gonna handle that or what?" he asked.

"You know I got you. Just be ready to handle your business when I call. And Esco?"

"Yeah?"

"After I do this for you, we're done. I want you out of my life for good," Yummi said.

"A'ight, ma, you got that."

Yummi hung up the phone in a daze. Could Toby have played her and convinced her that he was something that he wasn't? It was possible; anything was possible. After all, Yummi had been lying about who she was her whole life. She didn't, however, want to believe that Toby was lying. He'd told her of his gambling addiction. He'd assured her that gambling for him was just a means of coming up on some quick money. She'd in turn assured him that as long as he kept it real with her and loved her like she deserved to be loved, he would never have to worry about money. He'd given her his word that he would not only love her like no other man could, but he would work for a living and give up gambling, and that's what he'd been doing. She was torn, but she felt as though she owed it to her love for Toby to get the truth. If he told her that he'd done the things that Esco had accused him of, she'd simply walk away. If he denied it and she could read the truth in his eyes, then they would move forward. Until she knew the truth though, she couldn't even begin to think of a future with Toby. She loved him, but she wouldn't live her life with a rapist. Her hands trembled almost violently as she dialed Toby's cell number.

"Hello?" he answered.

"Hey babe, are you busy?" Yummi asked.

"I'm just trying to get ready for work, psyching myself up for this hour long bus ride. What's good?"

"Don't catch the bus. I'm going to come and pick you up and I'll take you to work."

"Okay, I'll wait. Is everything alright? You sound strange," Toby asked.

"Everything is fine. I just want to talk to you face to face." She hit the end button and left her hotel suite.

Yummi tried not to speed through the city streets en route to her lover, but it was next to impossible. She weaved in and out of traffic, bravely accelerating through yellow lights until she reached her destination. "I'm downstairs," she said, as Toby answered his phone.

Moments later, Toby emerged from the condo and jumped into the passenger's seat. "What's up, Pudding?" he asked and kissed her on the cheek.

Yummi smiled. She wasn't exactly sure how to bring the subject up, but it had to be discussed. "Do you love me, Toby?" she asked.

"Hell yeah, why?"

"Remember when we first met and - " she began, but Toby cut her off.

"Don't beat around the bush, baby, just come out with it," he urged.

"I want to ask you something and it's imperative that you're totally honest with me for the sake of our relationship, okay?" Yummi asked.

"I never lie to you, baby girl, so go ahead," he said.

"Do you know someone named Esco?"

The question took Toby by surprise. He didn't know whether to scream or whether to jump out of the car. Months earlier, his Aunt Ruth had called him and told him about the rude young man that had come by their home with a job offer for him. After she'd described him, Toby had known it was Esco. Now Yummi was mentioning him by name and it made him uneasy. "Why you ask me that?" he asked nervously.

"Because I've met him and he has it out for you. The question is why? He claims that you're a rapist, baby."

"That son of a bitch is lying, babe! You know why he wants me dead? Because I beat him out of a couple of racks on the poker table and I cheated to get it. When he caught me cheating he tried to kill me, but I dipped and came to Dallas. I'm not a rapist," he said.

The look in his eyes told Yummi everything that she needed to know. She explained to Toby how she and Esco had come to meet and also how Toby's name had come into the mix.

"If he knows where I work, I can't go back there, Yummi. Esco might be a loser, but he's also a killer," Toby said.

"Don't worry about that; I have a plan - that's if you're with it," she said.

"Oh yeah? And what's this plan?"

"All we have to do is get Esco to admit that he's trying to kill you on tape and then take it to the police. They'll lock him up and we'll be rid of him forever," Yummi said. Toby's laughter echoed throughout the small rental car. "What's so funny, Toby?" she asked.

"Because you're talking like this is an episode of *CSI: Miami* and this is real life. Baby, this dude is a killer, I told you that. The only things he's interested in are money and my blood, nothing else. He won't talk."

"So what are we supposed to do?" she asked as she pulled into the parking garage of her hotel. She wanted to get all of her things out of the hotel and find another one close to where Toby stayed before Esco had a chance to come for her. It was, as Toby said, their only means of making it out of the situation alive.

By the time they made it to her hotel room, the plan was hatched. Yummi would still turn Toby over to Esco, but instead of things going the way that Esco planned, it would be an ambush by both Yummi and Toby. They would be rid of him once and for all. Toby pulled Yummi close to him and kissed her passionately.

"You know I love you, right?" he asked.

Yummi stepped back and undressed slowly. "Why don't you show me?" she asked. Again Toby pulled Yummi to him, this time letting his fingers slip into her moistness. "Aren't you going to get undressed, baby?" Yummi asked with bated breath.

"No, baby, it's all about pleasing you right now. Are you ready for a mustache ride?" he asked with a sly, knowing grin on his face.

"A mustache ride? What's that?"

"I want you to sit on my tongue, sit on my face, and ride my mustache while I lick your soul," Toby said.

Chapter 22

Tristen couldn't relax. His Ferragamo loafers clicked and clacked against the clinically white tile floors of Parkland Memorial Hospital. He paced nervously, praying that Natalie would pull through. Nigel sat nearby with his hands clasped together, balled tightly in silent prayer. He finished praying and turned to Tristen.

"Are you going to make it, bro?" Nigel asked.

"Yes, I just feel like it's all my fault, like Brennen did this to her to get back at me," Tristen said.

"No, he didn't. Nat and Brennen had history, and although he may have been jealous of you, he did this to get back at Natalie for rejecting him. He's always wanted to control her and the fact that he can't drives him crazy," Nigel explained.

"Well excuse my language, but fuck him! I'm going to get them all for their little racist games. They hurt my baby, Nigel!" Tristen huffed.

"Are you sure that you're built for that, youngster?"

"I'm a nice guy, but even nice guys have a limit and I've reached mine. No more being nice; it's time for war!" Tristen snapped.

"I understand, but I need a favor, Tristen."

"What's that?" Tristen asked.

"Save Brennen for me. I have something special for that dude."

"Are you sure? I wouldn't want you to mess up anything between you and God," Tristen said honestly.

"You let me worry about that. He's not finished with me yet, so I'm not perfect. Yeah, I'm a soldier for Christ, but I'm also a rider for mine. Jesus knew what he was getting when I enlisted in the Christian Army."

There was nothing that Tristen could say. He'd never been overly religious. Fact was, he couldn't remember the last time he'd been to church before meeting Natalie and Nigel. "My mom once told me to use what God had blessed me with to get even and I never quite understood what she meant. I don't have much in the way of a killer's mentality, but my best weapon has always been my mind," Tristen said. He snapped his fingers as if he'd been struck with an epiphany. He hastily made his way toward the elevator.

"Where are you going, Tristen?" Nigel asked.

"I have a few ideas. I'll be back." The elevator opened and Tristen stepped inside. As the doors slid closed, he tripped the sensor to reopen the doors. "If she wakes up, tell her that I love her and that she was right, crying is cleansing," he said.

Tristen's mind was beyond clear, but his anger was mounting. Natalie was innocent. Sure she had a quick temper and a smart mouth, but she was innocent just the same. He accepted the reality that no matter how smart he was, no matter what he was able to bring to the table professionally, they would always see him as a nigger. He knew that they would always see him as someone beneath them in social ranking. In their eyesight, he wasn't worthy of the position that he held. It was bad enough that he had to deal with Frank, Sean, David, and Brennen, but Caleb Weeks was even in on it. Who was left to turn to if his boss was siding with the racists?

And then it hit him. Caleb was their corporate protection, so to speak. He had basically given them an executive license to operate with impunity. Tristen would eliminate Caleb first and he knew just how to do it. Caleb Weeks lived in Hayden Cross's shadow and he would use that to his advantage. The first thing that he needed was a dummy computer, an untraceable computer that he could use for his dirty work. He didn't trust the laptop that the company had given to him. Tristen pulled into the parking lot of Best Buy and ran inside. He purchased a laptop and headed towards Billionaire's Row. After he made it home, he rushed upstairs to his apartment and called the office.

"CrossTech, how may I direct your call?"

"Hello, Alice, this is Tristen Graham. There's been a death in the family. I'm going to need the rest of the week off," he lied.

"Hi, Tristen, okay, I will let Mr. Weeks know as soon as I see him. Have a nice day."

He hung up the phone and began his dastardly deed. It was simple – genius, actually. Tristen connected multiple proxy servers together, each from a different part of the world, from his new laptop. By stringing together more than twenty proxies, his IP address could never be traced. If by chance someone did try to trace the IP address, it would register to a random server somewhere in the Congo or perhaps France and so on. Tristen set up his phantom network and began his work.

First he set up an offshore account in Caleb Weeks's name. Next he hacked into Check Mark Inc. They were the company that handled payroll for CrossTech. He cross referenced the employees that had been there since the company's inception against the employees that had come and gone over the course of their twenty-five years in business. Over the years there had been more than four thousand employees to come and go through the doors of CrossTech. Tristen went into Check Mark's system and deducted ten cents per hour from each of those four thousand employees for the entire twenty-five years. He didn't care if they were gone or not, Tristen simply needed a red flag to go off in the offices of Check Mark. With the amount of employees that CrossTech employed, it wouldn't be long before Check Mark was alerted of fraud. They would in turn contact Raj Patel, who would launch a full scale investigation. He didn't particularly care for Caleb Weeks, so as soon as he got wind that the money had been funneled into an account owned by Caleb, he would contact the proper authorities. Yes, it wouldn't be long before Mr. Weeks was up shit's creek without a paddle. He'd set the wheels in motion for Caleb to spend a very long time in prison for the embezzlement of more than twenty million dollars in CrossTech funds. Tristen chuckled to himself. *Hopefully Bernie Madoff has room in his cell for this asshole*, he thought.

Chapter 23

Jealousy is one of the most powerful emotions known to man and Tristen knew this. After all that Natalie had told Tristen about Frank Trimble and his wife Heather, it wouldn't be hard to drive him to the brink of insanity. Tristen went to Photobucket and found several pictures that fit Natalie's description of Jamal. A tall, chocolate brother with long dreads and chiseled features graced the fake Facebook page that Tristen had created. He was unsure of how Heather's memory might be concerning Jamal so he didn't want to take the chance of naming him after Heather's Jamaican lover. He Googled names until he found someone who had a lot going for himself, but who lacked the photographic evidence of his existence. Patrick Mason was a young entrepreneur that, according to his profile on LinkedIn, preferred not to post pictures.

After he finished creating his fake profile, Tristen started searching for Heather Trimble's Facebook page. There were only twelve or so active profiles, but one of them had to be hers. She was young and beautiful and the world was hers for the taking. A woman of her caliber, whose husband didn't demand that she work, had way too much time on her hands. Heather had an affinity for cheating with black men, so she would most certainly be on Facebook. There were just too many beautiful people to see and interact with for Heather to not be on the largest social networking platform in the world.

Out of the twelve Heather Trimbles that he found, only two were from Dallas. Out of those two, one of them was fourteen years old, the other one was *his* Heather, and Natalie's description hadn't done her justice. He could see why Frank Trimble had fallen into her snare and was unable to let her go. For all intents and purposes, Heather was gorgeous, but she was still a whore and Tristen would use her to bait her husband. He sent her a Friend request along with several other people so that his page didn't look fake and then he waited.

Tristen went into the bathroom and removed the clothes that were soaked with Natalie's blood. While he showered, he attempted to hatch yet another plan to rid himself of David Ganzelle. He smiled as the water ran down and cascaded over his hard body. He heard the familiar ding of acceptance coming from his laptop. Still naked and wet, he went to the living room and looked at the computer screen. Heather Trimble had accepted his friend request. He sent a message directly to her inbox:

"Thanks for accepting my request, beautiful, don't be a stranger," he said, with a winky face after the sentence.

"I won't, handsome, and neither should YOU," was her response.

Those three capital letters spoke volumes to Tristen. She was most definitely feeling his fictitious character.

He chatted with her for what seemed like an eternity when she finally asked him if he had a girlfriend. Heather's conversation seemed borderline juvenile compared to the conversations that he'd had with Natalie, yet he indulged. "No, actually I'm single," he typed.

"Would you like a girlfriend?"

"How is that possible? Your status says that you're married."

"I am, but my status never said that I was happily married. So how about it, Patrick? Do you want to be my special friend?" she asked.

"I think I can handle that. You're hot, plus I think our bodies would mesh well together! So what do you like…in the bedroom?" Tristen asked.

"Everything!" she replied quickly.

For hours they chatted and by the end of their conversation, Heather was ready to meet Tristen – well, Patrick – and do everything that should have been reserved for her husband. She was sprung from their tête-à-tête, probably because Frank was so hell bent on keeping Heather hidden from the world that he never took time to *talk* to his wife. In the few hours that they'd talked, Tristen knew not only most of their personal business but he knew damn near everything about her. She loved black people - black men in particular. She hated her husband and his racist views against not only blacks, but anyone of color. She said that she cringed every time he talked about black people because there was never anything nice being said. She even told Tristen about Jamal and how Frank was never even half the man that he had been. She shared her hopes of one day owning her own chain of high-end sex boutiques that catered to women that felt trapped by their marriages and were looking for a way to spice up their lives. She would sell everything from lingerie to dildos and everything in between. She said that she'd even worked out a plan to partner with the Ashley Madison website to cater to women that might want a little extramarital action on the side.

Tristen and Heather had agreed to meet at 4:00 p.m. at a hotel near Tristen's fictitious address. He'd let Heather play the aggressor for most of the conversation, only agreeing with her and stroking her ego in an attempt to keep her typing. Heather said she wanted to have a few drinks to loosen up and then she wanted to swallow his cock. He agreed fully, furthering her anticipation by promising to suck her clitoris gently until she was ready to explode. He vowed to then ram his rigid 13" cock into her until she begged him to stop. Heather said that she was getting off of the computer to get ready for their "date" and Tristen agreed. He laughed to himself. Heather was so freaky that he found it hard to believe that she was real.

He closed his computer, dressed quickly, and left Billionaire's Row, en route to CrossTech. He needed a few tools from his lab if he was going to pull off his ruse without a hitch. Tristen walked into CrossTech and went straight to his laboratory. Both Brennen Goldstein and Frank Trimble were in the lab, but they immediately fell silent when Tristen entered the room. He pushed a button beneath his desk and a compression chamber was lifted on the work table behind him.

Inside of the glass chamber was a prototype of NR613 with its projector. The firing mechanism for the prototype was an ink pen - or so it seemed to be. After years of watching rerun episodes of *Get Smart*, the ink pen was the most logical choice. Building the tiny components needed to power the NR613 was the real challenge. To the naked, untrained eye it looked and functioned like an actual ink pen, minus the writing. When the top button was pressed, it exposed the tip of the NR613, which resembled a ball point. Once armed, the shooter simply needed to lift the pocket clip to fire the device into its intended target. Once it was implanted, the user could control the person injected via Bluetooth. The beautiful thing about the NR613 was its quietness. There was no sound associated with firing the projectile and Tristen had created it that way purposely. If Hayden Cross hoped to market it to the military, then its stealth nature would be a definite plus.

Tristen loaded a leather doctor's bag with the tools that he would need not only to complete the mission before him, but his next mission as well. Brennen and Frank were crouched over Brennen's desk whispering, probably about what he'd done to Natalie but, Tristen couldn't hear them.

"I have to drain the lizard, Frank, plus it's getting a little too dark in here for my tastes. I'll be right back," Brennen said, staring at Tristen as he left.

Tristen went over to Frank and put his hand on his shoulder. "I know what Brennen did, Frank, and he's going to pay for it," he said.

"First of all," Frank said, looking back over his shoulder at Tristen. "Get your dirty black hands off of me. Secondly, I don't know what you're talking about. Now if you don't mind..." Frank said, gesturing toward the door. He turned back to the desk and thumbed aimlessly through a fishing magazine.

Tristen quickly removed the NR613 from his shirt pocket, put it to the base of Frank's skull, and lifted the clip. Tristen had barely turned around to exit the lab when he heard Frank's hand slap the back of his neck.

"See, nigger, you've brought bugs with you!" Frank barked.

Tristen smiled to himself and put his Bluetooth into his ear. He walked to the door and paused. "You should really apologize to Tristen," he whispered into the headset.

Moments later after he'd left the lab, he heard footsteps running up behind him. Frank stopped him, panting and out of breath. "Tristen, I want to apologize. I was an asshole and I just want to say that I'm sorry," he said.

"Well, Frank, apology accepted. That was mighty white of you," Tristen said as he passed through the massive glass doors leading to the parking lot.

Tristen Googled Frank Trimble's address: 3081 Welborn Ave. He'd barely driven five miles before he reached his destination. As he pulled into the middle class neighborhood, he glanced at his watch, which read 2:23 p.m. *Heather should be leaving soon,* he thought.

Before the thought left his head, he saw Heather leaving the residence. She waved to the prepubescent children on their way home from school, backpacks in tow, laughing and playing along the way. Heather sashayed her way across the lawn to her C-class Mercedes Benz, very prim and proper. She looked expensive; her perfectly tanned skin shimmered as the sun bounced off of it seductively. Her dress barely covered her rear, which looked more like it should've belonged to a woman of color. Heather's hot pink stiletto heels matched her dress and lipstick perfectly. She bent over once she'd reached the car to pick up something from the floor board and Tristen gasped. She'd exposed an expertly shaven, smooth as a baby's butt nether area.

As soon as she started the car and was out of sight, Tristen went to work. He walked around to the back of the house, careful to go undetected. He peered through the sliding glass patio door. Tristen reached into his back pocket and grabbed the monogrammed handkerchief that his mother had given to him years earlier. He used the hanky to shield his fingerprints as he checked the lock on the patio door. Just as he suspected, the patio door was unlocked. Suburbanites often thought that if they stayed in a nice neighborhood, then locked doors were unnecessary, but Tristen knew different. He'd grown up in the suburbs, but his parents made sure that their doors were always locked. Even when everyone was at home, his father still made it a point to lock the doors. He'd grown up in the streets of Newark and didn't trust a soul.

Tristen slid the door open and stepped in cautiously. Directly in front of him on the coffee table was a Pepto Bismol-colored laptop. Next to it on the table was a towel and an extremely large ebony-colored dildo. The thing was massive, at least 12" in length and 2" in diameter. It looked as though someone had detached it from an unsuspecting Mandingo warrior. Heather hadn't even bothered to turn off the television. She'd merely muted it. A muscular black man with oversized man parts did his best to give a fair haired, green eyed white woman every inch that he'd been endowed with. Heather had undoubtedly "gotten ready" for their date by pleasuring herself to the sights of what she *thought* she had coming by meeting Patrick. Tristen could only shake his head and chuckle. *Nympho*, he thought.

He opened her laptop and much to his surprise, Heather's laptop was not password protected. The Facebook conversation that she'd been having with Patrick was still open in her browser. Tristen couldn't believe how easy the caper was coming along. He placed a small, eraser-sized microphone on the end table behind the lamp. He checked the computer one last time and exited the house. Once Tristen was safely inside of his car, he spoke into his Bluetooth, not loudly, but not quite a whisper either. "Something's not right! Heather sure has been acting strange. I bet she's cheating again. That's probably why she's always on the computer. If she's cheating with a black guy, you should kill her. She knows you hate blacks. She's not faithful, just wait, you'll see!" Tristen said.

Everything that he'd said into the Bluetooth registered to Frank Trimble as his subconscious mind. He undoubtedly thought by now that his mind was playing tricks on hm. Ten minutes later, Frank came speeding down Welborn Ave. and whipped into 3081. Frank jumped out of his car and looked around.

"See, her car is not here. Some big black, dread-wearing coon is fucking Heather right now!" Tristen said.

As if on cue, Frank turned and stormed into the house. Through the car speakers, Tristen could hear Frank's footsteps stomping through the house in search of his unfaithful wife. "This whore has been masturbating to jiggaboo porn!" Frank screamed.

"Because she wants a strong black man, not your short dicked old ass," Tristen said.

Frank balled his fist and pounded on his temples. The voices in his head would not cease. The sound of glass breaking and furniture crashing echoed through the car, reverberating from window to window. Tristen just hoped he didn't break her computer. Then he remembered that he controlled Frank Trimble.

"Look at her computer; she left it open for you," he whispered.

Frank began to cry, softly at first and then monstrous sobs bellowed through the speakers. "Why, why, why? I've done everything for her. Why would she do this to me?" he cried.

"Because she's an ungrateful, selfish whore, that's why," Tristen countered.

Heather pulled into the driveway with both a look of disappointment and alarm written on her face. She dashed inside to find Frank sitting in front of her computer crying. "What's wrong, baby?" she asked.

"You've been cheating on me again, that's what's wrong. With a nigger at that!" he screamed.

"Calm down, baby, it's not what you think. Sit down and let me explain."

Tristen heard silence and then slurping and then the sounds of faint moaning. She was pacifying him with sex and he was falling for it. "You're a dumbass! A little head and some pussy and you're right back in her clutches! Kill her, Frank, kill her!" Tristen ordered.

Frank pushed Heather to the ground and zipped up his slacks. He walked into the bedroom and got his .38 revolver. He went back into the living room and pointed the gun at Heather. Through the speakers, Tristen heard Heather beg for her life.

"Frank, please, I didn't do anything! I love you!" she screamed.

"She doesn't love you, Frank, she's just using you! Kill her, Frank," Tristen said.

"You don't love me; you love niggers with big dicks. You're just using me, I know that now. I read all of your messages to your lover Patrick! You just met the guy, for fuck's sake, and you're telling him how much I repulse you? How you'd love to be Mrs. Mason? Well, I hope his dick was fucking worth dying for!" Frank spat.

"That was just random conversation, baby, you're the one I love, daddy!" she lied.

"She's lying, Frank, kill her!" Tristen teased.

Frank squeezed a round from his pistol and it ripped through Heather's leg. She dropped to the couch, writhing in pain.

"Now you've done it, Frank. Pick up the phone and call the police! Tell them that you've killed your wife and you're going to kill yourself!" Tristen said.

"I don't want to die! Why are you in my head?" Frank screamed.

Heather lay moaning on the couch, unable to move.

"Finish her, Frank!" Tristen said.

"I'm sorry, Heather! I loved you - I mean I love you! I don't know what I mean!" Frank cried. He squeezed two more rounds into Heather, one in her chest and one in the center of her forehead. Blood and brain matter oozed from the coffee cup-sized hole in the crown of her skull. Frank collapsed next to her, sobbing with heavy grief.

"Frank, what have you done? You need to call the police. Heather was the only woman that ever loved you and you killed her!" Tristen said.

Frank sat next to Heather, holding her, rocking her dead, lifeless body. He dialed 911.

"Hello, 911, what's your emergency?" the operator asked.

"I've killed my wife and I think I want to kill myself!" Frank shouted into the phone.

"Sir, stay on the phone with me, we have an officer en route," she said, but before she could finish, Frank hung up the phone. Frank's wet, salty tears mixed with the blood on Heather's face as he kissed his wife for the last time. "I'm sorry, baby, I never wanted to hurt you!" he cried. "I just wanted you to love me like I loved you.

I told you, I warned you that if I couldn't have you no one would!" Frank said.

He put the .38 snub-nosed revolver in his mouth and pulled the trigger. As Frank slipped into eternal darkness, chunks of his brain glued themselves to the wall behind him. In a particular chunk of brain matter, the prototype for the NR613 lay embedded. Behind the layer of blood and goo, the light indicating good working condition grew dim and faded into obscurity at the same time that Frank stepped into the light.

Chapter 24

Tristen set his sights on Sean Westbury. He would be an easy mark because he only stayed three doors down from Tristen. The most elegant feature of Billionaire's Row was the balcony that wrapped around the entire structure. Originally it had been built with the intention of serving as a jogging path, so that the tenants could jog conveniently rain or shine. He glanced at his watch. It was just shy of 6:00 p.m. and he still had lots of work to do.

Tristen walked out onto the balcony and traveled the few steps to Sean's balcony. He walked past it and glanced inside. The apartment was dark save for a faint light coming from the kitchen. Again, just as he'd done at Frank Trimble's house, Tristen tried the patio door, but a shadow caused him to stop. He knocked on the door lightly.

Almost instantly, a slim, fair-skinned black man appeared. He was shirtless and wore pink gym shorts with matching sneakers. He came to the patio door and slid it open. "May I help you?" he asked. He was sweaty and sipping water from a champagne flute. If Tristen would have had to guess, he would have bet money that he'd been working out.

"Um, yeah, my name is Tristen, I work with Sean. Is he home, by chance?" he asked.

"Oh, hello, no, he's not home from work yet. I was just doing some aerobics. Is there something that I can help you with?" he asked flirtatiously.

"Actually, yes, I was wondering if I might borrow a couple of eggs. It's my cousin's birthday and I really want to bake him a cake. I'm just too lazy to go to the grocery store," Tristen lied.

"Sure, come in, it's mosquitoes out there. My name is Rory, by the way, nice to meet you," he said, extending his hand.

Tristen shook his hand and noticed that his hands were slender, almost ladylike, and extremely soft. Rory disappeared into the kitchen and yelled back to Tristen, "So how long have you been working with Sean?"

"Only a few months but, he seems nice," Tristen said.

"Oh, he's a sweetheart! Today is our three year anniversary and he's taking me out to a nice restaurant!" he said, handing Tristen three brown eggs.

Tristen could see the youth in Rory's excited eyes. He couldn't have been more than seventeen or eighteen years old, which meant that if he'd been with Sean Westbury for three years, then his affair had started with the boy when he was a tender thirteen or fourteen years old. "Cool. Well, I hope you guys have fun," Tristen said as he looked around to survey his surroundings.

"Okay, scoot, scoot, I have to shower, get ready, and put on my face before my boo makes it home. Tootles," Rory said.

Tristen exited the same way he came, through the patio. He listened for Rory to click the lock to the patio, but he didn't. He went to his apartment and dialed Toby's number, but it went to voicemail. "

"You've reached Toby, you know what to do," Toby's voice said through the cell.

"Toby, this is Tristen. Natalie's in the hospital. It's some real bad shit going on right now. Call me," Tristen said.

He took the iPad that CrossTech had given him and dismantled it. He had an idea tailored especially for David Ganzelle. He then took the iPhone apart as well. It would involve making one piece of equipment control the other, but first he would need to write an override program. Tristen sat down in front of his computer and began writing the outline for the program that he'd need. Before long, voices distracted him from his task. He went to the front door and listened closely. Sean and Rory were in the hallway giggling like two love-struck teenagers. Tristen cracked his door and peered through the tiny opening.

"I love you so much, Rory! I'm glad you're not like the rest of them," Sean said.

"Who is the *rest of them*?"

"You know, *those people*," Sean said.

"Well, honey child, I'm not like anyone else, but you do realize that I'm one of *those people,* right? So let me get this straight. You like to fuck young black boys, but you don't like black people, is that it?" Rory asked sarcastically.

"That's absurd! I just don't like niggers - you know, the ignorant kind with their pants sagging, showing their entire ass cracks and using the word nigger like it's going out of style. They get mad when we say it, but they call themselves niggers every day," Sean said.

Tristen heard the whir of the elevator humming up the shaft and then Rory speaking again. "What about your friend Tristen? He seems smart, plus he's cute," Rory cooed.

Tristen heard the ding of the elevator, but what he heard next made his blood run cold.

"You stay away from that spade - I mean it! He's not my fucking friend. A black man that is too smart is just as bad as a black man that's standing on the corner all day, so you stay away from him, Rory!"

"Did you hear the shit that came out of your mouth? How did you come to that dumb-ass conclusion?"

"Niggers that hang on the corner would love to see the white man eradicated and smart niggers want to rule the world!" Sean barked.

"That's ridiculous, baby," Rory laughed.

"Well, it might be ridiculous, but we've already taken care of his porch monkey girlfriend and he's next, so if you know like I know, you'll steer clear of him," Sean said as they disappeared into the elevator.

It angered Tristen to hear Sean speak those words because for a split second, he'd considered not seeking retribution against Sean for the racist views of his friends. Much to his chagrin, Sean was just as racist as his counterparts and to hear him speak of Natalie in such a manner only seemed to heighten his fury.

Tristen closed his door and locked it. He turned off all of his lights and eased out of his patio door. He crept down to Sean's condo and tried the sliding glass door. Just as he'd suspected, the door was unlocked. He went inside and stood perfectly still and tried to adjust his eyes to the light. Once he felt comfortable, he moved swiftly throughout the house, searching for Sean's laptop. He found it in Sean's bedroom, next to his bed on the nightstand. Tristen sat on the edge of the bed and opened Sean's computer. It amazed him how people never seemed to put much stock into security, especially cyber security. Tristen used several keywords that he knew would flag the FBI and lead them directly to Sean's IP address. From Google he typed *adolescent sex party, boys under 13 that like cock, 10 year olds with big boobs,* and so on. On each site that he clicked on, he downloaded dozens of pictures. He downloaded photos until there were literally thousands of photos of young kids in compromising positions on his laptop. Tristen sat for an hour categorizing the child pornography and distributing it to different folders with names like *treasure chest, tight butt, sweet kids,* etc. After he'd stored the photos and hidden them in Sean's computer, he cleaned the browsing history. He made sure to put everything back the way it was and then slinked out of the apartment.

Tristen pulled into the CrossTech parking lot and parked beneath the trees near an inconspicuous side door. There were no cars in the parking lot except for Mr. Wilkins's beat up Lincoln Town Car. Tristen wasn't worried about him though, Mr. Wilkins was cool. He didn't want the old man involved, however, so he would do his best to sneak in and out. On his way to CrossTech, Tristen had stopped at CVS and gotten more damaging material. He stood in the parking lot of the popular drug store and cut out pictures of children, nothing provocative or risqué, just something to add fuel to the fire. He used Natalie's company ID to enter the building and made a beeline for Sean Westbury's office. He planted the photos deep within his desk. Tristen sat down at Sean's computer and repeated his ritual from Sean's personal computer.

As he was leaving, Mr. Wilkins stopped him in the hallway. "What are you doing up here so late, youngster?" he asked.

"It's better if you don't know, Mr. Wilkins, that way you can't be implicated."

"I heard about Natalie, son. Is that what this is all about?"

"It's about righting wrongs and much deserved retribution, that's all I will say on the matter," Tristen said sadly.

"I understand. Just be careful, Tristen. I would hate to see you lose it all because of these peckerwoods. Don't get me wrong, I don't have a racist bone in my body, but these boys deserve whatever they get, so be careful."

"I will, I can promise you that," Tristen said as he made his way to David Ganzelle's office. He sat behind David's plush Victorian style desk and dialed the FBI. "Hello, I would like to report a crime," Tristen said.

"Sir, you may need to hang up and dial 911."

"This crime involves children. I think my coworker may be a pedophile. He's always thumbing through kiddie magazines and talking about how he wants his next lover to be preteen. It makes me feel uncomfortable," he lied.

"Although it makes you uncomfortable and it is highly inappropriate, sir, it's not a crime."

"Is it illegal to have images of half-dressed children in compromising positions? He's always showing me images of scantily clad little boys and girls on his computer at work," Tristen lied.

"Sir, if what you say is true, then yes, he's committed several crimes. I just need to get some general information so that I can get an agent on this as soon as possible. Now, what's his name?" she asked.

"His name is Sean Westbury and we work at CrossTech Industries."

"Okay, and what is your name, sir?"

"My name is David Ganzelle, but I don't want to be involved in this," Tristen said, hanging up the phone. No sooner as he had hung up the phone then it rang back, but Tristen didn't answer. He stood transfixed, afraid to move, as if they could somehow see him through the phone.

"Hi you've reached the desk of David Ganzelle. I'm either away from my desk or on the other line. Please leave your name, number, a brief description of the nature of your call, and I will be sure to get back to you," David Ganzelle's answering machine said.

The loud beep that followed caused Tristen to jump. He laughed to himself. He couldn't understand why he was so jumpy. No one was even at CrossTech besides Mr. Wilkins, but Tristen had never been comfortable doing wrong.

"Mr. Ganzelle, this is Agent Rutledge with the cyber-crimes division of the FBI. I understand that you have some information for us concerning a Mr. Westbury. Call me as soon as possible. My number is 214-555-"

The agent went on, but Tristen had tuned her out. He needed to figure out a way to get into David Ganzelle's phone and erase the message before he had the opportunity to hear it. Tristen frantically searched the computer's files for the program that controlled the phones. For fifteen minutes he searched. He finally stopped and looked around David's desk and silently cursed himself. The erase button glowed a magnificent apricot orange. He pressed the button and the answering machine beeped once.

"Message deleted," the machine said in its robotic female voice.

Tristen left David's office and headed toward the side door where his car was parked. His phone vibrated and it was Toby.

"Hello? Ay, Cuzzo, what's this about Natalie being in the hospital?" Toby said.

"Yeah, man, the dude Brennen beat her, bruh. It was him, but they were all in on it, I think."

"Oh, hell nah! So what you wanna do? I might be able to get my hands on some heat!" Toby exclaimed.

"No guns. That's what they expect us to do. Nah, I'm going to get them the best way I know how - with my brain," Tristen said.

"Man, I got some shit going on too. Remember the dude Esco that I told you about?"

"The one that you beat out of the money before you left Jersey?" Tristen asked.

"Yeah, him. Well, how about him and Yummi were on the plane together and this ol' pussy-ass nigga told her that I raped somebody close to him in Jersey and that he was going to kill me. It's a long story, but basically this clown knows where I work, the whole nine. I'm not as smart as you so I gots to get some heat," Toby said flatly.

"Don't get into any trouble. Just set him up and get him out of your hair."

"Yeah, that's what Yummi said but, this dude is crazy. Anyway, call me if you need me, Triz. I'm about to bounce. Yummi is taking me out to a fondue restaurant tonight," Toby gushed.

"Alright, be careful, Toby."

"You too, bruh," Toby said.

Tristen tossed his cell phone onto the passenger's seat and drove the short distance back to the condo. He had a lot of work to do on David Ganzelle's demise.

Chapter 25

The murder/suicide of Heather and Frank Trimble spread through CrossTech like wildfire. It had started as breaking news at 10 p.m. and spread into the morning. By the time the employees started to arrive, the Trimble's deaths were front page news and the only topic open for discussion. Hayden Cross had even cancelled one of his frequent trips in hopes of doing damage control. The news had attributed the deaths to everything from infidelity to stress and Hayden Cross had heard enough. If Frank Trimble was weak enough to kill himself then that was his business, but Hayden refused to let it disrupt his business. He walked through the halls of CrossTech, hoping to hear someone speaking of the Trimble ordeal. They would be fired on the spot because he hated gossip and he wouldn't feel the least bit guilty about doing it, no sir, not one bit.

As he made it to his office, Emily, his elderly personal assistant, came walking toward him briskly. Given her age, it was odd to see her move faster than a snail's pace. Now she was moving toward him swiftly, and where her demeanor was usually calm and laid back, it had been replaced with worry and dread. An almost cogent sense of foreboding overcame Hayden Cross.

"Morning, Mr. Cross, may I speak with you?"

"Sure, Emily, what'cha got?" he asked.

"Well, sir," she whispered, looking around to make sure no one was listening. "I'm sure you've heard about Frank and his wife, but there's more bad news. That wonderful girl Natalie was savagely beaten, Mr. Cross. She's still in ICU," Emily said.

"Wait, what? How is she? When did this happen?"

"Early Monday morning, I believe. She's stable, the poor baby. I went to visit her last night and her twin brother the preacher was there praying over her. I think she'll be fine," she said.

"Okay, send her some flowers from the company and keep me posted."

"I'm already on top of it but, Mr. Cross?" Emily said warily, stopping him in his tracks. "There's more, sir."

"What more could there possibly be, Emily?" he barked.

Emily winced under the sharpness of his tone. She had a mind to let him walk into an ambush, but he would surely fire her and she needed her job. Her Social Security benefits barely covered her rent and her late husband Edgar's veteran's benefits hadn't been much help with prices skyrocketing the way that they were. "Mr. Patel is in your office waiting for you with three men and a lady from the FBI. Mr. Patel looked really perturbed," Emily said.

"Thank you, Emily. Is there any more bad news that you wish to give me?" If she answered, Hayden Cross didn't hear her. His mind was preoccupied with the FBI. He didn't know what kind of business they had with him, but he did know that there was a fine line between good business and breaking the law. He'd done things not only on a business level that were less than scrupulous, but on a personal level as well. Within the last year, he'd made some personal decisions that weren't exactly lawful, and if discovered, could potentially land him in prison for a very long time.

Hayden took a deep breath and walked into his office. Raj Patel stood up, as did the agents when Hayden Cross entered the room.

"Greetings, Mr. Cross, allow me to introduce Agent Rutledge, Agent Gilley, Agent Turner and - " Raj started.

But Hayden cut him off. "Agent Monica Deitrich," Hayden said.

"Mr. Cross," Monica said, nodding at him.

"You two know each other?" Agent Rutledge asked.

"Oh yes, we have a rich history," Hayden said sarcastically.

Raj Patel cleared his throat, trying to cut some of the tension in the air. "Well, Mr. Cross, this is a two part meeting. First off, I was going over the books, as is customary for the quarter, checking for any discrepancies before payroll goes in. I noticed that we'd been red flagged by Check Mark. After a little more investigation, this is what they sent to us," Raj said, tossing a manila folder onto Hayden's desk.

As Hayden read, he grew angrier. According to Raj Patel's paperwork, Caleb Weeks had been stealing from the employees, from the company, hell, even from him since he'd started CrossTech - over $20,000,000 to be exact.

"The FBI was alerted at the same time that we were," Raj said.

"We have a search warrant for Sean Westbury's office and computer," Agent Gilley said.

"You think Sean is in on this crap with Caleb?" Hayden asked.

"No, but we do have reason to believe that he's not only attracted to young boys, that his computer may contain inappropriate photos of underage children," Agent Gilley said.

"That's absurd! He may be a little eccentric, hell, even downright fruity, but I don't believe that he's a pedophile. First Frank and his wife, now Caleb Weeks is embezzling company funds, now you're telling me that Sean Westbury may be a child molester who's using his work computer to look at kiddie porn? What's going on? Jesus Christ!" he exclaimed.

"Maybe it's a case of your proverbial chickens coming home to roost," Monica said sarcastically.

"At any rate, if there is nothing on his hard drive, then no harm, no foul, but we have to investigate those matters fully. Agent Turner is our cyber forensics lead, so if there's something there, he'll find it."

"I completely understand and you have my full cooperation. Excuse me, gentlemen, and lady," he said, nodding in Monica's direction. He walked to the door and summoned Emily. "Emily, come here please."

She appeared instantly with notepad in hand. She'd worked for Hayden Cross for the past eighteen years and she'd never witnessed this side of him. He wasn't angry, but rather calm under the circumstances. His face was a mixture of pain and disbelief.

"Emily, I want you to put out a companywide alert. I want everyone in the company in the Slaughter House for a meeting. Patch in the subsidiary locations via satellite. Make it clear to everyone that this meeting is mandatory and anyone not in attendance will be terminated," he said.

"What about the people that are off from work, sir?"

"They need to be here. Are you having a hard time grasping the term mandatory?" he asked harshly.

"No sir," she said and then ambled out of the office. Emily got onto the company PA system and put out the alert. Her small, dry voice cracked over the intercom as she made her announcement. "Attention, all employees need to report to the Slaughter House auditorium immediately. This meeting is mandatory and anyone not in attendance will be terminated," she announced.

"I want you agents to know that CrossTech will not tolerate these shenanigans and we will do whatever is necessary to help," Hayden said.

"Mr. Cross, that is greatly appreciated and I assure you that we will expedite this matter as quickly and efficiently as possible," Agent Gilley said.

Tristen was still working on his override program when his iPhone rang. "Hello?" he said.

"Tristen, this is Emily Bergstrom with CrossTech. Mr. Cross is calling an emergency meeting in the auditorium and he requests that every employee be in attendance. He's made it mandatory with the promise of termination if you don't show up, dear," she said.

"No problem. I was supposed to leave on a 9:30 a.m. flight to Newark, but I'll just reschedule," he lied.

"Okay, see you soon."

Tristen removed the earpiece from his ear and went back to work. His program looked and operated like any ordinary mobile app. The display screen was the iPad and the actual override controller was his iPhone. David Ganzelle wouldn't know what hit him. Tristen grabbed the iPhone with its connectors and headed for the parking garage where his car was parked.

Chapter 26

Hayden Cross led the FBI agents out of his office toward Sean Westbury's office. He let the agents walk ahead while he talked to Monica Deitrich. "Well, well, well, long time no see, Agent Deitrich," Hayden said.

"Indeed. How have you been?"

"About as well as can be expected. FBI? I thought you were DEA?" Hayden asked.

"I was, but the whole undercover agent situation drained me emotionally. After Kochese's death, I started to question if it was all worth it, you know?"

"I understand you knew him far better than I ever did. I was a terrible father to him, I know that. I only hope that I can be double the father to my other two boys, Khalil and Hayden Jr.," Hayden said.

"So Kochese had brothers?" Monica asked curiously.

Hayden didn't answer. He knew that Monica was trying to pry and he didn't know why. He wouldn't allow her to get any closer than she needed to be. Monica Deitrich was cunning and extremely manipulative, that much he knew for certain. "Yes, something like that," Hayden said.

The Slaughter House was buzzing with speculative chatter when Tristen walked in. Employees wondered aloud what the meeting could possibly pertain to. The rumors ranged from CrossTech Industries being sold to the Chinese to CrossTech Industries being bankrupt. If Tristen believed half of the things being said, then he would be a disgruntled worker, working under Chinese rule. His hours would be long and his pay would be dismal. By the time the rumors had subsided, Tristen's head was spinning. It was amazing how people could take something as small as a meeting and twist it until the rumors ran rampant. *I wonder if people listen to the shit that they say*, he thought with a chuckle.

Moments later, Hayden Cross stepped onto the stage to a heavy round of applause. He raised his hands to silence the crowd. "Hello, Techies, and welcome. There are a few things that I would like to clear up before we get started. CrossTech is not being sold and we are not bankrupt. We're actually more profitable than ever as we go into this third quarter. There are, however, a few problems that we must address. Caleb Weeks, could you come up on stage please," Hayden said.

There was an agent on each side of the stage. The other two were stationed near the entrance to the auditorium. Caleb got up from the front row and strutted to the stage proudly. He took position next to Hayden Cross with a huge smile on his face. Hayden Cross looked out into the audience and called for Sean Westbury to join them on stage. He too took the stage proudly, smiling from ear to ear.

Tristen's heart beat so loud and rapidly that he just knew that everyone present could hear it. He fidgeted in his seat uncomfortably, wondering why both Caleb and Sean were on stage at the same time. It couldn't be mere coincidence and then Tristen noticed the two men dressed like the *Men in Black* standing near the base of the stage. He shifted in his seat to look around the auditorium and saw a man and a woman in dark suits and dark sunglasses, inside no less, standing by the entrance, and then it all made sense. His plan had worked quicker than he'd expected.

Hayden Cross's voice caused Tristen to turn in his seat. "These two gentlemen are two of my top executives. Their combined salaries are a whopping $780,000," Hayden said. Caleb and Sean smiled at one another, proud to be in Hayden's company. "How long have you worked for CrossTech, Caleb?"

"I've been here since the beginning, boss, twenty-five years," Caleb said.

"And how long have you known me personally?"

"Well, we met in tenth grade when I was fifteen years old, so about thirty-five years," Caleb replied.

"In the thirty-five years that you've known me, what has always been my motto?"

"You've always said that you do what you want, when you want, how you want because rich men make the rules and don't take shit!" Caleb exclaimed loudly.

"So why then…" Hayden started as he aimed a remote control somewhere into the abyss. A large screen was illuminated behind the stage. "Why then would you ever believe that I would let you steal from me?" Hayden asked, turning toward the screen.

"What?" Caleb screamed, turning to see what had everyone so captivated. He tried to speak, but the sound of loud boos and hisses filled the auditorium. "This has to be a sick joke, Hayden, I've always been loyal to you!" he yelled.

"Don't you dare talk to me about loyalty! I was beyond good to you and you fucking stole from me. These folks work hard for their money and you stole from them. You took it upon yourself to help yourself to their hard-earned wages. I don't think so!" Hayden screamed.

Caleb was still pleading his case when Agent Gilley and Agent Turner led him away. Monica gestured toward Hayden, signaling that they had all of the information they needed to arrest Sean. She removed her dark Ray-Ban sunglasses and strolled down the aisle toward the stage. He turned to Sean Westbury, who was visibly shaken. He toyed with his hands nervously, peeling away layers of skin from his cuticles. He found it hard to make eye contact with Hayden Cross. He had never stolen from CrossTech - well, not much anyway. He'd stolen ink pens, note pads, sticky notes, markers, highlighters, even toilet paper and paper towels, but never had he embezzled funds. He couldn't for the life of him guess why Hayden had called him up on stage. He started sweating profusely, almost instantly soaking his Hugo Boss dress shirt.

"Now ladies and gentlemen, this young man here has shown real potential. He's one of my real bright spots here at CrossTech," Hayden began, and Sean relaxed a little bit, almost smiling at Hayden's kind words. His tone was soft and caring as he spoke of Sean's first day on the job. "We all thought he was a little too soft," Hayden said, laughing. The audience laughed along with Hayden Cross, openly ridiculing Sean Westbury. "And then the rumors started circulating about his sexuality and his antics," he said. His voice was all business and his face was stern. A calm, almost deadly hush fell over the crowd. "I never cared about your sexual preference, Sean, I actually embraced your difference because I felt like it brought a sense of diversity to the company," Hayden said.

"Mr. Cross, I've always tried to keep my sexual preference under wraps because I didn't think that it would be embraced."

"Would you agree, Sean, that CrossTech takes care of its employees and their families? That we try our hardest to cater to our employees, especially the parents? Before you answer, let me say this. We take pride in protecting our employees with children and those employees are more so a priority to us than those without because I am a father myself," Hayden said calmly.

"Yes, Mr. Cross, I believe that family is a top priority here, sir."

As Sean finished answering, Monica walked up to Hayden and whispered in his ear.

"If you agree, then you won't mind going with these fine FBI agents to explain to them why they found child pornography on your office computer. They also found multiple pictures inside your desk. There are agents at your condo in Billionaire's Row as we speak, and if they find child porn there, then you're in violation of the morals clause in your employment contract. If you've violated, Sean, you not only lose your condo, but you forfeit your company pension and your earnings from the employee profit sharing program," Hayden explained. He loved putting people on the spot in front of their peers, not because he wanted to embarrass them, but because he'd never liked rumors. An agent ran to the stage with Sean's home computer in his hand and whispered in Monica Deitrich's ear, who in turn whispered in Hayden Cross's ear. "Well then, it's settled. Do what you need to do, agents," Hayden said.

Sean collapsed onto the floor and wept like a small child. "I don't wanna go to jail, please, I didn't do this!" he cried. He struggled against the firm grip of the FBI agents.

They were finally able to stand Sean up but, his body was dead weight. He looked out at the audience and saw David Ganzelle and Brennen Goldstein sitting in the front row with disgusted looks on their faces. Maybe it was them who had set him up. They didn't particularly care for him anyway because he didn't fit their good ol' boy mold. Sean Westbury had no fight left in him. Possession was nine tenths of the law and they had caught him red-handed. Even if he pleaded his case, they would never believe him. When a sixth agent walked through the doors of the auditorium with Rory handcuffed, Sean lost it.

"Okay! Whatever you need me to do or say, I'll do. Just let Rory go; he didn't have anything to do with any of this," Sean whined.

Not only did each picture on Sean's computer carry a separate charge, but he would also be charged for statutory rape. Rory had been a minor when they'd met and Sean had slept with him anyway. He'd taken advantage of the fact that Rory was a runaway teen with nowhere to go and had used that to his advantage. He'd wined and dined the young boy, keeping him hidden from the world, using him to fulfill his own perverted sexual fantasies. It wasn't until Rory came to him and threatened to leave him that Sean began to treat him better.

To a certain extent, Sean was happy that he was made to leave Rory alone because he was addicted to the young boy. Rory had come into his life and made him feel things that no woman or man for that matter had ever been able to and he was grateful. The love that he had for him, however, was a sick love. He would've rather killed Rory than to let another man savor the love that they shared. Now those days were over. As they escorted him up the aisle of the auditorium toward the entrance/exit, he caught Tristen's eyes trained of him.

Tristen sat in his seat with a demented smirk on his face. As he passed, Tristen winked at him and then it registered to him what had gone on. Tristen had played him like a winning hand of poker. He hadn't actually personally done anything to Tristen, but he understood. He and the rest of his friends had tried everything possible to make him miserable in hopes that he would quit. It hadn't worked and evidently they had underestimated Tristen. He silently wondered whether he had anything to do with what happened to Frank and Heather and then just as quickly dismissed it. It had to be strictly coincidence, but Tristen deserved a nod. Sean passed and underneath his breath, with his eyes still locked on Tristen he mouthed the words, *"Well played, Tristen."*

"Well, now that we have the thieves and pedophiles out of the way, I have an announcement to make. My son Khalil will be taking over the daily operations of CrossTech. Many of you know my son Hayden Jr., but you've yet to meet my son Khalil. He was stationed overseas in the military. After his tour of duty he wanted to stay abroad, so I obliged. I want you all to get to know him and embrace him as your leader. I'm getting old and I would like to enjoy my money before I die," Hayden Cross said.

The auditorium broke into raucous laughter and applause. He was a stern and strict company owner, but he was fair and he took extremely good care of his employees. Their wages were on average 15% higher than other companies in their field. They also accrued sick time rather quickly. On average, they were entitled to two weeks sick leave and up to three weeks' vacation. Raj Patel had tried to encourage Hayden Cross to combine sick time and vacation time to maximize production from the workers, but Hayden had resisted, saying that a man or woman deserved their vacation and that they shouldn't have to choose between being sick and going on vacation to enjoy with their families.

The things that he did with his company were a direct reflection of how he had been treated when he'd gotten his first job. He was treated like shit, working long hours for low pay. The last straw for him was when his mother had taken sick and he needed to be by her side. He'd gone to his supervisor with tears in his eyes, almost begging for time off because the doctors hadn't given his mother much time to live. He'd been told that if he took off work that his job wouldn't be there when he came back. He'd accepted his boss's terms and kept working and when his mother died, he was working a double shift. When his grandparents buried his mother, he was also working a double shift. Hayden Cross had been working on the line at his job at Texas Instruments when it hit him. He had let his mother slip away from him and he would never see her again. He took off his apron and his gloves and he removed his goggles while still on the line, knowing that it would draw his supervisor Milton onto the floor.

"Cross, you need to put your PPE (personal protection equipment) back on and get back to work or your lazy ass is fired!" Milton screamed.

Hayden laughed loudly. He reached into his shirt pocket and removed a non-filtered Camel cigarette. He lit it right there on the production floor. He took a long drag, inhaled the smoke deeply, and blew it into Milton's face. He heaved up as much phlegm as he possibly could and spit it into Milton's face. "That's for making me feel like shit for wanting to be with my mother on her death bed, asshole. And don't worry about firing me, you son of a bitch, because I quit!" Hayden had said.

And that was that. He'd walked off of that job and never looked back. When he'd started CrossTech, he'd vowed that he would take care of his employees and he'd lived up to that promise.

As Hayden Cross talked, Monica Deitrich stopped and stared at him. Kochese hadn't said anything to her about two brothers. He'd only said that he watched Hayden Cross from a distance throwing a football around with his son. She remembered because he'd said that it made him feel like his life didn't matter. Now he was talking about a second son. Maybe Hayden Cross was a rolling stone that made children wherever he went. *Oh well*, Monica thought, shrugging it off and exiting the building.

Hayden continued to talk and once he was sure that Monica had exited the building he introduced his son. "Without further ado, I present to you the future of CrossTech Industries, my son Khalil Cross." A tall, younger replica of Hayden Cross emerged from back stage. There were very few differences between Hayden and Khalil. It almost looked like Hayden Cross had paid a doctor to create a perfect clone of himself.

Brennen Goldstein and David Ganzelle exchanged wary glances. They had never heard of Khalil Cross, and in their arrogance, they'd both believed that they were in contention for the position.

"My name is Khalil Cross, as my father stated. I want everyone to know that when I take over, I will continue the same rich traditions that my father started. No worries, ladies and gentlemen. I can't wait to meet each one of you on a personal basis. Thank you."

"Okay, ladies and gentlemen, this concludes this meeting. Please return to your work stations. Tristen Graham, if you're in the audience, I need to see you, son. Meet me back stage in ten minutes," Hayden Cross said.

Tristen raised his hand so that Hayden would know that he was present, but he had already disappeared back stage with Khalil. By the time Tristen made it to the curtains that led back stage, he'd walked up on a heated discussion between Hayden and Khalil.

"You better fuckin' hope so, Pop!" Khalil said.

"She doesn't suspect shit; calm the fuck down," Hayden said, but he let his voice trail off when he noticed Tristen standing nearby.

"You wanted to see me, sir?" Tristen said sheepishly.

"Yes, Tristen. How are the tests for the NR613 coming along?"

"Very well, actually. I'm pleased to announce that I have ten prototypes ready for testing and we should be ready for full production as soon as the tests are done," Tristen said.

Hayden reached into his inside jacket pocket and removed an envelope. "This is a little incentive to keep you going strong. This is $50,000. Have you ever had this kind of money in your hands, Tristen?"

Tristen was speechless. He didn't know why Mr. Cross was giving him that kind of money, but he was more than appreciative. "No sir, never," Tristen said.

Khalil studied Tristen's face closely. He barely looked like he was out of high school, let alone old enough to be working at a Fortune 500 corporation.

"Do you know why I've given you this money, Tristen?" Hayden asked.

"Um, as an incentive? Like a bonus?" Tristen asked.

Both Hayden and Khalil laughed uncontrollably. Khalil found that statement to be so funny that he was doubled over in raucous laughter. "No, son, it's not a bonus, its hush money. Whatever happens at CrossTech stays at CrossTech, do you understand?" Hayden asked.

Tristen nodded; there was no need for words. He didn't know what Hayden Cross was talking about, but for $50,000, anything short of murdering his mother and they had his full attention.

"I hope you understand, Travis - I mean Tristen - because the last two employees were terminated. But in this case, if you run your mouth about anything that you may have seen or heard, you'll be *exterminated* instead of terminated." Khalil snickered.

Chapter 27

Tristen sat in his car in the parking garage of Billionaire's Row, waiting on David Ganzelle to park his car. He turned on the radio and listened while Michael Jackson sang in his nasally but melodic voice.

"Where did you come from, baby, and oh, won't you take me there

Right away, won't you, baby, tenderoni you've got to be

Spark my nature and fly with me."

He had barely made it to the second verse when David Ganzelle pulled in. Tristen slumped in his seat so as to not be detected. Seconds later, Brennen Goldstein pulled in beside David's car. They stood at the rear of their cars as Tristen watched through his windshield. He cracked the window to his car and listened.

"Why are you so fucking nervous, David?" Brennen asked.

"Are you serious? Are you that stupid, Brennen? Do you honestly believe that all of this shit is coincidence? First Frank, then Caleb and Sean. Are we fucking next?"

"Next for what? You've been watching too many horror movies and drinking too much scotch." Brennen laughed.

"The shit ain't funny! I'm telling you, something's not right."

"You need to have a drink and calm the fuck down. On another note, when those FBI agents came in, man, I just knew that they were there for me because of that nigger bitch Natalie," Brennen said.

Tristen fought the urge to get out and try his hand with Brennen, but he held his composure.

"Brennen, fuck that bitch and your little nigger loving fetish! I'm telling you that some seriously spooky shit is going on. Did you know when I got back to my office there was an agent named Rutledge waiting for me, saying that he was anxious to talk to me and that they wanted to thank me for the tip on Sean?" David said.

"All I know is you're acting really strange and its making me nervous. Are you going to rat us out, David? The other three guys are gone and I'll be damned if I go down because you're nervous and can't keep your mouth closed."

"I have never said shit about any of the hateful shit that we've done. I knew I should've walked away from you guys when we beat that old man Wilkins. I stuck around through all of the rapes and beatings, all of those young black girls," David Ganzelle said as if reflecting from some faraway place. "I've been here, loyal to you guys. When you hanged that young college kid from the oak tree behind SMU, I was there. When I bombed the

Muslim mosque in the West End, you were there. We have dirt on each other, so why would I rat?" David said.

Brennen began to chuckle until his chuckle turned into hearty laughter.

"What's so fucking funny, Brennen?"

"Remember Christmas of last year when we caught the old nigger lady getting off of the bus with all of those gifts? Remember when Frank kicked her in the stomach and she shit on herself and Caleb whipped his dick out and pissed on her? That was classic."

"That was somebody's grandmother, Brennen, I had nightmares after that bullshit," David said.

"It wasn't my grandmother, and since when are you so sensitive when it comes to the blacks?" Brennen asked.

But David didn't answer; he'd heard enough. Brennen was sick, and either he'd never noticed or had been too blinded by their friendship to really care. Between David, Brennen, and the other horsemen, they had wreaked havoc on the streets of Dallas for years with their hate crimes. A typical Saturday night for the five of them consisted of riding through the streets searching for victims. People often thought that the poorer white population was the ones that committed the hate crimes, assuming that their impoverished state of existence caused them to lash out in hopes that minorities might feel their pain, or that they blamed the minorities for their financial state. In reality, hatred knew no boundaries. Rich whites hated blacks, Mexicans, and poor whites equally. Poor whites hated rich whites and a lot of other people. Blacks hated Mexicans and Mexicans hated everybody. It was the way of the world. Frank had convinced them that they were doing the world a service by making the blacks and Mexicans miserable. They'd even gone so far as to go into the trailer park and beat their own kind. No one was safe when it came to these men. At one time, Brennen's Jewish roots had threatened to have him meet the same fate, until he reminded his brothers in hate that they had all been watered down with something or another. There were, as Brennen put it, no pure Aryans left. They had done it all together: murder, mayhem, rape, and plunder.

Brennen caught up with David at the elevator and they disappeared. Tristen gave it a few minutes and then got out of his car, moving slowly toward David Ganzelle's car. Tristen tried the door on David Ganzelle's Chevrolet Suburban. It was locked, but he had neglected to lock the back hatch. He lifted it and climbed inside and closed the hatch softly, making sure to leave it cracked just a little bit. He wasn't sure if opening one of the doors would set off the alarm, but he didn't want to take the chance.

Tristen crawled to the front of the SUV and reached beneath the dash. He removed the cover that housed the fuse box and the truck's computer. He hardwired the iPhone into the power source to keep it charged. He then plugged a USB connection into the phone and the other end into the truck computer's mainframe, which was known as the CAN (Controller Area Network). It was the nerve center of the car and it would allow Tristen to control the car without ever touching it. Car companies thought that they were making cars more efficient and advanced by making them more computerized, but in reality, they were making them more susceptible to hackers and engineers alike. Lastly he plugged a jack where headphones would normally go into the wiring harness. He spliced it into the wire that controlled the clock so that he could control the car in real time. Tristen replaced the cover and emerged from the truck sweating. It had taken him longer than he expected. It had only been a little under five minutes, but he was disappointed in himself. His talents and intelligence were his only sense of pride and he scolded himself. *What if they had forgotten something and come back, Tristen? Ugh, stupid*! he thought to himself.

He walked to his car and grabbed his backpack from the back seat. He climbed onto the trunk and sat back, resting his back against the rear window. Tristen reached into the backpack and removed the iPad. He found his override program and switched it on. From the control console of the program, Tristen hit the ignition button on his iPad and David's Suburban hummed to life. He hit the horn button and the horn button blew. Tristen turned his iPad to the left and the tires on the Suburban turned left. He was giddy with excitement. He wanted to scream from happiness. He had successfully turned David Ganzelle's 7500 pound mammoth vehicle into a remote control car. As one last test, Tristen switched the windshield wipers on and off, and the SUV did the exact same thing. He nodded his approval and then switched the program off.

The Suburban fell silent as if it had never run at all. Tristen got into his car and drove away from the parking garage. He had one last stop to make before he went to Parkland Hospital to spend time with Natalie.

Chapter 28

Tristen pulled into Turtle Creek Liquors and parked. He'd never once in his life been in a liquor store - not that he thought that he was too good, he'd just never had a reason to enter one. His mother and father always kept a full bar packed with anything that a drinker might want. Growing up, Toby had been the drinker, calling Tristen a lightweight. Toby loved to drink and Tristen loved to make money, a match that had been made in proverbial heaven. Tristen and Toby had started selling shots of liquor to the neighborhood kids when they were only twelve years old. It have been a lucrative business until Chester Graham had gotten that phone call. They'd sold a double shot of Peppermint Schnapps to Cody Barnes, who, after downing it like water, promptly went home and hugged the porcelain throne. When his mother asked him what was wrong with him, he snitched on Tristen and Toby in his drunken state. Mary Barnes called Chester Graham, demanding Tristen and Toby's heads mounted on a spike for corrupting her only son. Chester had laughed insanely and then kindly reminded Mary Barnes that her son had, in his fourteen years, already failed seventh grade twice and that he had been to juvenile at least twelve times for multiple petty crimes.

"So you see, Mary, I will discipline my boys, but your son is already corrupted so you can miss me with that bullshit," Chester had said.

Tristen smiled at the memory. Sure, Chester had whipped them both, but it had been well deserved.

Tristen stepped into the liquor store, clutching the envelope that Hayden Cross had given him, and went to the cashier. "Excuse me, what's the most expensive bottle of scotch that you carry?" Tristen asked.

The cashier gave Tristen a once over. Black people didn't really frequent the liquor store much and when they did, they were buppies (black yuppies). Tristen looked more like a college kid with his Polo sweater and matching Polo sneakers. "Let me get a manager for you, sir," she said. She disappeared into the back of the store and resurfaced moments later with the manager in tow.

"How can I help you, young man?" the manager asked.

Tristen turned on his best charm. "Yes sir, it's my parent's twenty-fifth wedding anniversary and I wanted to do something really special for them. My dad is always talking about scotch, so I wanted to get him a really nice and expensive bottle," Tristen lied.

"Well, you've come to the right place. We have the largest selection of liquor in Dallas County, so if you can't find it here, you won't find it anywhere, son. C'mon, let's go to my office," the manager said.

They went into the manager's office, where the manager turned his computer on and turned it toward

Tristen so that he could see the vast inventory of scotches. Tristen's mind was blown. He'd never known that scotch could be so expensive. In the list that the store manager showed him were bottles of scotch that ranged from $12,500 for a fifty-five year old bottle of Macallan Lalique in a crystal decanter to a $6.2 million bottle of Isabella's Islay single malt scotch. The extremely luxurious crystal decanter was adorned with a whopping 8,500 diamonds and even featured a handsome amount of white gold, along with a generous spread of some 300 rubies encrusted all over the bottle.

Tristen could not believe his eyes. *Who would pay that?* he thought. Maybe the Jay-Z's and Beyonce's of the world, but not Tristen. He settled for a bottle of fifty year old Highland Park single malt scotch that cost him a staggering $17,500. He winced at the price, but two things helped Tristen reach his decision to purchase the expensive liquor. First, the money was free money to him, and second, he would spend all that he had to avenge Natalie. "I think I'll take this Highland Park," Tristen said.

The manager looked at the computer screen and then at Tristen, then back to the computer screen. "You *do* know that that's $17,500, right?" he asked.

"Yeah, I can count. You just get that bottle and put it in a nice gift bag with a bow on it," Tristen said.

The manager vanished into a vault like storage room and reappeared a few minutes later. He led Tristen to the register, where he counted out one hundred and seventy-five crispy one hundred dollar bills. When he exited the store, he looked back to see the manager and the cashier looking at the money hungrily. They hadn't bothered to ring him up on a register and Tristen silently wondered if the manager even had plans of recording the sale.

He dialed Toby's cell number as he got into the car. "Hey, Toby, you said if I needed you that I needed to call. Well, I need you now."

"What you need, Cuzzo?" Toby asked.

"I need you to be here in the morning by the time I leave for work."

"You got it, man. I think I'm going to just have Yummi bring me home now, man. We've been doing the nasty all day and I know she has to be tired," Toby said.

"Man, I don't want to hear about your sexual conquests. I hope you have your key because I'm on my way to the hospital to see Natalie."

"Alright, I'll chill for a while because I think I left my key on my dresser. Just hit me when you get to the crib."

"Okay."

"How do you know I'm ready to let you go home, Toby," Yummi said, reaching over and stroking Toby's cock. His tool immediately grew rigidly stiff.

"Don't start none, won't be none," Toby said seductively.

"Can I ask you something, babe?"

"You can ask me anything. What's on your mind?" Toby asked.

"We've been together for a little bit and we've stopped using condoms. What are we going to do if I get pregnant, babe?" Yummi asked.

"What do you mean? We're going to take care of it, love it and raise it."

Yummi climbed on top of Toby and kissed him. He looked into Yummi's eyes. He'd never been attracted to anyone outside of his race, but she had him. She was Oriental to the fullest, but her demeanor was that of a black woman. She was sassy, beautiful, confident, and courageous. Toby flipped her over playfully and ripped her panties from her petite frame.

"I hear you callin', Here I come, baby

To save you oh oh

Baby, no more stallin'

These hands have been longing to touch you, baby

And now that you've come around to seeing it my wayyyyyyy..."

R. Kelly sang in his smooth and sensuous tenor. Toby kissed Yummi's neck and then her chest. He expertly circled her nipples with the tip of his tongue. He left a trail of wet kisses down the center of her flat, olive-colored stomach until he reached his destination. He buried his tongue deep within her moisture. Her juices flowed like the sweetest nectar, like it had been sent from heaven, as he tongue kissed her love box. He sucked her clitoris to the beat of Trey Song's "Neighbors Know My Name".

"Oh my God, baby, I can't take it!" Yummi screamed.

"Open up and take it like it like a big girl," Toby said.

He forced her legs open and back so that she couldn't run. Toby had her entire lower extremities exposed and he took full advantage. He sucked and licked until he felt her small frame shudder and shake into an intense orgasm. He bit both of her butt cheeks softly and then let his tongue slide past her asshole.

"Oooooh," she moaned in pleasure.

He let her body rest on the mattress as he took her clit into his mouth, once more circling it with the tip of his tongue.

"Wait, baby, wait, wait!" Yummi cried. "Let me get on top."

Toby lay down with his legs spread eagle. Yummi approached him much like a leopard that was stalking her prey. She took his dick into her hands and tried her best to swallow him whole. She moaned and purred as she bobbed and slurped on Toby's man pole.

"Do you know how much I love you?" she asked.

But Toby was unable to answer, for he was lost in a world of utter ecstasy and blissful euphoria. Yummi turned her back to Toby and straddled him as Marques Houston crooned "Sex with You". She swiveled, gyrated and wiggled her hips, taking all of Toby inside of her. He reached up to touch her and she trembled and arched her back. Toby felt her wetness running down his leg as she came. She grinded in circular rotation until she came again.

"Hold up, baby," Toby said. When Yummi lifted herself from him, he grabbed her and guided her round, firm ass to just above his face, leaving his phallus fully exposed for her to do as she pleased.

"I don't think I can handle the 69, baby," Yummi cooed.

"You can handle it, baby, see?" he said, burying his tongue deep within her.

Yummi tried to concentrate on the task at hand, licking around the head and then dropping down onto his shaft, allowing her tongue to tease his balls. She pulled his cock from her mouth and let her tiny hands stroke the length of it while she fondled his sack with the other. Toby licked her clit ferociously and then spread her butt cheeks apart as far as they would go and plunged his tongue back into her wetness, wiggling it around her insides.

"Oh…my…God…Toby…I'm…c-c-c-c-cummming again!" she screamed.

Toby felt the wet sticky sweetness of her ejaculation running down his goatee. "Let me up, baby," he instructed.

Toby stood up and positioned himself over her at the edge of the bed. He loved the hotel bed; it was perfect for his height and he had the ultimate leverage. He had Yummi rest her legs on his chest. Toby pulled her to the edge of the bed, where she was almost hanging from the edge, and entered her slowly. Her body shivered as he buried his fullness within her. He pumped to the rhythm of the Isley Brothers. He had a goal of at least six full songs before he would allow himself to cum. After each artist, he would change positions, ensuring that their sexcapade would run its course. He'd read the *Kama Sutra* front to back twice and one of the lessons that it taught was that men came fast because they usually refused to change positions for fear of losing that magical feeling.

Maxwell came on and Toby pulled out of her with a wet plop. He lay her down and climbed on top of her, putting her legs on his shoulders. He brought his body close to hers and kissed her deeply. "We're going to make that baby tonight; I feel it," he whispered. He grinded into her deeply, burying himself within her up to his pelvis.

Yummi rubbed Toby's chest softly. "I love you, baby, my God, I love you so much. You're all up in this pussy, daddy, I can feel you in my tummy!" she moaned.

That did it. Toby felt his testicles swell with the full weight of his manhood. He spewed his love seed deep inside of Yummi. At the exact same time that he came, so did she, spraying her hot wet gooey liquid all over him. He felt her insides tighten and squeeze, milking him for the last of his thick, liquescent expulsion.

"That was a baby right there, baby girl," Toby said.

Chapter 29

"I'm making this shit right, Natalie," Tristen said to an unresponsive Natalie.

She was still in ICU, not exactly fighting for her life, but in critical condition just the same. He held her hand tightly and wept. He'd never felt this way for any woman and it scared him. The more he thought about the situation, the heavier his sobs became. He felt helpless, as if somehow he had allowed this to happen to her. He wiped his tears away and kissed her hand.

"Three down, two to go, baby. I think Nigel wants Brennen for himself, so I'll keep you posted," he said.

She didn't move. It was almost as if she was comatose, but she wasn't. For the few days that Natalie had been in the hospital, Tristen hadn't stayed long during his visitations. He couldn't bear to see her unresponsive and laid up. Her lips were chapped and cracked from dehydration and her hair was a mess. The bruises around her eyes where Brennen had beaten her were now a dark purplish blue and puffy. The sounds in the room threatened to drive Tristen insane. It was mostly the oxygen regulator and the heart rate monitor. The constant whoosh, beep, whoosh, beep, whoosh, beep, whoosh, beep was monotonous, to say the least.

Tristen rubbed the back of Natalie's hand against his cheek and closed his eyes. He imagined the softness of her gentle touch and grew angry. He'd thought that getting even with the men that hurt Natalie would give him some measure of comfort, but it hadn't. Even knowing that the racist maggots had gotten what they deserved didn't seem to cajole Tristen into believing that he hadn't done something wrong. He stood and kissed Natalie on the forehead and exited the room.

Nigel was walking toward Tristen with a pained look on his face. He looked at Tristen as if he'd done something terrible; there were demons in his eyes. Tristen didn't know much about the Bible, but he was sure that pastors and reverends weren't above reproach. He gave Nigel a once over. His knuckles were bloody and badly bruised and his clothes were torn and dirty. It looked as though he'd been fighting, or at the very least in a scuffle.

"What's up Nigel? Are you okay, man?" Tristen asked.

"I'm fine, Tristen, how's Nat? Are you leaving?"

"Yeah, I gotta get out of here, man, I hate seeing her like this," Tristen said sadly, then added, "You look like you've been boxing."

"Don't worry about me, playboy, I'm fine. You look like shit. You need to go home and get some rest. Hit me tomorrow," Nigel said, dismissing Tristen. He turned his back to him and disappeared into Natalie's hospital room.

Tristen awoke to the sounds of a light rap at his front door. He'd fallen asleep on the couch with all of his clothes on. "Who is it?" he said groggily.

"It's Toby, nigga, open the door."

He let Toby into the apartment and collapsed onto the couch. For whatever reason, Tristen was beyond exhausted.

"Get up, Cuzz. It's seven-thirty already," Toby said.

Tristen snapped to attention and jumped off of the couch. "Shit, alright, let me jump in the shower right quick. All I need you to do is drive for me, Toby, just drive and do what I tell you. Can you do that?" Tristen asked as he made his way to the bathroom to shower.

"Yeah, I got you, my dude. Ay, I need a favor though, if you can."

"What's up?" Tristen asked.

"I need to borrow a few dollars until I get my little last check. Yummi has been covering me for everything and it would be nice for me to look out for her for once, you know?"

"I got you; just take my bank card. There should be enough on there to do what you need to do!" Tristen yelled from the shower.

Toby looked around and saw Tristen's wallet on the bookshelf next to a book that he'd been reading. He picked up the book *The 48 Laws of Power.*

"Do Not Go Past The Mark You Aim For. In Victory, Learn When To Stop.

The moment of victory is often the moment of greatest peril. In the heat of victory, arrogance and overconfidence can push you past the goal you had aimed for, and by going too far, you make more enemies than you defeat. Do not allow success to go to your head. There is no substitute for strategy and careful planning. Set a goal, and when you reach it, stop."

"I see you found my secret weapon, Toby," Tristen said as he appeared from nowhere.

"Yeah, I'd picked it up before, but I never made it this far. Dude be speaking some real shit."

"Yeah, I know. Did you get the bank card?" Tristen asked.

Toby nodded. "So where do you need me to drive you to?"

"I'm going to let you keep my car, but I need you in the parking lot of my job at exactly 4:30 p.m. Don't be late; it's very important that you're there on time," Tristen said.

They left the condo in high spirits. Even though Tristen had been conflicted about his special brand of justice, he knew that he had to see his task through to the end. "Never start a task and not finish strong," Tristen's father would often tell him when he was just a kid, and it had always been a part of his personality.

Tristen pulled into the CrossTech parking lot and threw his car into park. He reached down next to his seat and pressed the trunk pop button and the trunk sprang open. Tristen walked around to the trunk and removed the expensive bottle of scotch in its decorative bag. He slammed the trunk and stared at Toby, who was walking around to the driver's side of the car. "Don't forgot, Toby, 4:30 sharp!" Tristen said.

Toby smiled and shooed him toward the building. He didn't understand why Tristen was so adamant about 4:30 p.m., but he would be there. He had a little business to attend before he came back to get his cousin, but he would be sitting in the parking lot when Tristen got off of work…unless he was dead.

Chapter 30

Yummi rode through the streets of south Dallas searching. She wouldn't take any chances with hers or Toby's safety and they needed protection. She rode from block to block and hood to hood until she saw what she was looking for. She pulled into a shopping plaza on the corner of Hatcher Street and Second Avenue and parked her rental. The majority of the stores were either closed or abandoned and for a split second she felt a twinge of fear, but fear had no room to dwell where love resided. She wouldn't lose Toby to the likes of Esco.

Yummi got out of her car and walked up to a man that looked like he'd done too many drugs in his time on earth. He smelled of stale urine, rot gut whiskey, and old cigarettes. Yummi winced at the smell, but remembered that she had come from these very streets. She had smelled a lot worse in the time that she had been in Yellow Shoe's stable of whores. Some of her johns had smelled much worse, preferring to come directly to the whorehouse after work to reduce their wives' suspicions. If they came and got their rocks off after work, they could go home and shower with nothing said, but if they went home and showered then went back out, there was no way they could explain taking another shower. It was real grease ball shit, but Yummi understood. She ran her slender fingers through her jet black hair, straightened the wrinkles in her white Herve Leger mini dress, and pulled her white Chanel sunglasses from her eyes.

"Excuse me, sir, may I speak with you for a second?" Yummi asked.

The bum lifted his head and thought that he had died and gone to heaven, not because Yummi was gorgeous, but because she had on all white and her back was to the sun. He squinted to see her face, but the sun was in his eyes.

"You can ask me any gotdamn thang you want to, baby, looking like a sexy-ass angel. Are you an angel, pudding?" he asked.

"I don't think so," Yummi said as she moved to block the sunlight from the elderly man's eyes.

"What can I do you for, little lady?" He was sitting with his back against the wall, staring up in Yummi's direction, and she didn't know whether he was looking at her or trying to look under her short mini dress.

"Could you stand up so that we can be face to face, sir?"

He struggled to stand, undoubtedly still feeling the effects of whatever bottle of three dollar rot gut that he'd been drinking. He was barely taller than Yummi's 5'3" frame, not much bigger either - with the exception of his stomach, that is. On his spritely frame sat a stomach bloated from junk food and cheap liquor.

"Do you know where I might find a pistol?" Yummi asked.

"I might. What's in it for me?"

"I'm willing to pay you for your time if things go smoothly," she said.

"Okay, China doll, I'm going to trust you. You see them little niggas down at the end of the strip mall? Go down there and ask for Icky Rat. If he ain't got a pistol for sale, then they don't make pistols no mo'."

"What's your name sweetie?" Yummi asked.

"My mama named me Charles, but the streets named me Shame."

"Okay, Shame, I'm Yummi," she said, extending her hand to the man.

His hands were extremely rough and calloused. His fingernails were cruddy and too long for a man. "Hot damn, baby, you got the right name!" Shame said, licking his crusty lips.

"Well, thank you, you're too sweet. I'm going to tell Mr. Rat that you sent me."

Yummi walked toward the end of the sidewalk where the young hustlers were congregated. Broken glass and gravel crunched and crackled underneath her Charlotte Olympia heels as she made her way to the men. She tried to picture which one of them would and could possibly have the name Icky Rat.

The picture was made clear as she got closer. Within the group of young men there was one that the name seemed to fit so perfectly. His skin, although dark, was an ashen grey. His ears sat high, almost too high on his head, and were pointed at the tips. The hair that made up his goatee was sparse and looked more like whiskers than an actual goatee. All of that combined with the fact that his two front teeth were extremely pronounced and seemed to overshadow the rest of his teeth made him look like a rat.

"You always stare at niggas you don't know, Kung Fu?" he said.

"The name is Yummi, not Kung Fu. I'm looking for Icky Rat," she said.

"You found him, Choong Chong, fuck you want?"

"I need to speak with you privately if that's possible, Mr. Rudeness," Yummi said.

Icky Rat blushed as his friends began taunting him.

"Oooooh shit, she checked your ass, Rat!" one kid said.

"Little mama sound like she don't play that shit, Rat," said another.

"Let's step over here, shawty. What you need?" Icky Rat asked.

"I need a pistol, something small but powerful."

"Shit, for a small fee and a piece of pussy, I will kill the nigga. He must be stupid to let you get away."

"It's not like that. Let's stick to the business, please. Can you help me or not?" Yummi asked.

Icky walked away and disappeared behind the liquor store where he and his friends had been hustling. Yummi looked around anxiously, her nervousness growing with every waiting moment. Icky Rat knew that she wanted to buy a pistol so it was obvious that she had money on her. If he decided to rob her, there was nothing that she could do. He reappeared suddenly with a brown paper bag in his hand.

"Look out, shawty. I got this little .380. It's not too big and if you shoot a nigga right, then it's powerful. It's some extra bullets in the bag too," Icky Rat said. He handed the bag to Yummi, who looked inside to inspect the merchandise.

It was a rusty black contraption that looked old and worn. There was no telling how many lives might have already been on the gun, but that didn't matter because she didn't plan on getting caught with it. "How much do you want for it, sweetie?" Yummi asked. She turned on her sex appeal full steam. One thing for certain, men couldn't resist a pretty face. She batted her eyelashes and tossed her hair seductively.

"Shit, I usually charge two hunnit for something like this. You's a fine ma'fucka though. Just don't forget about a nigga. Maybe when you swang through again we can get up and kick it. Throw me fitty bones and it's yours," Icky Rat said.

"Really, daddy? Aw, you're the best!" Yummi said. She leaned in and kissed him on the cheek. Yummi removed a wad of bills from her white Charlotte Olympia clutch and peeled off a crispy fifty dollar bill. She winked at him and strolled off.

"You a trickin'-ass nigga, Rat. You see all that money? She ain't even let you sniff the pussy and you breaking bread," someone said.

Yummi heard him, but she didn't stop. She smiled to herself. Men were easy to manipulate. All it took was a bright smile, a tight dress, and a fat ass and they were putty in her hands.

"Here you go, Shame, thank you, baby." Yummi handed Shame a new one hundred dollar bill. Before he could thank her for it, she jumped into her car and disappeared into the south Dallas streets, headed toward her Toby.

"Meet me at 12:00 p.m. at the Meridian Motel, room 5. I'll have Toby with me," Yummi said.

"Fa sho', Yummi. It's almost done, then you'll be rid of a nigga for good, yo," Esco said.

"Yeah, forever." She pressed the end button and dialed Toby's cell. "Where are you, baby?"

"I'm leaving the condo, I was going to head your way, what's up?" Toby asked.

"Meet me in south Dallas at this place called the Meridian Motel. It's right off of the freeway. Take I-45 south and exit on Lamar. Make a left and come all the way down. You'll see it on the right. I'll be waiting in room 5. Get here soon, baby, that lame Esco will be here at noon and I want you here before him," Yummi said.

"Okay, baby, I'm on my way now. We have to get this shit over with because I have to be back to get Tristen by 4:30 p.m.," Toby said.

Toby placed his cell phone into the cup holder and fired up a Newport cigarette. He turned the air conditioner off so that the smoke wouldn't get into the filters. Tristen would never let him live it down if he smelled smoke in his car. He needed the cigarette though. He felt like he was going into battle, not to mention he had no idea how he and Yummi were going to handle the situation with Esco. He'd known Esco long enough to know that there was no reasoning with him. He understood blood - nothing more, nothing less. If the price was right maybe, just maybe, but in a situation like this, Toby knew that Esco would not only be pissed about losing the money but he would feel like it was Toby's fault that he had to kill his friends. Toby drove the whole forty-five minutes wondering if he could even make it out of the situation alive. He didn't like going naked, but Yummi had assured him that it wouldn't come to that.

He pulled into the Meridian Motel and its name belied what lay in front of him. It was an out of the way place where crack smoke-induced zombies seemed to roam free. There was nothing else around as though these were the forgotten, the people that society had relegated to this small section of the city, condemned to smoke until they died of either drug overdoses or some incurable communicable disease. Mindless drones milled about searching for their next hit. It reminded Toby of the worst parts of Newark. Nearby, an overfilled dumpster reeked of rotten food and used Pampers.

A woman seemed to materialize from thin air. She was beyond thin, almost emaciated, with a faraway dazed look in her eyes. Toby looked down at his watch: 11:35. He did it to break the gaze that she held on him. He made the mistake of looking up and caught her eye again. She held a small child by the hand and Toby's heart sank. The child couldn't have been older than one year old. Her little legs were bowed outward as if she'd been forced to learn to walk far too soon. She was barefoot and her tiny feet were black on the bottoms. She only wore a urine and feces filled Pamper that sagged in the back, threatening to snap the tape on the sides that held it to her delicate frame. Her face was dirty and her tears had streaked her face, carving out deep ravines of muddy sadness. Her hair was matted on her head; only remnants of a faded hairstyle still remained, as if her mother had only combed her hair in the distant past to serve as evidence to a wary grandparent that she was taking care of her child.

The crackhead walked up to Toby, scratching, fidgeting, and shifting from one foot to the next. "Excuse me, cutie, you think I can get a couple of dollars? I'm tryna get my baby somethin' to eat," she lied.

"I ain't got no cash on me, ma. Let me handle this business and see what I can do."

"We can spend a little time together if you want, or I can pay you back on the first. You holding?" she asked.

"Um, no, I don't think so, shorty, and nah, I'm not holding shit. I'm not here for that."

"Oh, you with the bourgeois Chink bitch in room 5, huh?" she asked snottily. "Yeah, you look like one of them niggas that don't like yo' own kind." She snorted.

"Shit, if I wasn't with her, I still wouldn't fuck with your skank ass. Fuck you mean, yo? You need to take care of this baby and get your raggedy ass somewhere and sit down. I ain't got time for this shit."

"Fuck you, ol' uppity-ass nigga!" she barked and scurried off, dragging the child behind her like a rag doll.

The child looked at Toby as if begging him to save her from the wretched beast that had been named her mother. Toby turned his head for fear that his tears would flow freely in protest of the baby girl's treatment.

He knocked softly on the door of room 5. Yummi answered the door looking splendid in her all-white attire. She looked like money and Toby silently wondered how he'd gotten so lucky. "Hey, baby," he said as he walked into the motel room and kissed her on the cheek.

"Hey honey. Listen, he'll be here in fifteen minutes so this is the deal. I'm going to tell him that we're in love and I'm going to try and pay him back what he lost to you, plus a little interest," Yummi said.

"And what if he doesn't go for that, baby?"

She produced the .380, cocked it, and smirked at Toby. "Then I'm going to blow his fucking head off," she said seriously.

Toby smiled and shook his head. He could believe that not only was she gorgeous, but she was a little gangster as well. He walked to the window and peeped through the thick curtains. He saw Esco walking toward the room through the pothole-filled parking lot. He had a fiendish scowl on his face, and when Miss Crackhead with the baby tried to stop him, he mushed her in the face, sending her crashing clumsily to the ground. Her daughter giggled as if seeing her mommy feel some pain gave her the greatest pleasure.

"He's coming, baby!" Toby said excitedly.

"Okay, come over here, sit by me. Let me talk, baby, okay?"

Toby nodded. He didn't think that he could form any words anyway. He was terrified of Esco, so the less he had to talk, the better. Esco knocked on the door hard, causing Toby to jump slightly. Yummi answered the door and Toby instinctively moved back a few paces.

Esco stepped inside and tried to stare a hole through Toby. "What's up, bitch boy?" he barked.

"Now, now, Esco, no need for name calling. We're here to come to an amicable solution for everyone," Yummi said.

"We? Oh, it's 'we' now? Bitch, fuck you and this little bitch-ass nigga then! You two can die together for all I care."

"I have a solution. You lied to me and told me that he was a rapist. I now know that he cheated you out of money. Let me pay you what he owes you plus a little extra and we'll be done with all of this," Yummi reasoned.

"And why should I let you do that? You fucking this nigga? You wouldn't put me in the pussy, but you fucking this clown-ass nigga?" Esco barked.

"Man, f-f-fuck you, Esco!" Toby managed to say. He wasn't even convinced that he meant it.

Esco's laughter boomed through the small, low budget motel room. "Fuck me? Nah, fuck you!" he said, producing a chrome snub nose .38. "First I'm gonna fuck your bitch while you watch, then I'm going to shove the barrel of this pistol up her ass and pull the trigger. After I'm finished with her, I'm going to fuck you with the barrel of my gun, and just when your gay ass is about to cum, I'm going to blow your bowels through your throat." Esco had a mad look in his eyes. The sadistic thoughts swirling through his head had somehow given him a sick sense of gratification. "Bend over the bed, bitch, I'm finna show you how men fuck, since you ain't had a good fucking because you been fucking this needle dick little nigga!" Esco sneered.

Yummi backed up in protest and stumbled slightly. Her clumsiness drew Esco's attention and Toby pounced. He tackled Esco, knocking the gun from his hand as they tumbled to the ground wrestling. Toby hit Esco across the bridge of his nose and blood leapt from the gash. It only seemed to make Esco angrier. He unleashed a flurry of blows to Toby's ribs and he doubled over in pain.

"Get him, baby!" Yummi screamed.

He couldn't get him though. Toby had never been in real combat, especially not with a battle tested, prison seasoned veteran.

Esco scrambled to his feet. He looked around fervently for his pistol. He spotted it at the edge of the bed, but his mistake, as was the mistake of most who were overzealous, was talking instead of doing. "You see that gun right there, bitch? You should have picked it up and shot me with it because I'm going to use it to kill your little boy toy. Then we can have that little date I promised you," he said, laughing.

Toby tried to make it to the gun, but Esco was too close to it. Esco stood up with the gun in his hand and before he was able to take aim, Yummi fired a shot into his temple, sending brain matter and skull fragments splashing against the wall. The point blank range threw his body toward the door, and before he hit the ground, Yummi fired another shot into his jaw. The two shots rang throughout the room, commingling with the sound of Esco's fading breath. Esco fell, still looking at Yummi from somewhere beyond life.

"Let's go, Toby baby, our work is done here," Yummi said.

Chapter 31

David wasn't the classic racist. He'd learned his hatred. Whereas other racists hated everyone of color, his hate was unique in that it was specifically targeted at African Americans. There were no "good kind" in his eyesight. At nine years old, his father had lost his job at Boeing Aircraft after nearly two decades and his family had been thrown into financial ruin. Including his mother and father, they were a family of seven. David had three older sisters and a younger brother that for whatever reason that floated around in his little head seemed to worship the ground that David walked on.

On a particularly crisp autumn evening after finishing their meal of salmon patties, rice, and pan bread, his father stood and announced that they had to move. David and his younger brother had been born in the large brick home on Linden Blvd. It was a sprawling neighborhood with spacious homes, lush landscaping, and manicured lawns. They lived in a close knit community where bake sales and PTA meetings were the norm.

Nine-year-old David Ganzelle didn't want to move. As a matter of fact, he was staunchly against it. He had plenty of friends and he was somewhat popular in school. When his father had come in a few days later and somberly announced that he'd found a new home for his family, the reality of the severity of their financial woes hit home. After nearly two days of packing, they'd loaded the U-Haul truck and the family station wagon and moved to a small, wood framed house on Myrtle Avenue. They'd moved in the dead of night and David had ridden with his mother in the station wagon while his father trailed in the U-Haul.

"Mom, why do we have to move at night?" he'd asked.

"So that people can't see what we take inside of our new home," his mother had said.

"I don't understand, Mom, why do we have to hide what we have?"

"We're not hiding, doofus, we're moving into a neighborhood full of niggers!" his sister screamed.

"Elizabeth Ganzelle! You are to never use that word, do you understand? It's vulgar and disgusting and no daughter of mine will speak that way. Do I make myself clear?"

"Yes ma'am," Elizabeth said. She stared out of the window, ashamed to meet her mother's gaze.

After their move, David had been optimistic about his surroundings. He'd never had much trouble making friends. His father and mother had enrolled him and his younger brother Dalton into Phyllis Wheatley Elementary School and it was "different", to say the least. David and Dalton were the only white faces in the school. The children were extremely cruel to them, often taunting them, calling them unspeakable names like honky, peckerwood, and cracker, but they would never call them by their names. They were picked on, beat up, and chased home almost every day, and the more they tried to fight back, the more blacks would join in on their beating. By high school, David was a pothead and dedicated alcoholic who chose to self-medicate in order to escape the torture of the constant ridicule and ass whippings.

Dalton, who was two years David's junior, had been mortified by the prospect of starting Robert T. Hill Junior High School alone. After all of the horror stories that David had shared with him, he couldn't do it alone. It was David's tenth grade year when he'd walked into their house to find the entire family sitting in their living room crying. Two of his sisters had graduated and the youngest girl, Christi, was a senior and home from work early. She never left work early so something had to be wrong.

"What's wrong with you guys? Why's everyone crying?" he asked, but no one said a word. They just sat there zombiefied, staring into outer space. "Where's Dalton?" he asked, but his questions only seemed to agitate their crying. In all of his sixteen years, David had never once witnessed his father shed a tear, not when he'd lost his job and moved their family of seven to a two bedroom, cold water flat in the slums, not even when his oldest sister Elizabeth had proudly announced at eighteen that she was pregnant with the star quarterback's baby, who just happened to be black. David asked again, this time more forcefully, "Where's Dally?"

"He's gone, David. He's in heaven with Nanny and Paw Paw," his mother said.

"What? Don't talk to me like I'm a child, mother, where's Dalton?"

His father stood and handed him a crumpled piece of paper soaked with tears. David opened it and read it slowly.

Dear Mom and Dad,

I can't do this anymore. They treat me like I have the plague. Nobody plays with me, nobody wants to be my friend, and I feel like an alien here. I wish that we could just move away but I know we can't afford it. Maybe things will be better if you guys have one less mouth to feed. I don't want to fight anymore and I'm tired of being sad every day. I'm sorry.

Love Always,

Dally

A boater had found his young body hanging from a bridge above the Trinity River, dangling by his neck, swaying in the breeze. He'd been so disparaged by life that he'd felt his only way out was to end it all. His father had had the great displeasure of carrying his youngest child's limp, lifeless body to the coroner's van.

That catastrophic event had been the catalyst to David's hatred and he fed on it. He clung to that hatred for dear life because in reality, that was the only thing that he had to remember his kid brother by. So when Tristen Graham knocked on his office door fifteen minutes prior to quitting time in hopes of reconciling their differences, he wasn't exactly keen on the idea.

"Excuse me, David, do you have a minute?" Tristen asked.

"Make it quick."

"Well, I know that we didn't get off to the best of starts so I was hoping that we could start over," Tristen said. He extended the gift bag to David, who promptly snatched it up and peered inside. His eyes lit up like headlights at half past midnight. "Yeah, I noticed that night at the bar that you only ordered scotch, so I wanted to get you a nice peace offering," Tristen said.

"This shit is like fifteen grand a bottle, how did you afford this? Are you a dope peddler on the side, nig - I mean, Tristen?"

"It's actually seventeen five a bottle, and no, I'm not. Mr. Cross gave me a bonus for delivering my prototype early and coming in under budget," he lied.

"Well, this calls for a toast. I've never met a darkie with such exquisite tastes. A malt like this is to be savored, and since you paid for it, I'm going to savor it in one big gulp," he said, pouring two glasses.

"I don't drink, but we can talk while you savor the flavor - if that's okay with you," Tristen said.

David gulped both drinks and poured another and then another. He told Tristen about his childhood and how he had come to hate black people. He told him about Dally and how that had been the deciding factor for his hatred. He shared how he despised black people for their defensive nature, when they were in fact one of the most racist groups of people on earth. He cried like most drunks and totally contradicted himself, stating that he'd always believed that because of the things blacks had gone through, it made them the most caring and most nurturing people he'd ever met. His tears continued to flow as he confessed how he'd asked Tara Hill, a black cheerleader who'd just transferred to his school, to the prom. She'd said yes, but after pressure from the other black students at school, she'd called and abruptly cancelled.

"Why?" he'd asked.

"Because if I go to the prom with you, they are going to kick me off of the cheerleading squad. I'm sorry," she'd said and hung up the phone.

He'd skipped the prom, unbeknownst to his parents. He'd dressed up in his tuxedo, borrowed their station wagon, and parked outside of the school. He watched sharply dressed young men and scantily clad young women enter the school gymnasium in stellar moods. Then David saw her. Tara Hill had turned him down only to back door and go to the prom with Arnolf Mobley, or Mr. Basketball, as they called him, and he lived up to the name. He was 6'6" of pure muscle and athleticism and David hated his guts.

He waited until after the prom and followed them and much to his surprise, Arnolf Mobley was the perfect gentleman. He took Tara directly home after the prom, only kissing her on the cheek and then leaving. As soon as Arnolf's tail lights were out of sight, David made his move. He reached into the glove compartment and removed the box cutter that his mother kept there. He crept up on Tara as she climbed the stairs to her small second floor apartment.

"Tara!" he said.

She jumped, obviously startled by his intrusion. "Oh, hi, David, you scared me! What are you doing here?"

"You said you weren't going to the prom! You're a liar. You can't just hurt people and think it's okay!" David said calmly.

"I never said I wasn't going to the prom. I said I wasn't going with you and I don't have to explain shit to you!" she screamed.

The glint of the box cutter shone brilliantly against the moonlight as David slashed quickly across Tara's cheek. "If you scream, I'm going to kill you, then I'll go into your house and kill everyone in your family."

Fearing for her eight-year-old sister's life, Tara nodded her understanding. David grabbed a handful of Tara's freshly pressed hair and dragged her to the wood line that bordered the back of her apartment complex. "Take off your clothes!" he barked. Tara did as she was told. "Everything, you black bitch! Your panties and bra too!"

Tara stepped out of her matching bra and panties and began to cry. "David, please don't do this! I'm a virgin."

"Not after tonight," he said as he stepped out of his tuxedo pants.

He raped Tara repeatedly, and by the time he was done, Tara lay in a motionless state of shock. He hadn't planned on killing her until she began to cry again and said adamantly that she would tell when she made it home. She never made it home. David cut her throat from ear to ear. He covered her body with fallen leaves as best he could and then fled. A couple of weeks later, a group of teenagers stumbled upon her body during their annual Senior Skip Day. Every year, thousands of students across the state of Texas (not just seniors) played hooky from school.

The news spread throughout school like a bad case of the measles and south Dallas went into panic mode. They assumed that the Atlanta child murderer Wayne

Williams had either found his way to Dallas or had a copycat. Soon after Tara's murder, David enlisted in the military and continued his depravity. No matter where the Army stationed David Ganzelle, he raped and sometimes murdered black women. He'd never in his life found a need for conversation to get women, and as he told Tristen in his drunken state, "I hate black people, but I love black pussy and it loves me."

"If it loves you, then why take it? Why not just marry a black woman?" Tristen asked.

"Are you fucking crazy? And have little chocolatey nigglets running around my house? No thank you!" he slurred.

"It's been nice talking to you, David. Be careful driving and wear your seatbelt. You look a little wasted."

"Don't worry about me, jig - you mind if I call you jig? I've been doing this since you were a tadpole in your nigger pappy's nut sack, boy!" David garbled.

He and Tristen left his office together. David Ganzelle stumbled as he walked. He put his hand on the wall to steady himself.

"Are you okay, David?"

"Yeah, I'm fine. You know, you're alright, jig. I mean, for a nigger, that is."

Tristen didn't say a word. David Ganzelle would get his soon enough. They stepped outside into the warm autumn breeze and David cursed at the brightness of the midday sun. Tristen saw Toby sitting nearby in his car with a bewildered look on his face. Tristen slapped the passenger's side door with the palm of his hand and Toby trembled and shook as if he'd seen a ghost.

"What's wrong with you, dude?" Tristen asked.

"Man, it's a long story. Where are we headed?"

"You see that Suburban right there? Follow it, but be careful because he's drunk."

"Gotcha. Yeah, I watched him walk to his truck. Dude gives a whole new meaning to white boy wasted," Toby said.

They followed David, and much to Tristen's excitement, he bypassed Billionaire's Row. He drove down Mockingbird Lane, heading for the congested North Dallas rush hour traffic. "Stay with him, Toby!" Tristen shouted as he removed the iPad from his backpack.

"I'm on him, Cuzzo."

Tristen watched David's progress on the iPad and smiled at how well his program was working. He made David switch lanes, cutting off another SUV in the process. He swiped his finger across the screen in a figure eight motion and his SUV swerved recklessly. Horns blared, people cursed, waving fists and displaying upturned middle fingers. Tristen increased David's speed to a brisk 58mph in the 35mph zone that he was driving in. It kept increasing the speed of David's SUV until it reached 72mph. He swiped the brake button and David's vehicle skidded through a red light. Tristen laughed aloud at the thought of what must be going through David Ganzelle's mind. Five hundred feet ahead of them a Mexican vendor walked to his truck to replenish his fruit stock and Tristen saw an opportunity. He increased the Suburban's speed to 90 mph and sent it careening through the small fruit stand.

In the distance, Tristen heard sirens approaching quickly from behind them. A Dallas Police cruiser gave chase and then another joined, then another. Before long, Tristen heard helicopters overhead. Tristen backed off of the speed of the SUV to 55mph and cruised in the far left lane, careful to keep David's vehicle in his sights. He swiped the screen to the right and the vehicle jumped the curb, riding the sidewalk. At a Dunkin Donut ahead of them, a young cop was exiting the donut shop with a box of donuts and two coffees for him and his partner. Tristen decreased the speed to 45 mph and jumped the curb again with a swipe of his finger. He swiped the screen one last time and hit the brake button.

David Ganzelle's Chevrolet Suburban crashed into the waiting police cruiser. The young donut-wielding cop dropped his donuts and coffee and drew his weapon. The police officers that had been pursuing David's vehicle stopped abruptly, leaping from their cars with guns drawn. Tristen had Toby slow down. An officer was ripping David Ganzelle from the driver's seat. As they passed, Tristen rolled his window down and smiled at David. It took him a minute to focus, but when he did, the realization of what had just happened registered deep within his drunken brain.

Tristen winked at him and David knew then that he'd been played. He'd tried to warn Brennen Goldstein that something wasn't right and he'd blown him off. Texas laws were some of the stiffest in the nation, and if he was convicted of DUI, they could also charge him with attempted murder on a police officer because he had crashed into the police cruiser while he was intoxicated. David Ganzelle's hatred and arrogance would cost him everything that he held dear. The irony of it all was the fact that the very thing that he loved the most had also been used to bring about his demise.

Chapter 32

Brennen tried to call David Ganzelle, and when he didn't get an answer, he instinctively dialed Frank Trimble's number, only to realize that he would never answer. He tried David's number again - nothing. Slight panic began to set in with Brennen. He'd thought that David was just being paranoid, but maybe he was on to something. His boys had been picked off one by one, which meant that he had to be next.

Brennen felt a pinprick on his neck and then the breeze of someone passing him. A gorgeous Chinese or Korean woman sat next to him. He didn't know exactly what part of the Orient she had come from, but she was a classic Oriental beauty. She wore a black and gold kimono which seemed to accent her jet black hair. Her long straight locks hung past her shoulders and framed her oval-shaped face. She smelled like love, a light summery scent that wafted into Brennen's nostrils and intoxicated him instantly. Her smile was radiant and her dark, smoldering eyes sparkled like those of a woman in love. When she whispered a sweet "hello" in Brennen's direction, his heart fluttered. He was smitten.

In a dark corner booth tucked away neatly in the back of the tavern, Toby texted Tristen: NR613 IS ACTIVE. Tristen was sitting in a dark alley with Nigel not two blocks from the bar in a black unmarked van. He exited the van, strolled casually from the alley, and took his position across the street from City Tavern. He wore all black from head to toe. He also wore a Japanese Kindei Hannya mask. It was a golden mask of a demon's face, popular in Japanese folklore. Toby left the bar and headed toward the alley, but bypassed it and took up position a couple of blocks north of the alley. He pulled his golden Japanese Deijya demon mask from his backpack and put it on.

Tristen whispered into his Bluetooth, "She's a demon goddess, Brennen, leave! She got Frank already; you're next," he said.

Brennen tried to see her face, but her back was turned to him. "Excuse me," Brennen said, touching her shoulder.

Yummi spun around. Her once radiant smile had been replaced by jagged fangs and her smoldering eyes were now golden slits. Brennen jumped from sheer fright and almost fell off of his bar stool.

"I want your soul, Brennen. Frank Trimble says hello from hell," Yummi said.

Brennen couldn't believe his eyes or ears. He threw a fifty dollar bill onto the bar and walked out into the mild autumn darkness. The streetlights glowed brightly, but only in sketchy spots, shimmering against the metallic-like asphalt. Brennen shoved his hands deep into his pockets and looked back. Standing in the doorway of City Tavern was the Chinese demon, staring at him with her golden eyes, smiling with her wolf like teeth.

"Walk, don't run!" the voice in his head said. "There are more of them."

Brennen wanted to run, but he was afraid. He walked briskly toward the parking garage where his car was parked.

"Look to your left, across the street," the voice said.

Brennen looked to his left and saw a lean, demon-faced figure in all black crossing the street. He met the demon queen on the sidewalk and headed towards him quickly.

"There's another one in front of you. They know that you're trying to get to your car, Brennen," the voice said.

Toby was dressed in all black also, crouched low and heading directly toward Brennen.

"He's a soul eater, Brennen, he wants to eat your soul. Look for the man in white - the man in white, Brennen!" the voice said. Brennen looked around frantically, searching for some sign of the man in white. He approached the alley quickly. "There, Brennen, there, down the alley!"

Brennen looked to his right and at the end of the alley, standing beneath a streetlight, stood Nigel in a white robe.

"Go to him, Brennen, run!" the voice said.

Brennen ran toward the man in white. "Help!" he screamed. The streetlight overhead flickered on and off.

It clicked and crackled as bug after bug flew into its luminous clutches.

Nigel stood with outstretched arms, welcoming him, inviting him to refuge. "What's wrong, my child?" Nigel asked.

"Demons all around, demons are chasing me!"

"Get into my van, child, I will take you to the safety of the Lord's house." Nigel offered, extending his hand toward the van.

"Either go with him or face the demons behind you. Look!" the voice said.

Brennen looked toward the entrance to the alley and saw the three demons standing there, taunting him with their infernal laughter ringing in his head. They were talking about him, arguing over who would devour his brain, who would devour his heart, and who would claim his soul. They all seemed to be in agreement that they would equally share in the privilege of ripping his body to shreds and eating his flesh together. He could hear every word and then the laughter started again - loud, sinister laughter. Brennen snatched the back door of the van open and climbed inside. He grabbed his head and began to beat it viciously, trying to make the voices in his head stop. He rocked to and fro as if somehow inwardly consoling himself. Nigel backed the van out of the alley and drove toward east Dallas.

Tristen, Toby, and Yummi removed their costumes after the van was out of sight. Their work was done; the rest was up to Nigel. He'd wanted to simply kidnap Brennen, but Tristen had convinced him otherwise.

"Why forcibly kidnap him and draw unwanted and unneeded attention when we can *lead* him to you?" Tristen had said, and it had made perfect sense to Nigel.

Yummi removed her gold, catlike contact lenses and jagged fangs and smiled. "When I told him that I wanted his soul, I thought that he would shit himself," she said.

She and Tristen laughed, but Toby was stoic.

"What's wrong, baby?" Yummi asked.

"What's wrong? Are we going to pretend that today didn't happen?" Toby asked.

"We didn't have a choice. It was either him or us. I'm not pretending."

"Wait, what happened today?" Tristen asked.

"We killed Esco. It was either kill or be killed!" Yummi said.

"*We* didn't kill shit, *you* blew his brains out!" Toby screamed.

"First of all, lower your fucking voice, Toby. I did that for you! Do you not understand that he was going to murder us both?" Yummi snapped and then added, "Now it's all on me though, right? Okay, babe, I'll take that."

"This isn't me, baby that's all I'm saying, I'm nobody's killer. It's easy to pretend that you're about that life. When it's all said and done, though, you're either built for it or you're not and it seemed to come really easy for you. I don't know," Toby said sadly. He dropped his disguise at their feet and walked in the opposite direction. Toby was conflicted. He'd honestly thought that Dallas would be a new start for him. He loved Yummi and she'd saved his life in more ways than one, but murder was serious. He removed his cell phone and dialed Sister Mattie's number.

"Greetings and God bless you. Which one of God's children am I speaking with?" she asked.

"It's Toby, Mother Mattie."

"Hey baby, how are you, child?" she asked sweetly, but Toby didn't answer. "Is everything okay, baby?"

"I'm sad. I don't know where my life is headed. I mean, I want to do right, but I feel lost, like I'm in over my head," Toby rambled.

"Have you been praying, honey?"

"I've done something terrible, Mother Mattie!" he cried.

"There is nothing that you can't take to Jesus, baby, He can fix it!"

"Even murder?"

"Even murder. Although the Bible says 'Thou shalt not kill', in Mark, chapter 3 verses 28 and 29, the Lord says, 'Assuredly I say unto you, all sins will be forgiven the sons of men, and whatever blasphemies they may utter; but he who blasphemes against the Holy Spirit never has forgiveness, but eternal condemnation'. So you see, baby, as long as you don't speak against God, you're covered by the blood of the lamb," she said, rattling off the Bible verses from the top of her head.

"Thank you, Mother Mattie."

"Anytime, baby. You get down on your knees, be still, and listen when you pray, honey, He'll give you the answers. You just have to be quiet long enough to hear the answer, Toby."

Nigel pulled behind the dilapidated building that used to be Our Lady of Grace Catholic Church. It was an imposing brick structure that had once housed some of Dallas's most prominent Cardinals, Priests and Archbishops. Now it was an abandoned building used to house derelicts and drug users. Nigel pulled into the edifice through an opening where a section of the building had collapsed from bad weather and old age. He killed the engine and the lights and turned to Brennen. "You're home, Brennen," he said.

"W-w-what? How do you know my name?" Brennen asked.

Nigel didn't say a word. He exited the truck and walked to a table covered with a black cloak. There were candles circling the table with a candlelit path leading to an altar. The table contained an array of knives of different types and sizes. The candles flickered menacingly against the cold steel of the shiny blades. Shhhrit, shhhrit, shhhrit, shhhrit echoed throughout the hallowed halls as Nigel scraped two of the blades together diabolically.

The sound sent shivers down Brennen's spine and drew him from his perch inside of the van. When Brennen saw the sight before him, his knees grew weak. No longer were his savior's features soft and inviting.

No, they had become the features of an intimidating and deadly tormentor.

"Come to me, Brennen!" Nigel shouted, but Brennen stood paralyzed. "If I have to come and get you, you'll regret it!" Nigel said in a singsong type manner. Brennen walked to Nigel slowly until he was mere inches from him. "Do you know me, Brennen?"

"You saved my life; that's all I know," Brennen said, choking back tears from fear.

"Take a really good look at my face, Brennen Goldstein. Look at me!" His voice boomed and bellowed throughout the church.

And then it registered; it was Natalie's twin brother! It dawned on him a split second too late. Nigel buried his blade deep within Brennen's bowels. He squealed in agony as Nigel yanked the knife from his gut. He wanted to run but, he couldn't feel his legs. Nigel picked Brennen up by the collar of his shirt and slammed him onto the altar. It was a crude wooden contraption in the shape of a cross. Brennen tried to fight back, but he had no strength. Nigel reached onto a nearby table and retrieved a nail gun while still applying pressure to Brennen's windpipe.

"You should have never touched Natalie," Nigel said calmly.

"You're a man of God, Nigel!"

"Key word in that sentence is '*man*'. You have to pay for your transgressions against my sister!" he said as he nailed his left hand to the cross.

Brennen screamed in pain, squirming, struggling against the firm grasp of his captor. "Please, please, I'm sorry!" Brennen shouted.

"'Please, please, I'm sorry!'" Nigel mimicked. "I know you're sorry. God forgives; I don't!" Nigel shouted, nailing Brennen's other hand to the cross.

"Just kill me! Oh my God!"

"In due time, Brennen, in due time. The fun has just begun."

Nigel ripped Brennen's shirt open, revealing his pale, less than muscular chest. The blood bubbled and gurgled from the wound that Nigel had inflicted and Brennen struggled to catch his breath. Nigel carefully removed Brennen's shoes, then his pants, and finally his underwear. Brennen bucked and thrashed, angering Nigel who, as punishment, nailed both of his legs to the cross via his ankles.

"Aaaaargh!" Brennen screamed.

"Aaaaargh!" Nigel mimicked. "No one can hear your screams. You may want to save your energy," Nigel taunted.

He walked to his van and got a large container with no label. He approached Brennen and removed the top from the canister. He took a large meat cleaver from the knife table and began spreading peanut butter on Brennen. He spread it on his chest, on his thighs, on his genitals, and on his eyelids.

"You know the beautiful thing about peanut butter, Brennen? Rats love peanut butter, and believe it or not, they're attracted to the smell of human blood too!" Nigel said, slicing into Brennen's thigh with the meat cleaver.

He took a scalpel from the knife table and sliced the corners of Brennen's mouth up to his ears on both sides of his face. "I want you to look happy when you get to hell so that Satan knows that you're happy to be there," Nigel said, tossing the scalpel to the ground.

Brennen blinked rapidly. The peanut butter had mixed with his sweat and tears and had begun to run into his eyes. Brennen could smell his own blood mixed with his terror. He heard the sound of tires against gravel as Nigel drove away. He heard the sound of tiny squeaks coming from somewhere beyond the darkness. He turned his head to the left and saw dozens of beady red eyes staring at him. He turned his head to the right and they were already emerging from the darkness en route to their feast. Brennen closed his eyes and said a silent prayer and the squeaks grew closer. Before Brennen could open his eyes, he felt the first set of teeth rip into his peanut butter-covered flesh, then another and another until his silent prayers turned into desperate plea's for death to take him.

Chapter 33

Tristen, Nigel, Toby, and Yummi sat in Natalie's hospital room in more than jovial moods. Natalie was stable and in high spirits, which in turn lifted everyone else's mood. Toby and Yummi had just announced their plans for marriage when two well-dressed, middle aged white men entered Natalie's hospital room. They stood near the back, close to the door, observing the young African Americans.

"Which one of you young men is Tristen Graham?"

"Who wants to know?" Nigel asked.

"Are you Tristen Graham?"

"Why?" Nigel asked, standing up.

"Everyone calm down," the other man said, producing his badge. "I'm Detective Alvarez and this is Detective Hall. We have a few questions for Tristen Graham, that's all."

"Why didn't he just say that then?" Nigel asked.

"He just did," Detective Hall said.

"I'm Tristen Graham. How may I help you, Detectives?"

"You're a wanted man, Mr. Graham!" Detective Hall said excitedly.

"Wanted? What is it that I've supposedly done?"

"Stand up and put your hands behind your back, please," Detective Alvarez said.

"I need to know what I'm being arrested for, sir," Tristen said.

"You'll find out everything that you need to know when we get downtown!" Detective Hall barked.

"Aw, give the kid a break, Hall. After all, he's going away for a long time. We might as well get the ball rolling," Alvarez said.

Tristen's head was spinning. He'd been careful to cover his tracks. He'd planned out everything that he did. It had been calculating and brilliant, and the thought of two gumshoe police officers breaking the case was beyond his comprehension. Besides, the crimes that he'd committed weren't state charges, his crimes had been federal, so he was even more confused.

"Well, Mr. Graham, do you know a man by the name of Edmondo Bonitez?"

"No, why? Should I?" Tristen asked, honestly perplexed.

"I think his street name is Esco. He was found dead in a hotel and we have reason to believe that you may be our shooter."

Tristen laughed. It was actually funny because according to the timeframe that Toby said that they committed the crime, Tristen had an airtight alibi. He was at work, and the best thing about it was that they were required to check in and out by their company ID's and they were time stamped. "Sir, I'd love to help you out but, there's a problem with your theory," Tristen said.

"Oh yeah, genius? And what's that?"

Toby was mortified. Tristen was about to incriminate himself and he didn't even know it. By telling the detectives that the murder was committed while he was at work, it would let them know that he knew something about the murder. Tristen was smart, but he didn't have common sense all the time. The detectives had never mentioned what time they believed the murder took place. At best, he was looking at accessory after the fact. If the judge was an asshole and the DA was a crack shot, it was highly possible that they could charge him with a simple accessory to the crime, and unbeknownst to Tristen, in the state of Texas, the accessory and the murderer often garnered the same sentence. Toby had prayed something fierce since his conversation with Sister Mattie and he knew in his heart that he had been forgiven. He'd asked for forgiveness even though he hadn't been the one to pull the trigger.

"Well, according to your - " Tristen started, but Toby cut him off.

"I'm the man you're looking for, officer," Toby confessed.

"Is that so? Tell us something that we don't know," Hall said.

"Okay, you're fat, he's gay, and you both suck as police officers," Toby said sarcastically.

"Fuck this! Let's take them both," Hall said.

"Okay, wait, wait. Okay you found his body at the Meridian Motel," Toby said, standing up.

"What's your name, son?" Alvarez asked.

"My name is Toby Graham."

"Okay, Toby Graham, sit your black ass down," Alvarez said.

"Am I under arrest?"

"Yes, you're under arrest, now sit the fuck down!" Hall growled.

Toby did as he was told. He sat and he began giving the details of the crime, careful to keep Yummi's name out of it. He told them how he'd cheated Esco out of money in Jersey and how Esco had followed him to Texas. He gave them all of the details and some made up details as well to steer them away from Yummi.

"So tell me this: how did Tristen's Bank of America card get to the murder scene?" Alvarez asked.

Toby cursed himself silently. He'd gone to that meeting with sweat pants on and must have dropped it during the scuffle. "Tristen gave it to me to get lunch because I hadn't gotten my check from the sandwich shop," Toby said.

"Okay, I think we have enough. I'm no lawyer, but this sounds like self-defense, young man," Alvarez said.

"Well, partner, you know this is Texas and his black ass is going down for a long, long time," Hall said.

Upon hearing, that Yummi began bawling. She sobbed heavily, unable to contain her emotions.

"Can I kiss my girl before y'all take me? I was honest with y'all and cooperated. Can't y'all do that for me?" Toby begged.

"Make it quick, goddammit, this ain't *Love Connection*," Hall said impatiently, anxious to put another black man behind bars.

Yummi and Toby stood up and faced each other. He hugged her tight and kissed her deeply, and then he whispered in her ear as soft as his voice would carry. "Don't worry, baby, get me a lawyer. I'll be out by morning because these assholes arrested me, let me confess, and they didn't Mirandize me, they never read me my rights. I love you."

Made in the USA
Charleston, SC
27 September 2016